About the Author

Rob has co-written two full-length musicals and written two plays, all of which have been staged. Rob wrote a book about his English Channel swim in 2012 called *From Starr to Starrfish*, which was published in 2013. Rob lives in Brighton with his wife Sharon and their three children, Asher, Mia and Jesse. Rob's passion is open water swimming and he swims every morning at 6:30am throughout the year from the Palace Pier in Brighton. This is Rob's second novel.

Also by Rob Starr

Fiction:
What the Tide Brings Back

Non-fiction:
From Starr to Starrfish

ROB STARR

THE FIRST WIDOW

JUST ONCE
PUBLISHING

First published in 2024 by Just Once Publishing Ltd
Copyright © Rob Starr 2024

Rob Starr has asserted his right to be identified as the author of this Work in accordance with the Copyright, Designs and Patents Act 1988.

ISBN: 978-1-7394101-1-7

Editing and design by Fuzzy Flamingo
www.fuzzyflamingo.co.uk

A catalogue for this book is available from the British Library.

Dedicated as always to my four Starrs:
my wife Sharon and my most beautiful children Asher, Mia and Jesse

My thanks go to Jen Parker at Fuzzy Flamingo, my editor Scott Pack,
Lizzie Gardiner for the illustration and everyone at MIDAS for their
help in helping this book reach my readers.

Brighton – Greyfriars Close

11th May 2012

The heat was relentless, and the air was thick with smoke. Despite it being early evening, a small crowd had already gathered in the Brighton cul-de-sac to watch the action firsthand. The lights of the fire engines drew them in like children to a firework display.

The atmosphere around the crowd quickly became a mixture of fumes and fear. As the heat intensified, they all took a step back, making the street look like it was the setting for a flashmob dance.

Fortunately for its neighbours, the burning house was detached, with at least ten feet separating them on each side. It meant that whilst the toxic smoke would most definitely make its way around the streets and into open windows, the fire itself could be contained to the one single home.

"Keep back!"

"Stay back!"

"Move away!"

The screams of the police kept the crowd moving back to safer distances, whilst the frontline firefighters fought a battle that had become about containment rather than control.

The front door to the house burst open as two firefighters, blackened by soot and flames, came staggering out. Between them they dragged a burning body into the night air and rolled it over on the grass to dampen the flames.

The fire marshal rushed forward, grabbing a water-soaked fire cloth from the back of the unit as he ran and threw it over the head, where the flames had started to take hold. The two firefighters dropped to their knees with exhaustion and rolled the body one final time before falling backwards next to it, gasping for air.

"She's alive, medic, medic, she's alive!" the marshal screamed above the noise, taking in a lungful of acrid smoke himself.

A lady rushed forward from the crowd, trying to ignore the smoke that instantly made her gag. Before she reached the body, she was grabbed by a policewoman and held back.

"Let me through!" She fought against the woman holding her back. "I'm a nurse, I can help," she said with a wheeze as the smoke started to dig deep in her chest.

"It's not safe, stay back!" the policewoman shouted at her.

"I said I'm a nurse!" she screamed back, her cries seemingly ignored. "I know her. She's my friend!" She continued to push forward, but the policewoman was too strong. She had no choice but to give up and let herself be pushed back to safety amongst the crowd.

She watched from over the road as a team of paramedics rushed forward. The first one to reach the body pulled the damp cloth off its head and forced a mask over the half-burnt face. Carefully and slowly, he pumped fresh oxygen into the charred and empty lungs.

"Is anyone else in there?" the marshal asked the final firefighter as he stumbled from the house and joined his comrades fallen on the front garden.

The fireman raised his mask so he could be heard and coughed a barely audible reply. "I saw a body near the stairs, sir, but it was too hot in there, we just couldn't get back to him, it was impossible."

"It's all right, son," the marshal replied, putting a hand onto the younger man's shoulder, "you did good, Geoff, you did good. Keep your mask down," he said as he adjusted the man's mask over his mouth and eyes, whilst also checking his own was still safely in place.

He walked back to the burnt figure on the ground as the medic was preparing it for the ambulance. He knelt down. He could see it was clearly a woman, he could tell by her figure, but with all her hair burnt off her head and her face blackened by smoke, there was no way of knowing what she would have looked like just thirty minutes earlier.

He lifted his mask just enough so that he could be heard by the woman. "Can you hear me, miss?" Whilst he spoke with authority, the wobble in his voice gave away the distress he felt. "It's important, I need to ask you a question. I need to know who else was in the house with you."

"Leave him," she replied. Her voice box was so damaged that barely a sound came out from under her oxygen mask.

The marshal leant in closer, trying to make out what she was saying.

"Please, miss, we need to know, who else was in there?" he repeated. "Is it your husband, is he still in the house?"

"My... husband..." The words came out slowly, her accent clouded by her damaged lungs making the reply barely legible, but he managed to just about understand her.

"I'm so sorry, we can't go back, we can't save him." He gently lifted the mask from her face whilst the tears ran down his own face.

"Buono," was the last thing she said before she passed out.

Before her eyes closed, the marshal swore he saw a smile at the edge of her mouth and just the slightest sparkle in her eyes.

That was certainly what he told the judge at the inquest into her husband's murder.

CHAPTER 1

Edinburgh – The Royal Mile

15th January 2022

"Christ!"

The word barely escaped his lips as the pain tore into his gut for what seemed like the hundredth time that morning. Taking a deep breath, he managed to force himself away from his desk and crawl the twenty feet to the door before the burning sensation eased enough that he could pull himself to standing. He leant heavily against the glass panel separating his room from the main office and took in another breath to try to slow down his racing pulse.

He had designed the office himself and had put his own room right in the back corner, behind the panelled bookcases and as far as he could away from the prying eyes of his staff. Today that privacy had come at a price.

"Anyone. Please…" He had only just got the words out before the pain returned in all its intensity, forcing him back to his knees and into a ball on the floor.

"Mr Powers, is that you?"

He heard Sheila's voice somewhere near, but the words didn't quite register over the pain.

"Oh my God!" Sheila rushed through his door and knelt beside him. "Mr Powers, can you hear me? Mr Powers?"

As the pain eased once again, he was able to open his eyes and see his secretary squatting next to him. "Get me some water," he said to her.

"I'll get help, stay right there, Mr Powers, I'll be as quick as I can."

Sheila sprang into action, leaving him barely able to catch his breath.

"Just get me some water," he whimpered. "Please," he said to the empty room as he pulled his eighteen-stone bulk up from the floor.

After another short reprieve from the pain, he regained just enough strength to walk unsteadily into the main open space.

"My water, please," he gasped, looking around for his secretary but not able to see her.

"Fuck!" he screamed into the empty office as the pain took hold once again. It forced him into the nearest chair. He squeezed his overflowing bum cheeks into the small, round swivel seat and lowered his head onto his round stomach.

Since starting his own investment brokerage over two decades before, Martin Powers had lived on rich food, fine wines and his nerves. The result was severe IBS. It meant he was as familiar with the men's toilet on the second floor as he was with his own office on the third; something that had not gone unnoticed by his staff.

But as bad as his IBS had been over the years, he'd never experienced anything as crippling as this. He knew this had to be something else; a hernia maybe, or food poisoning.

Sitting in the swivel chair, the sweat forming around his middle, he was already trying to work out if there was someone to blame for making him so ill. Maybe it was the fault of his office chef – it could easily have been the undercooked sausage and egg roll he'd had at the canteen this morning. But then again, it could have been last night's dinner. He had told Jane the chicken looked undercooked, but she had insisted it was fine. Whoever's fault it was, he'd still make sure Jane also suffered for the pain he was in.

She had tried to convince him to lose at least two stone before their next holiday, but she never realised how hard it was for a man of his size to do that. It was easy for her, she was a natural size eight and could eat whatever she wanted, but for him everything he touched seemed to add another inch onto his waist. The other thing was that he never wanted to lose weight, he was happy as he was. She said she was only trying to protect him from himself, but it made him angry when she would tell him she was worried about his heart giving up. *The stupid woman doesn't care about my heart, she is only worried about my wallet*, he thought to himself.

Before he could continue his thoughts, another shot of pain hit him harder than the last, forcing his head down onto the desk.

"Sheila, get me the damn water," he croaked, leaving the words to sink into the cheap wooden desk before they could find his secretary's ears.

The pain had first started as he'd sat down at his desk and taken a swig of cola from the bottle he'd started yesterday. Warm cola in the morning was another habit Jane told him he had to cut out. At first, it was like a lightning bolt in his colon, literally sending him to his knees, then second by second, it increased in intensity until it was almost impossible to even roll himself back up straight. Every minute or so, he'd get a reprieve, but then it would come back, each time more painful than the last.

He knew he had to get out of the office fast and get back home, or maybe even go straight to the hospital. If he could just make it to the car, he'd be fine, it was only a short drive to either, and then...

"Christ, not again!"

The intensity of the shockwave that ran though his bowel threw him back further into the chair, forcing him to crunch his head down into his lap.

He stayed like that for a good thirty seconds before it eased again. Leaning forward onto the desk, he pushed himself out of the chair and weaved across the main floor, past the broken lift and through the end door. He went down the stairs as quickly as he was able to, banging heavily into each wall with every turn he took. After fifty-eight unsteady steps, he eventually crashed through the final door and into the lobby, sailing past Sheila as she was making her way back to the stairwell with a cold bottle of water in one hand and dragging their finance officer Evan with her in the other.

"Mr Powers, I've got help," she called to him as he went past. "Mr Powers…" she continued as she turned back and ran after him. "Your water!" she shouted to his now deaf ears.

He burst through the front door onto the street, knocking through half a dozen people making their way into the building and scattering another half a dozen heading into the city, carrying cups of scalding coffee.

"Hey, man!"

"What the hell!"

"Watch out!"

"Fuck, man, my coffee!"

He ignored everyone and just kept going forward.

He sucked in as much fresh air as his nicotine-damaged thirty-five-year-old lungs could handle and tried to focus on exactly where he was. He now had to get to a hospital fast, but he knew there was no way he was going to be able to drive in this state. He needed a taxi, and he needed it right away. As if in an answer to his prayers, a bright neon light came through the lights and swept down the road towards him.

The pain was so bad now, even his eyes were starting to hurt. He didn't know his eyes could hurt. His brain told him that was crazy and that the noise heading his way had to be stopped before his head exploded.

As the light on top of the car came closer, he realised that this could be his only chance of getting help, that there was no way he could afford to miss this opportunity and wait for another taxi, no way! He stumbled forward with his hand outstretched, totally misjudging the gap between the pavement and the road and fell forward.

"Mr Powers!" Sheila's scream was lost in the noise of the busy road.

Ironically, Martin Powers fell directly into the path of a speeding ambulance.

The very last thing he felt was the pain subside in his stomach. The very first thing the ambulance driver felt was the impact of the blood splashing onto the front windscreen as Martin's head exploded on the speeding vehicle.

CHAPTER 2

Edinburgh

Three Weeks Later – Funeral of Martin Powers

The rain was so strong it cascaded off Kiara's hair in mini waterfalls down onto her glasses, blurring her vision. It made it almost impossible to see definition in anyone, especially as she was surrounded by a sea of oversized black umbrellas.

She would have loved to have had her eyes lasered this year, but she knew they had an expensive few months coming up, what with Asher's thirtieth birthday party to plan and then their house move. But glasses, how she hated wearing glasses. Right now, she was almost blind from the rain, and it was near impossible to spot the client. She really needed to find her in the next few minutes, offer the obligatory 'sorry' and then get going. Otherwise, she'd miss her return flight to Gatwick and then she'd really be in trouble.

If she hadn't been so anal about her job, she would have been at home with Ash and the kids right now, enjoying a relaxing Saturday afternoon in the garden, rather than being in Edinburgh, attending yet another funeral of someone she knew intimately, but had never met.

Kiara hated funerals at the best of times, but travelling to Edinburgh on a Saturday morning, especially on a wet and miserable day like today, really made her understand why the other investigators did their completions from the comfort of their offices instead of going to site to meet the clients for a final sign off.

When she had first joined the claims department at Seico Life Insurance as a fraud investigator, she thought it would be a nice, cushy office job. The description had sounded perfect:

Fraud Investigator – Life Claims

Office-based job liaising with the underwriting department and, where necessary, the national and international fraud offices to establish the validity of life insurance claims. Reporting directly to the board of directors. Full training given in-house. The successful candidate will be based in our local Brighton office and reporting to the board of directors in our UK head office in London. Starting salary, dependent on experience, between £50,000 – £75,000 plus benefits.

Nowhere in the job description did it say: 'and you will get to spend your weekends away from your family getting soaked to the skin in an Edinburgh cemetery'. Maybe that was the benefits part, she thought ironically.

The truth, however, was far simpler than that. Kiara was obsessive when it came to her work. Most of her cases were simple, a life insurance claim off the back of a car accident or death from an unknown medical condition that had been carried around by someone since childhood that eventually had its way. Not that it made them any easier emotionally for her; she felt equally sad about all her cases and most left her in tears by the time she settled them. But sometimes, especially on the larger sums insured and when the reason for the death had something unexplained attached to them, it became much more about the numbers than the lives involved. As soon as there was a question mark, her instincts would go crazy and she became obsessed with solving it. One could say that this was the perfect trait for an investigator to have, but it did mean she would find herself going to extreme lengths to find the truth, even if it meant travelling to Scotland to ask one more question face-to-face to see the reaction she got.

Brushing the water from the face of her watch, she was dismayed to see it was already nearing two o'clock. She really needed to be home on time tonight. She'd promised Asher she wouldn't be late. Tonight, his parents were hanging out with the twins so that they could have their first date night of the year and she was desperate not to miss it.

"It was kind of you to come."

The lilting Scottish accent brought her straight back to the present, to the cold and wet funeral of Martin Powers. Kiara wiped the rain from her glasses and stared straight into the face of the archetypal *Scottish Widow*, straight from the old television adverts. Standing at five feet ten, with long, straight, black hair, piercing green eyes and a fashion model's waist, Jane Powers was a stunning vision in black.

Kiara didn't usually find herself lost for words, but Jane Powers had somehow made her feel vulnerable and uneasy. There was something about the way she spoke. Kiara had picked up on that the first time she had called her. She never seemed to use any colourful or expressive words, she always sounded so clipped and to the point, seeming never to say more than she needed to. It was as if she was attached to a word count programme and was limited to a certain number per sentence.

"Really, it was no problem," Kiara replied. "I'm sorry I had to ask you so many questions at such a hard time."

"You were just doing your job," Jane said as she wiped away the tears that had gathered under her eyes. "I'm sorry, I promised myself I wouldn't cry today, but it's hard for me, and for Martin's

8

parents, of course. Martin was not the easiest of people and I never really understood his business, or much of what he did. That was why it wasn't easy to answer all your questions. You see, our marriage was, perhaps, difficult at times, but I did love him, and…"

She abruptly ended the conversation mid-flow.

In the short seconds she had spoken, Kiara had seen a completely different person to the one she had been talking with these last few weeks. Despite the wind, rain and dark atmosphere, there had suddenly been colour and expression in her face, and the conversation had, for the first time, lost its clipped tone. Kiara wanted to speak with her longer, to keep this stranger talking, so she could understand more about the man she had just seen buried and what impact it was having on his wife.

But, in the splittest of seconds, the stranger was gone and the beautiful but lifeless voice of Jane Powers returned. "Join us back at the house for a drink, if you wish." It was an invitation delivered without intent. Her eyes had already left Kiara's face and were looking over her shoulder, signalling that the conversation was finished.

Realising that the moment had passed, and she may never actually meet the *real* Jane Powers, Kiara decided to make her excuses and leave. "I really need to get the next flight out, otherwise I'll be late home, and I promised my husband…"

"The payment?"

"Excuse me?" Kiara said, thrown by the interruption and the curtness of the question.

"My husband's life insurance. Will you be able to make the payment now?"

"Erm, well yes, of course. First thing Monday."

"Thank you," Jane Powers replied, her eyes holding Kiara's once again. "Thank you."

Kiara could have sworn in that shortest of moments she saw

a small slump of the shoulders and a sadness in her eyes. They were gone as quickly as they had appeared, but they were there, she was certain. She desperately wanted another few days to work on the case, to probe just a little more. Not because she thought she would find anything untoward – Martin Powers had clearly stumbled into the road by accident – but because she knew that there was a different Jane Powers somewhere in there and the investigator in her desperately wanted to see who was hiding away.

"Monday then," Jane Powers said as she turned and joined the throng of black umbrellas making their way up the path towards the Powers' manor house in the distance.

"Yes, Monday," Kiara whispered as she watched the widow walk away.

CHAPTER 3

Brighton

On the short flight home from Edinburgh, Kiara settled back and read the latest copy of *220 Triathlon Magazine*. Having recently signed up for her next Ironman event, she needed to restart her training. The Ironman consisted of a 3.9km swim, then a 180.2km bicycle ride and finishing with a 42.2km full marathon run. Less than one percent of the population actually completes an Ironman in their lifetime, which was why it was considered one of the hardest single day events in the world. It fitted Kiara's obsessive nature perfectly.

Keeping fit and pushing herself in triathlons was the way Kiara cleared her head from the tougher cases she worked on; none more so than the Martin Powers case, which had left her with a constant question mark that she couldn't quite answer. She knew that a long training session would help clear her mind, giving her the clarity she needed to work out what was bothering her about this case. She checked the calendar on her phone and popped in a long run on Sunday morning. Training for such a big event took up a lot of her spare time and could easily take a toll on the family relationships, but Asher was so supportive of everything she did that he never once complained if she was out training for the entire morning. The twins were the same, not once did they moan about the hours she put in for her triathlons, and in fact Mia, being the other sporty one in the household, often joined her for the shorter runs. Kiara smiled to herself, thinking how lucky she was to have such an incredible and supportive family. She opened her phone again and moved the run on Sunday from 8am to 5am. That way she would be home at just about the time they were all getting up for breakfast; give and take, that was what made the Foxes such a tight litter.

With perfect timing, just as she finished the last page of her magazine, the pilot announced the descent into London. She took those last few minutes of the flight to close her eyes and try to put any more thoughts of the Powers family aside.

It didn't work.

The short drive from Gatwick Airport to her home in Brighton also did nothing to abate the feeling she had that Jane Powers was holding back some vital information about her husband's death. Something important that could affect the claim she was about to settle.

The autopsy had shown nothing unusual in his body, but that totally went against the witness statement of his secretary who swore blind that he was suffering from some kind of food poisoning and had stumbled into the road in a body *wracked with pain*. She recalled the secretary's exact words from the police statement taken at the scene of the accident. The medical examiner had found nothing to corroborate the secretary's statement. This had raised an alarm bell with Kiara right from the start.

The coroner had ignored the statement and simply listed the death as accidental, only having assumed Martin Powers had just lost his footing and tripped. He had ordered the release of the body within two weeks of the death, and everyone had assumed that the insurance claim would be wrapped up within days of that.

But Kiara had remained unsettled and couldn't just file it away as quickly as that. Her female intuition was like that of her namesake, a fox. She could sense when something was wrong from a mile away and, nine out of ten times, she was able to prove it. During her five years at Seico, Kiara had saved the company millions of pounds in fraudulent claims, whilst helping the police lock up numerous criminals, including those who had committed the worst crime of all: murder. That was the job of a fraud investigator, and she was one of the best in the business. But try as she might, she could find nothing out of the ordinary in the Powers case. Everything, with the exception of the strange symptoms he apparently had, plus her gut feeling, ticked all the boxes. At the end of the day, she had no choice but to concede that maybe this time her instincts were off, and Martin Powers' death was by natural causes, if of course one can call being run over by an ambulance natural.

It was why, three weeks after her husband's death, held up only by an autopsy that showed nothing untoward in his system, that Jane Powers was at last able to hold the funeral.

And it was also why Kiara was under extreme pressure by her bosses to pay the claim and close the file once and for all. Contrary to popular belief, the insurance companies wanted to pay claims as soon as they were able to as otherwise it affected their general financial rating with the regulators and it could tarnish their reputation in the marketplace. So Kiara needed to pay the claim as soon as she could to avoid the management coming down hard on her.

The ringing of her mobile phone interrupted Mellow Magic, her favourite radio station, just as she left the M23 and took the tight bend round to join the A23 to Brighton.

"Are you nearly home? My mum and dad have been here half an hour already and we're going to miss our booking if we don't leave soon," Asher said as soon as she picked up.

Kiara heard the annoyance in his voice but understood exactly why that was. She had told him she wouldn't go to the funerals of her cases any more, as she had been asked not to by her office and he had wholeheartedly agreed with them. But then she had broken that promise on the very next case.

"I'm really sorry, darling, I'm nearly home, I've just turned onto the A23 and the road looks pretty clear. Twenty minutes max, okay? This will be the last one, I promise."

"Did you really need to go? I thought we had agreed it wasn't part of your job."

"I know, I'm sorry. I just really wanted to meet her. We've spoken a lot on the phone and I just always thought she was holding back. I hoped meeting her in person would get rid of my worries and I could settle it and move on."

"And did it?"

"I'm not sure it did to be honest. I mean, she has been pretty consistent throughout, no emotion, just very concise. And I could tell she didn't want me there."

"I'm amazed she even let you attend. I mean, if it wasn't for you, she would have received her claim money by now."

"Exactly! So why then didn't she at least give me the cold shoulder? Sure, she was kind of cold towards me, but I wouldn't say she was really unfriendly. And then there was this moment when she seemed to forget who she was talking to and almost told me something that seemed important, but then she kind of recovered herself and went back to that odd politeness again. It was just weird, that's all. And my stomach keeps telling me I'm missing something."

"But your bosses want you to pay it, and it is their money. So shouldn't you now just do it? You've been stressing about it too much, you were awake all last night, weren't you? I really think you should pay it and be done."

Kiara didn't think it was as simple as that. It was her job to find the truth, and if the truth was a natural or accidental death then she would pay a claim right away, and even add interest if it was a few days late. But she hated being forced to settle when she knew in her gut that something was wrong.

"I know, you're right. I just hate paying out their money when I'm not a hundred percent certain," she said.

"It's just another reason why I love you. But darling, if you don't get home soon and let me take you to dinner, I'll change the locks and find a more dishonest – and perhaps younger – wife to eat with."

"Now that's just mean! I'll see you in fifteen minutes and you can apologise for that with a kiss!"

She ended the call smiling. She loved Asher so much. He would always give her another perspective to think about, and yet would still support her if she chose to do something her own way. She couldn't begin to imagine her life without him, he really was her calm in every storm.

Her phone rang again.

"Hello?" she answered with some trepidation. She recognised the number of her head office as it sprang onto her car's dashboard.

"I'm sorry, Kiara, but I just don't get it," Gemma launched straight into her complaint before Kiara had a chance to ask why she calling so late in the day. "Did I or did I not ask you to clear the Powers' case off last week?"

Gemma was her line manager, and she was clearly not pleased.

"Why is it still not paid? It'll mess up next month's stats if we don't get it done this week, and I've got accounts crawling all over me again."

"Yes, I know, but…"

"Well, if you know that, then why is it still in pending for Christ's sake?" Gemma's voice went up another octave as she continued talking without giving Kiara a chance to reply. "When you're asked to settle a case, it should be settled. I don't need MJ chewing my arse out just because you couldn't be bothered to finish your paperwork."

"I was working on it today, Gem, I promise…"

"Your caseload is growing and growing, and I've now got the

head of the fraud office shouting at me for wasting his time as well as the accounts department. For Christ's sake just pay the claim, will you?"

"It's a two-million-pound claim, Gem. And something just feels odd about it. I wanted to look the wife in the eye before signing it off, that's all. It'll be my neck on the line if I pay a fraudulent claim!"

"You went to the funeral! Really, even after both MJ and I told you not to?"

"I'm sorry, I should have told you I was going."

Kiara could hear Gemma take a deep breath and calm herself down before speaking again. She knew Gemma hated talking to her like that and she was only doing it because she was under orders from the management above her.

"All right, I get it. I know you always do the best job, that's why you get the big cases, but sometimes we've got to take instructions from upstairs and just pay a case when they want a case paid."

"Okay, I get it, I do, you're right. I was going to do it Monday, anyway."

"I'm sorry, but I need it done today."

"I'll do it Monday first thing, I promise."

"Please just get it done now. Honestly, it'll make both of our lives so much easier."

"Okay, but if Ash divorces me over this then it'll be you I blame."

"I'll always be here if he leaves you," Gemma said with a smirk.

"I'll do it, but only because it's you," Kiara replied, really not wanting to cause Gemma any trouble with the bosses. "I'll shoot to the Brighton office now and get it paid today, but I'll have to finish up the paperwork on Monday. All right?"

"Thanks. And I'll see you at the office next week, and lunch on me, agreed?"

"Agreed."

Kiara hung up the phone and carried on driving straight

through towards the turnoff on the A23 to central Brighton instead of taking a right up Mill Hill, heading to Hove and down to the seafront to her house. She was at the Brighton office just a few minutes later, pulling up into the private parking bay directly outside. Before heading out of the car, she whizzed off a short SMS to Ash telling him she'd be no more than half an hour and that she'd explain later. She sent it with a dozen kisses and a sorry emoji.

She'd never known Gemma to be so uptight with her, but as she said, sometimes head office could really put the pressure on when the numbers were that big.

Ever since Kiara had found three fraud cases in a row, all in excess of one million pounds, the company had rewarded her by increasing her workload by around a hundred percent, which in turn meant that Gemma's workload had increased by the same amount.

And to make matters worse, she was always at least two cases behind everyone else on completions, but no one seemed to acknowledge she was also holding more cases than them all. And, as usual in large companies, she was already in a battle to be heard over all her male counterparts, who would never quite accept that she was more successful than them.

Her phoned pinged back almost immediately.

You said you wouldn't be late tonight. I'm going out for this romantic dinner in the next fifteen minutes, WHETHER YOU COME HOME OR NOT.

They really needed a holiday right now, just a short romantic city break for the two of them. She would suggest it when she got home. Maybe Rome, where they had gone on their honeymoon all those years ago or perhaps Barcelona, she loved it there, it held great memories as it was the first city she had ever completed a full triathlon.

Lol. I'll be back soon, I promise. Love you.

She was sitting at her desk in the office in under a minute with the laptop open and logged into Seico HQ, searching the database for her case. Without wasting valuable time rereading her notes, she went straight into the claim authorisation screen and was about to press the settle button when she noticed the screen looked a different colour to its usual black and white. She paused just a fraction before pressing the button and took a closer look at the screen.

The database had taken her to the Seico Bristol site instead of Seico Brighton. Whilst each office could handle claims out of their region, the client codes still described which office was the handling office. Brighton, for instance, always ended in 'Btn'. All the databases of the company sat in one secure location, but each were colour coded to the region or country where the claim existed. Brighton was black and white, whilst other parts of the UK were made up of a number of different colours or shades. For some reason, her search, which was '@PwsMartBtn' had brought up two options, defaulting to the one that was dated a week earlier and was last viewed. It was highly unusual to have two cases with the same search codes. She took a deep breath, sat back in her chair and closed her eyes. She had almost sent two million pounds to the wrong beneficiary account.

She waited until her heartbeat had settled to its normal rhythm and then logged out of the payment gateway and straight back into the main database.

She slowly retyped the case name and waited the three seconds for the correct case to pop up. Once again, it highlighted the same two cases, both carrying the same case references. One was her case of Martin Powers, and the other was a case in the name of Martin Davenport.

She pulled her chair closer to the desk and leant in as close to the screen as her eyes would allow. She clicked on the notes for the Davenport case and started to skim read them.

The first thing she noticed was that the filename throughout the document was '@DavMartBst'. But someone had then manually changed the search name in the database to match that of her Martin Powers case.

"That's odd," she said under her breath. "Why would someone do that?"

She carried on reading, with butterflies in her stomach the more she read on. It was unbelievable. It was as if the two cases were almost an identical match. Both were men aged in their mid-thirties. Both married with no children. Both died after being in obvious pain but with no sign of ingesting anything. Martin Powers had run into the road whilst Martin Davenport had fallen from a balcony, but both seemingly after suffering unexplainable and unprovable stomach pains. And both claims were for exactly two million pounds. The similarities were too much for Kiara to just ignore.

Someone else had clearly spotted them as well and tied the two files together by amending the search passwords. She wondered why the Bristol office hadn't simply called or emailed her rather than linking the two cases on the system. That seemed an odd thing to do.

She knew Gemma would be mad with her, but she was not willing to settle the claim tonight without at least speaking to her counterpart in Bristol first. She scrolled to the bottom of the notes and saw the name of the investigator – Michael Hall.

She sent him a short internal email asking to speak on Monday, before then shutting off her laptop. She looked up at the clock on the wall opposite her desk and was dismayed to see she had been almost an hour. Asher would be furious with her.

Without another pause, she headed out of the office and back to her car, ready to face the music at home.

CHAPTER 4

Seico Insurance Co Head Office – London

Gemma sat back in her chair and took a long drag on her cigarette, before dropping it into the half-filled plastic cup by the phone. To hell with office rules, if she was going to be here after hours chasing down Kiara then she'd smoke a cigarette if she wanted to.

It was now time to go to the wine bar and meet her girlfriend; she had done all she could for tonight. Come Monday morning, the Powers case would be settled and she could get back to pushing Kiara to start clearing her backlog, and get MJ off her arse.

Gemma liked Kiara a lot. More than a lot, in fact. She was funny, charming, fit and utterly gorgeous. And she was by far the best investigator in the entire company; always totally focused on the job and hardly ever wrong about a case. She was also everything Gemma loved in a woman: slim and toned, short dark hair, legs so long you could never see where they ended and glistening olive skin that made her look as if she had just come back from a Royal Caribbean cruise.

It was only the fact that Kiara was not interested in women in that way that made Gemma hold back from declaring her undying love. *Why are all the good ones straight?* she thought to herself.

It made shouting at Kiara difficult and why she always fought so hard to protect her when head office called complaining about the back up of her cases. She knew one of these days she'd have to call Kiara into head office for an official warning. She dreaded that day happening, as Kiara could simply walk out and join another firm. Kiara was very aware of how good she was at her job and the value she brought to the company. And she was aware her talents would be snapped up by a competitor right away. Gemma was not so sure the same could be said for herself. The problem at Seico was that the accountants at the top ran the show and they were all about the SLAs (service level agreements), how many claims came in and how quickly they were paid out; speed and turnaround were key to the success of Seico Insurance and their reputation as the best claims payer in the industry. And Kiara was not helping those numbers at the moment.

As she went to turn out the lights and set the alarm, her phone vibrated. She'd forgotten to take it off silent when she was on the Tube this afternoon. She hesitated for a second, wondering if she could leave it, but she knew it was Mary-Jayne the moment she felt it jiggle around in her pocket, and she knew MJ would keep ringing until she picked it up.

"Hi, MJ. I was just leaving the office, can I call you back in a minute?"

"I told you to get the Powers case settled, didn't I, so why the fuck is it still pending?"

"That's impossible. Kiara just told me she was going straight to the office to pay it. She'd never lie to me about something like that."

"Then tell me why the hell I can see it still pending in the system?"

"One minute, just let me log on," Gemma said. She'd never heard MJ quite so mad before. If Kiara hadn't settled it like she'd promised, there would be hell to pay, for both of them.

"Well?" MJ shouted at her down the line.

"I don't understand it. She promised it was done."

"I can tell you myself from the logs that it isn't. She opened the case about half an hour ago, but then closed it without paying it. And then she went into another case with a similar name that belongs to the Bristol office. What the hell's happening here? It's a fucking shit show!"

"Bristol? I don't understand. Why would she need to contact the Bristol office?"

"Take a look for yourself!" MJ shouted down the phone. "She opened a case that she had no authority to look at, sent them an email that she had no authority to send, didn't pay the case you told her to pay and then logged off the system. So, you know nothing about this, is that what you're telling me?"

"I'm sorry, MJ, I really don't. I simply asked her to settle Powers today, and then come in on Monday and do the paperwork. I also told her she needed to clear up her other cases, as they were building up."

"I want you both in my office first thing Monday morning, you got that?"

"Yes, of course."

"Monday first thing, here, you understand?"

"Yes, we'll be there. She'll get it settled, I promised."

The phone went dead. Gemma sat back in her chair, cursing under her breath.

"For fuck's sake, K, why can't you just for once do what you're asked?"

As she left the office, she decided that she'd try to get to the meeting even earlier on Monday and have a few minutes with MJ before Kiara joined them. She needed to smooth the way first as she knew Kiara hated to be shouted at and it would really start the week on a negative footing. Also, she wanted to ask MJ why this particular case was causing her so much aggro. Kiara had about half a dozen cases still pending and the other investigators in the office must have two dozen cases between them that still needed settling, yet it seemed that it was always the Powers case that was being talked about at head office. Maybe she was missing something, perhaps Kiara had a point that something was off. *I'll get to the office half an hour early, maybe even bring MJ a coffee and croissant to relax things before I ask if she can help me understand what's really going on*, she decided.

CHAPTER 5

Brittany Road, Hove Seafront

"You want coffee, Ash?" Kiara called from the kitchen, loud enough that her voice would carry out of the window to the bottom of the garden.

Although Asher heard her clearly, he pretended not to notice and just carried on tying the new daffodils into small bunches with the help of Mia and Jasmin, their fifteen-year-old twins.

"Ash, coffee darling?" Kiara tried again, this time with a little more force.

"Dad, Mum's asking you if you want coffee," Mia said.

"I can hear her, sweetheart, but your mum and I are not talking at the moment."

"What's she done?" chipped in Jasmin.

"She's probably broken something of Dad's again, maybe one of his precious records," Mia replied, laughing.

"I made you one anyway," Kiara said, walking down the garden with a steaming hot mug of coffee in her hand. "Hey girls, you helping Dad in the garden? That's a nice change to just sitting and watching nonsense on your phones."

"What did you break, Mum?" Mia asked.

"Leave Mum alone, she's broken nothing," Jasmin said, leaping up and shoving her arms around her mum in a bear hug, forcing her to hold the hot drink up high to stop it from spilling.

ROB STARR

Jasmin always went to her mum's defence, whilst Mia was very much the daddy's girl.

The twins were so much alike in personality, but so different in looks. Jasmin, like her dad, carried a little extra weight around the edges and her skin, despite its olive tones, still somehow looked pale compared to her sister's.

Mia, on the other hand, carried her mum's olive skin in a much more pronounced way than her sister did and she stood a good inch taller. And like her mum, she had not an ounce of fat to be seen. People who saw the girls together assumed that they were best friends from school rather than sisters who were born less than a minute apart. 'Genetics are a weird thing that only brilliant scientists can understand', Kiara and Asher had said many times to the girls to try to explain it as best as they could. It still made no sense to them that twin girls could look so very different.

"At least one of my family still loves me," Kiara said, giving Jasmin and Ash a wry grin.

"I didn't want a coffee," Asher said with an edge to his voice without looking up.

"Oh, come on, Ash, I was only an hour late, and you could have waited for me."

Asher looked up at her, trying to not find it funny, even though the girls were both grinning from ear to ear. They knew that in the end their mum would win him over.

"And at least you and your dad got to have a father-son night out together and your mum got to hang out with the twins for a change. That must have been nice for all of you."

"It was, obviously. But I was really looking forward to just us having a night together. When was the last time we managed to grab a date night without your work getting in the way?"

"Girls, can you give me and Dad a few minutes?"

"Sure," said Mia, grabbing Jasmin's arm. "Come on, sis, seems we're not needed any more. Call us if you need us, Dad," Mia shot back as she pulled her sister back up the garden and into the house.

Once the girls had left, Ash put the mug on the grass and took Kiara in his arms. "I just wanted to have you to myself for a change. If we don't get some *us* time soon…"

Kiara cut off his words with a passionate kiss.

"Get a room!" Mia called from the top of the garden as Jasmin pulled her into the conservatory.

Kiara broke off the kiss and sat down on an old tree stump that was at the edge of the grass. Asher picked up his coffee and took a deep drink. They both couldn't help but laugh at Mia, she really was a funny one.

"I tried my best to get back," Kiara said, looking at him. "But Gemma called me, and I had to go to the office to pay the claim, she wouldn't take no for an answer."

"Surely it could've waited until Monday. I mean, it was already late, wasn't it, so a couple more days would have been all right."

"I think Gemma's been getting it in the neck from MJ. To be fair, I have been procrastinating over it, so I thought I'd give her a break and just go in to pay it, but…"

She stopped short of finishing the sentence; she wasn't sure she wanted to tell him the case was still live.

But Asher could see in her face what she'd done. "You didn't pay it, did you?"

"I was about to, honestly, but then something really odd came up." Kiara told him about the two similar cases and the email she'd sent.

"MJ is going to be so pissed off at you over this, and I doubt Gemma will be able to smooth it over this time. It's not the first time you've done this to her, is it?"

Kiara thought back to the last time. She had been told to settle a claim within the next twenty-four hours by MJ, but she'd refused.

MJ had told her the board would go crazy and she was right. They almost went nuclear on her. They took away her bonus for the year and she was only a breath away from resigning and moving companies.

"But I was right about that case, wasn't I? If I'd just settled it they would have lost over five million pounds, and a murderer would have got away with it. This is the same, I can feel it. I just know something's not right. And when I read that other file, I knew something was up. The other investigator in Bristol knows it as well, it's why he's linked our cases together."

"Why didn't he just call you?"

"I don't know, I thought that was odd."

"Maybe it's best if you don't get caught up in that as well. You need to settle your case and move on. The last thing we need is for you to lose your bonus again. We can't pay the mortgage on my teacher's salary alone."

"If anything, when I save them another two million, they might even promote me to lead investigator and I'll get a pay rise."

"Let's hope you're right about it, then."

"I'm always right, you know that... Listen, I wanted to ask you about the skydive next weekend. Are you still coming to watch?"

"Of course I am, I'm looking forward to it."

"I'm shitting myself."

"You'll be fine. I'll be watching you every step of the way, I promise."

"Seriously, I might be a bit of an adrenalin junkie, but you know much I hate heights. How the hell am I going to jump out of a plane?"

"You don't jump, they push you."

"Oh great, that's comforting."

"Have you organised the girls? They've got a netball game and someone will have to take them and bring them back."

"It's been cancelled. So they can come now."

"Excellent. A Fox family outing."

"It'll be an adventure. And maybe spending the weekend with MJ and Gemma will ease the tensions at work as well."

"Assuming you survive falling from a plane?" Asher said with a smirk.

"You'd better hope I survive, or you'll be bringing up twin girls on your own, just as they reach their peak teenage years."

"God help me!"

"Even God would struggle to help you with the twins on your own," she said as she pulled him in close again and planted another huge kiss on his lips.

"I was thinking," she said once they'd pulled apart, "do you fancy a city break next month, just the two of us?"

"Oh my God I'd love that," Asher replied, all memories about her missing dinner last night now fading away. "Where shall we go? Rome, maybe?"

"I thought that. Or Barcelona."

"Don't tell me there's another race on," he said suspiciously.

"Ooh, maybe there will be," she said, smiling her best smile at him.

"Come here," he said, pulling her in again, "get this claim settled, keep your bonus and then I'll let you take me away, but maybe somewhere different, a place where triathlons don't exist."

"Deal," she said, giving him yet another kiss, before turning away and heading back up the garden. "And bring the mug back with you when you're done."

"Yes darling, will do," he replied, his mind now jumping forward to a weekend away at last and wondering where they could head off to.

CHAPTER 6

Seico Head Office

M ary-Jayne sat at her desk and took a deep breath before logging on to her iPad. She clicked on the 'widows' icon that was almost invisible unless you knew it was there and waited until she heard the triple beep to confirm the call had gone through the security programme before she was patched through.

Even though they had been best friends since university, and she had been saved from a life of pain by her, she still felt nervous seeing her. She took a final deep breath before the picture came into focus.

"Mary-Jayne, it is so lovely to see you. It's been too long since you called me."

Slowly, MJ raised her head until she was looking straight ahead, doing her best not to see the prison cell her friend was answering from. Seeing her locked up in a cage broke her heart. She knew she should call her more often, but it was just too painful to see her friend like that.

As usual, her friend was wearing a red hooded cloak to cover the disfigurement to one side of her face. Mary-Jayne was amazed that, even after being locked up for so many years, Sophia still radiated the beauty and allure of a woman in her thirties rather than the early fifties that they had both recently turned.

29

"You look tired, MJ, is everything okay?" Sophia asked. As usual, she was more worried about her friend on the outside than how she fared locked away in the dull grey prison cell.

"I'm fine. It's just work, you know how I like to complain about my life," she said, suddenly feeling bad for being so selfish. Her friend had far more to complain about than she did. "Are you okay to talk? I always worry what would happen if you were found with that phone."

"Oh don't worry about that. They indulge me in here, I make sure they are well compensated, they'll leave me alone if they hear me talking. So go on then, tell me what's wrong, I can always tell when there's something you have to tell me but are putting it off."

MJ took a deep breath before she spoke.

"It's the investigator from Bristol. He's found another of our cases and has attached it to his own login on the system. I'm not sure what his intentions are in doing that, but I'm worried he'll expose us…"

Sophia looked deeply into the screen before replying, her tone suddenly much more serious and businesslike. "Has anyone else seen it?" she asked.

"It was pretty well hidden, and I deleted it as soon as I was able to."

"But it was still there long enough for you to find it?"

"It wasn't me who found it."

"I see. So someone else did see it then. Who was it?"

"It was one of my team, luckily. She was investigating Jane Powers' claim. He'd attached that file to Jane's file. My worry is that if she starts piecing things together… Kiara's smart and a bit like a dog with a bone when something seems out of place." She stopped talking and waited for the response.

Sophia lowered the cloak from around her face, exposing the scarred tissue. She took her time before she replied. MJ would not speak first; she knew better than to interrupt Sophia when she was thinking.

"You told me that the Bristol problem was taken care of, I thought he had been spoken to?" Her voice remained the same, but MJ knew her friend well enough to pick up the seriousness of her tone.

"He has, I'll call him again, it's in hand. But I can't rush it, we need to know exactly what he knows and if he's told anyone else what he's found."

"Well, it seems he knows more than we think. Do I need to remind you that we are all together in this, there can't be any loose ends? *Se cade uno, cadiamo tutti*, if one falls, we all fall."

When she was angry, her Italian accent came through stronger than usual and the words she needed were always found in her native tongue.

"I know that. I just never thought he was smart enough to manipulate the system. If I had thought he was capable of doing that I would have gone in stronger..."

"So, what are you going to do about it now?" Her voice was soft again, but behind it, MJ could hear the stress she was suddenly feeling.

"I'll make sure it's taken care of right away and I'll check the system to make sure he hasn't left any other trails."

"And your investigator, what about her?"

"Kiara? Oh, she's no trouble. I can get her to walk away from this without any suspicions."

"*Sei sicuro*, are you sure? Do you honestly believe that?"

"She'll leave it alone, I promise you. She's coming into the office to see me tomorrow. I'll make certain it's sorted."

"I'm sure you will. You can take care of her, but I'll deal with Bristol myself. So you don't have to worry about him. I just need you to take care of things your side. We can't have any loose ends catching up with us, can we?"

"I'll sort it."

"Call me after your meeting, just to put my mind at rest. And please, MJ, get some sleep. You've bags under your eyes. You need to look after yourself."

The screen went black as the connection was ended. MJ let out the breath that she didn't realise she had been holding. She could feel her heart beating in her chest like a racehorse rushing into the final furlong. She loved her friend, like a sister, but she knew better than to cross her.

She picked up her mobile phone and sent a quick text to Gemma: *'Gemma, 9am in my office tomorrow, with Kiara. DO NOT BE LATE.'*

CHAPTER 7

Seico London Office

Kiara got to the London office a little earlier than needed as she wanted to check her emails before she and Gemma met with MJ. She was desperate to see if Michael Hall had replied to her. She was disappointed to see MJ and Gemma already in a deep discussion. She assumed they were talking about her. Both were meant to be more than just work colleagues to her, they had both been round her house for dinner on multiple occasions and her twins thought of them both as surrogate aunties. Her first instinct was to march over there and confront them head on, but she knew that would not go down as she would want it to, so she would have to wait for the meeting, by which time she hoped she would have calmed herself down.

So instead, she headed to one of the smaller meetings rooms and opened her laptop, clicking on Microsoft Outlook. She was disappointed to see nothing from him. Her inbox, as usual, contained a few late-night chase emails from families checking up on the position of their claims. Before she did anything else, she replied to each and every one of them.

Having been so focused on the Powers' case, she had neglected her other ones for too long. She knew how important these claims were to people; literally life changing for so many who were now facing hard financial decisions since losing their partner. Gemma was right, she needed to get them agreed and paid immediately, it wasn't fair to keep them hanging on for so long.

There were eight in all, a mixture of life claims ranging from ten thousand pounds at the lowest up to a hundred and fifty thousand pounds at the top end, none anywhere near as large as the Powers case, but each one as important to the families involved. The reason they had been sent to her to look at was because all of them had information missing, or forms not signed in the correct place. This meant that they had been flagged up by the claims department as possible fraud, even though they were mostly just errors made by grieving families or inept solicitors. Kiara knew she should be sending them all back for completion and interviewing all the families to ensure there was nothing more untoward than poor paperwork. But she had delayed them long enough and she hated being the reason a genuine claim was delayed. Having already looked at each file when they originally came in she was a hundred percent sure that every one was genuine. So she took a decision that she was certain would come back and bite her, and paid every one of them there and then. For good measure, she also added a five percent additional payment to each one to make up for the delays she had caused. Doing that was probably going to get her into more bad books at work, but unlike the Powers case, her instincts told her that these were all honest people just caught up in the crazy amount of red tape that the insurance industry was drowning their clients in, and she would rather have a few more uncomfortable discussions with MJ than put them through any more pain.

Once she had closed them all down, she looked up at the clock above her desk and saw that is was time for her meeting. She pulled her mouse down to the lock screen just as an email pinged into her inbox. She looked at the clock again, knowing she really should look at this later rather than keep MJ and Gemma waiting, but equally she knew she would end up sitting in the meeting with them desperately wanting to come back and see if it was the reply she had been waiting for.

She made her decision and clicked the mail open. It had the usual internal Seico email address she was familiar with, but the colours were different. It was from the Bristol office.

From: *Michael J Hall*
Sent: *27 March 2022 11:50*
To: *Kiara Fox*
Subject: *Our Cases!*
Mrs Fox,

Thank you for your mail. Nice to be in touch with another investigator in the company.

I'm currently working on that case you mentioned. I'm not entirely sure how it became attached to yours, it was not intentional on my part. I'll speak with IT. I do agree with your email that both cases look similar, it is odd, isn't it? But I am sure it's all just semantics. I'll keep working on my case, but if anything comes up, I'll give you a shout and then maybe we can talk about it further.

Thanks,
Michael
Michael J Hall
Senior Fraud Investigator
Seico Life Insurance Co LLP

She sat perfectly still for a minute deciding on the best way to answer his email. Her instincts once again told her that he was lying. His email just seemed to brush her off, which didn't feel right. She decided she needed to meet him face-to-face, as was her way. She could call him, it would certainly be quicker, but she was always happier looking someone in the eye when asking them a direct question. Voices could hide a multitude of things, but eyes never lied.

She replied to the email right away:

From: *Kiara Fox*
Sent: *27 March 2022 11:50*
To: *Michael J Hall*
Subject: *Our Cases!*
Hi Michael,

> *Thanks for your reply.*

> *No worries at all, I'm sure it's all just a mistake. Out of interest, I'll be in Bristol in a few days seeing a friend, so if okay with you, I'll pop into your office and just say hi. It's always nice to meet my colleagues and talk about the job.*

> *See you soon, I hope.*

> *Thanks,*

> *Kiara*

> *Kiara Fox*

> *Senior Fraud Investigator*

> *Seico Life Insurance Co LLP*

"Kiara, are you ready?"

She looked up as Gemma walked through the door. Clearly this meeting was going to be very formal as Gemma hardly ever called her by her full name, usually preferring the abbreviated and more friendly 'K'.

"I saw you and MJ deep in discussion a few minutes ago. I assume it was about me."

"Not exactly."

"What does that mean?"

"I wanted to talk to her about the Powers case."

"So it was about me."

"No, it was about your case! You're starting to sound paranoid."

"Can you blame me? We're about to all meet, which is because

36

of what I have, or haven't done, and I see you two in a deep chat before I even get here."

"I wanted to understand why this case has got her so wound up, and I thought it would be easier to ask that if you were not in the room with us."

"Fair enough," Kiara said, giving her friend an apologetic look in the process.

"I wouldn't do that to you, you should know that."

"I do, and it's appreciated, really. So, did she give you a reason?"

"Kind of. She made it about the usual, late paying gives us a bad reputation, and all that stuff."

"But it's not the only late case. I've only just paid all my others, and I know I'm not the only one behind at the moment"

"I said as much to her. But she just brushed me off and said to come get you."

"Okay then. Let's go face the music, shall we, and I'll be good, I promise you."

Gemma led the way. MJ was sitting behind her desk concentrating on the computer screen as they let themselves in and each took a seat in front of her.

"Before you both start, can I at least tell you why I need just a little more time on the Powers case? I'm the one who's met Jane Powers face-to-face and I'm the one who's spent hours poring over the reports…" Kiara launched in, hoping to take control of the meeting before MJ did.

"Kiara, for Christ's sake!" Gemma interrupted her before she got them both into even more trouble. "Where did *being good* suddenly vanish to?"

"It's all right, Gemma, let her finish. She clearly thinks she knows more about what head office wants than I do. Go on, carry on, dig yourself into an even deeper hole," MJ snapped.

Kiara realised she had overstepped the mark and stopped talking immediately.

"Oh, is that it?" said MJ sarcastically. "Nothing else to say? Do you mind if I have a go now? I mean, it wasn't as if I called this friggin' meeting, was it?!"

"All right, I'm sorry. I won't say another word. It's your meeting, you go first."

"How kind of you. What the fuck, Kiara?!"

Her change of tone threw Kiara completely and she sat back straight in her chair. Gemma had been better prepared and was already trying to play the chameleon and blend in with her surroundings, trying to stay out of the line of fire.

"You were told to settle the Powers case. And then Saturday, after you took an unauthorised trip to the funeral, which you know I don't like you doing, you still ignored Gemma's instructions, which, by the way, came directly from me, your boss. Seico is not your company, Kiara, it is not your money…"

Kiara couldn't help herself, she had to say something to that. "It's not your money either, but…"

"Will you shut the fuck up for once and just listen," MJ carried on, her voice now two octaves higher. "You have no idea what goes on at head office or even why we need to sometimes overrule an investigator's advice. Sometimes they want to pay a case simply because it's good for our business reputation. Sometimes we are asked by the authorities to pay a case, so that they can follow the payment trail themselves and investigate a family who feel they are maybe out of the woods and then let their guards down. Sometimes our re-insurers decide to instruct us to pay a claim just so that their own statistics make them look good. And sometimes we just decide to pay a fucking claim without asking permission from our investigators. Do. You. Understand?!"

"Yes, of course I do. But…"

"But! Seriously, you have a but!"

"Look, I get it, I'm not always given the full picture. But, surely, it's my job to stop fraud. I've saved this company millions since I joined. More than anyone else. So, sometimes you just have to trust me."

MJ took a deep breath and let herself calm down before she replied. Shouting at Kiara clearly wasn't going to work, but she needed her to back away, for her own safety. And for the safety of them all.

"Listen, I really like you, you know that. I think of you as one of my closest friends. And I champion you all the time to the top brass, you know I do. But please, just this once, can you ask no more questions. Just let this one go. I've made the payment already this morning, so now I just need you to close the file and move on to the next case, okay? No more arguing, no more pushing back, just accept it, close the file and start clearing your other cases."

Kiara almost exploded. She leapt out of the chair and leant straight into the desk as close to MJ's face as she dared. "You paid it?!" she shouted directly into her face. "How can you do that without talking to me first? I've worked months on this...!"

MJ matched her in volume as she also rose from her chair and stared right back at her. Gemma stayed seated and quiet throughout the whole exchange, happy to not be in the middle of these two confrontational and passionate women.

"You would do well to remember whose office this is. Sit the fuck down!"

"Screw this. I want no part of it. If Mrs Powers killed her husband and you let her go..."

"You'll do what?! Phone the papers? Report it to the police? Who the hell do you think is in charge here? We are all just doing what we are told to do, and what proof do you have that Mrs Powers killed anyone...?"

Kiara had already stormed out of the room before MJ had finished the sentence.

"Go find her, Gemma," MJ said, a worried look etched on her face. "And, for her own sake, I really hope she listens to you as clearly I can't get through to her."

39

Gemma stood up and faced her boss. "Are you going to sack her over this? You know she's still the best investigator we've got here…"

MJ picked up her phone and pretended to make an internal call. "Just speak to her, Gemma. Now I've got work to get on with, and so have you," she said, finishing the meeting before Gemma challenged her further. As soon as she was left alone, MJ slumped back down into her chair and closed her eyes in frustration.

Gemma walked over to Kiara's desk and found her at the computer replying to an email.

"Well, that went well," she said without any irony in her voice.

"What the hell was that about? She basically paid my case out behind my back and then what, warned me to walk away and not do my job? What the hell's going on here?"

"I have no idea. But I can tell you she was super serious about it. You need to let it go this time. Whatever is happening, it's way above our pay grade."

Kiara's email sent and the noise as it left her outbox drew Gemma's eyes to the screen. Kiara caught her looking and pushed the screen down.

"Who was that to?"

"It was nothing. I was just sending an email to Mrs Powers to say the payment has now been made."

"Let it go, please. I'm serious, I've never seen MJ react like that before. She's going to fire you if you open this up again."

"It's done, okay? I know when I'm beaten. I'll close the file now, all right?"

"All right," Gemma said, not sure if she could believe her friend or not.

Kiara turned off the laptop and popped it into her rucksack. She gave Gemma a quick hug and promised her she'd go home, take the rest of the day off and start again tomorrow with a better attitude, and that she'd find the time to make up with MJ.

Gemma wanted desperately to believe her. She couldn't bear to think of the office without her there. She looked at the clock and decided ten-thirty in the morning was probably too early for a drink, so instead she headed off to find something to eat at the office canteen, stopping briefly at MJ's office to tell her that Kiara was definitely on board now, and that she would hear no more about this.

She felt sure that MJ believed her, and all was going to be okay, although in her own mind, she knew Kiara well enough to know that it was most probably far from over.

CHAPTER 8

Hotel du Vin – Bristol

Michael Hall had chosen a table in the corner facing the door. He sat waiting nervously for the lady to arrive. He looked around the bar, trying to spot her, but he had no idea what she actually looked like, as they'd only ever spoken on the phone. He had told her exactly where he'd be sitting, but so far no one had come up to him. He drained his entire glass of Merlot like it was a shot of whisky, before signalling for the barman to bring him another.

The waiting was causing havoc with his nerves and he was twitching more than usual. His nickname at school had been 'Elvis' due to his upper lip pulling to the left whenever he was feeling nervous or uptight. It had been years since he'd last felt this nervous, and about thirty years since the lip had made the energetic moves it did right now.

But tonight, it was no teenage angst causing the wobble; tonight was going to be a life-changing meeting and Elvis was most definitely leaving the building, but this time a lot richer than when he had come in.

Michael was a man who loved living life to the full, his ample waistline and reddened face stood testament to that. When once asked by a colleague what he would like on his epitaph, he easily replied, "Here lies Michael J Hall, he drank and ate himself to death and would do it all over again if given the chance."

The bar at the Hotel du Vin, apart from conveniently being directly opposite his office, was one of Bristol's most popular meeting places for company executives, certainly out of reach of someone on his pay grade, but with what he had coming to him, he reckoned that after tonight the barman would no longer have to ask him what he wanted to drink, it would be aged Johnnie Walker Blue Label every night.

The office of Seico Insurance was also just a stone's throw away from the art gallery where his wife worked. The thought of Rosie being just around the corner whilst he was negotiating a life-changing deal only made his lip twitch even more fiercely.

His office desk was nestled by the window directly opposite the hotel entrance and he'd been staring out at it all day, just counting down the minutes until the mysterious lady would arrive. At exactly seven forty-five, he had left his office and walked over the road to the hotel and then directly through the lobby, to the bar. He was fully ready for the seven-thirty meeting, having planned to be fashionably late, only to find that she was better at that game than he was.

Bloody woman, Michael thought to himself as he gulped down his second glass of red and checked his watch for the tenth time. No one had ever managed to intimidate him like she had.

He was pleased Rosie couldn't see him now, the sweat gathering on his forehead and the nerves reducing him to a twitching wreck. His wife of ten years was just about everything he had ever dreamt about but never expected in a wife. He'd never understood how he had landed her. It wasn't as if he was handsome, or particularly funny, and she certainly hadn't married him for his money. He was almost ten years older than her, which meant their childhoods were nearly a whole childhood apart. But, nonetheless, she had still fallen in love with him. And he was determined that one day he would be able to prove to her how successful he could be and that he could buy her any piece of artwork her heart desired. If he was her first love, then art was a very close second.

He gave the barman a nod to signal he was ready for his next drink.

"I'll have a large Black Label, lots of ice and a splash of water, in a tall glass please," he said, opting for a change of drink.

The barman nodded and went off to fetch it for him.

He leant back into the dark leather chair and reflected on the craziness that had brought him to this moment. Here he was, sitting in an overpriced bar, with no more than a few pounds left in his pocket, spending the last of their rent money on expensive alcohol, whilst his wife was just around the corner having to work extra shifts at the gallery just to help make ends meet. Not that she actually minded, the gallery to her was like the children they never had. Her love for art simply knew no bounds.

And yet, despite all that was unfair in their world, in the next few minutes, he was about to do a deal that would change their lives in an instant, a deal that would make all these people thinking he was just another loser drinking alone to take another look at him and realise he was a somebody, a real player.

It rankled him that he couldn't tell any of these strangers how rich he was about to become. He couldn't even tell Rosie. She was far too honest and would never have accepted money made from blackmail, unlike him, who had no qualms about doing to them what they were obviously doing to others.

But even if Rosie would have supported him, he still would not have been able to tell her. He had an agreement with the lady who had phoned him. It was the first thing she had said when she'd contacted him: complete secrecy was vital to the deal 'or else'. The meaning of 'or else' had come through very clearly in her tone.

Now that he'd proven to her that he'd deleted the file, tonight she was going to meet him face-to-face and then transfer the money to his account. He had no idea why she insisted on meeting him in person, but as he held all the cards, he decided he had nothing to lose. Also, he wondered who she was, if it was even someone from work. The curiosity had got the better of him and he had agreed to meet her in the flesh.

Once he'd seen her make the transfer of funds, all he'd have to then do was put together a story he could tell Rosie; that it was some kind of share windfall at work, or a gamble on the horses that went massively too well. He was sure he could convince her that their luck had finally changed.

The bartender put the whisky in front of him. Without looking up at the man, he instead glanced at his watch. His stomach turned. It was already past eight thirty, she should have been here an hour ago. The bloody woman. If she didn't show up soon, he'd have to wait for her to call him again, as he didn't have any numbers for her, only an email address that seemed to no longer be working. He needed the money now; he'd already spent most of this month's rent and he couldn't face Rosie and tell her how stupid he had been. The lady had to turn up or his life was about to get even harder.

He took a deep breath and pushed the negative thoughts away. Everything was going to be amazing. They had to pay him, he knew that they had no choice, otherwise he would report the case to the authorities and then she'd get nothing and likely be arrested for fraud.

He picked up the whisky and knocked it back in one go.

Why she thought he would actually delete the file, he had no idea. He was way too smart to just delete everything. Instead, he had kept a copy of his case on the main system and attached it to another case that was still open; a case that he'd found after hours of searching that was so similar to his one that it had to be another fraudulent one. They were clearly working on more than just his case and he wanted a fair share of them all.

He thought back to their last call; he was sure he'd been clear to her that he was no fool.

"Is it done?" she had asked.

"Yes. The file's completely gone from the mainframe."

"Only from the mainframe?"

"What do you mean?"

"Michael, please don't play with me. I can have the system checked if I need to. So, I'll ask you again, is it done?"

Michael had paused. He still wasn't sure how dangerous this lady was and even if she actually had access to the entire company data. Saving a copy of the file had been a last-minute decision at best. And hiding it in the main system by attaching it to another case seemed at the time a stroke of genius. He was sure it would stay hidden like that long enough for him to get his money.

"Michael…" she pushed.

He decided to gamble. "Let's just say I might have copied it onto another file as a precaution. Just until you pay me."

She replied without a pause, "You disappoint me, Michael. I thought we had an agreement. You would remove all trace of the claim and we would pay you a bonus to any account of your choosing. A million pounds is a lot of money. And now you renege on our agreement? So, what am I supposed to do now?"

"You were lucky it was me who found it and not one of my colleagues. If it had been any of the others, you could be sitting in a jail cell right now. It's only because I'm a little greedy that you'll get anything at all. But don't let my greed make you think I'm a fool. If I had deleted it all then you'd have no reason to pay me, would you? I'll delete it as soon as I have my money."

"And what about the other file you say it's attached to? What if that investigator sees it and starts asking questions?"

"I've already thought of that. If they see it, then they'll come to me first, won't they? And all I have to do is tell them it was an admin error. Unless, of course, they can't get hold of me, then I guess they'll start looking for another reason, won't they?"

"You're playing dangerous games, Michael."

"I'm just protecting myself, that's all. If anything happens to me, then your case will be investigated by someone you don't even know. But if you pay me my money, then I'll delete the case completely and no one will have known it even existed in the first place."

"So, we are at a stalemate, it seems."

"I just want what I'm due, that's all. If I get caught paying a fraudulent claim, then I'm the one who'll go to prison for this…"

She cut him off. "I understand, I really do. We don't know each other; we've not even met each other yet. So, how about we meet, in person, in a public place of your choice? I will transfer the money to you there and then, you can check it to make sure it is received and then you can delete the copy you took in front of me. Okay?"

He thought about it for a few seconds, playing it through in his head. A public place would give him security if she was out to harm him. And only he knew where the file was hidden, so would she really take such a chance? It was the perfect solution.

"Fine," he said, "but don't mess me around. All it would take is one call and…"

"I get it. You're the boss, Michael. You found us out. You're smart, no one has ever caught us before. We thought we were being so careful, but we never figured on someone like you. We could use a smart man like you in the firm. So, let's work together now, okay? We are very keen to do more, and you could be our partner. We need someone on the inside with brains and, quite frankly, the balls to be working with us. So, meet me at seven-thirty at the Hotel du Vin opposite your office tomorrow night and let's talk about the much bigger opportunity here, okay?"

He knew he should never have agreed to it, but a million pounds was so much money and all he had to do was settle a claim that he might have settled anyway had he not suspected fraud. And then he could delete the file or store a copy for extra safety. Literally a five-minute job and he would be set for life. And no one loses. Well, the insurance company would lose, but screw them, right? They'd never miss a few million, it was pocket change to them.

And maybe she was telling the truth, maybe this could be the first deal of many for him. She had sounded genuinely impressed with him. Perhaps this was the first of many jobs he could do for them. And what did it really matter? So, his company paid out a few more life claims than they needed to, who'd really notice, who'd really care?

He looked at his watch again. He'd give her another thirty minutes. He had enough money in his pocket for one more drink and, after tonight, he and Rosie would never have to worry about money again. Rosie would never give up her job at the gallery, though, she loved it too much, but for him work would soon be a thing of the past. He'd done enough for the company. He'd given Seico the better part of his working life and now it was time for his payoff. He'd do maybe two or three more jobs for her and then he would walk away from the job for ever, a rich man. He would spend his time sitting back in luxury whilst his wife could continue looking after her artwork, but without the pressure of the pound constantly bearing down on them.

"Sir, can I get you another drink?" the bartender asked over his shoulder.

"Eh, sure, but just a small single this time." He pulled out his debit card and just hoped he had enough credit left to pay the bill if the lady never turned up.

His phone rang on the bar, disturbing the few drinkers around him, drawing looks of disdain. He didn't care. Pretty soon, he'd no longer have to worry about what other people thought about him. He picked the phone up and looked at the screen. He didn't recognise the number, but he knew it would be her.

"You're late," he said with the bravado of someone who thought they were in charge.

"I'm sorry, I've been held up."

"You knew our arrangement. If I don't get my money today, I'll share the link with the authorities and the other investigator, and then it's over for all of you."

"There's no need for anything so drastic, Michael," she cut in. "I was held up on an important call, that's all. I'm now stuck at my office. Can you maybe jump in a taxi? I'll text you the address in a moment."

"You said we'd meet in a public place."

"If we are going to be having a business relationship going forward, then perhaps we should get to know each other, in, shall we say, a less public place. We need to start trusting each other now, don't you agree?"

Maybe it was the drink, but the way she said that... she sounded genuine enough.

"Okay, I'll come, but I want the money sent now. Otherwise, this is over."

"Check your account. I made a deposit earlier today, just to show good faith."

With shaking hands, he tapped on his banking app and pulled up the private account he'd set up in his own name just a week before. His heart almost leapt out of his chest when he saw a credit of a hundred thousand pounds in there. He was rich. His shoulders dropped as he felt the release of pressure, and for the first time in a long time, a smile started to form on his face.

"Michael, are you still there?"

He brought the phone back to his ear and looked around him to make sure no one else was eavesdropping on his call.

"I'm here. You only sent a hundred thousand, though," he said, the bravado having already returned.

"Of course. I needed to make sure you would do the right thing. I need to see the file deleted. You'll get the balance as soon as we meet. Then, well, we can celebrate our new partnership. There's a lot we can do together after this."

49

"Okay, send the address," he said, the endorphins suddenly surging through his bloodstream as he started to envisage the money that would flow after tonight.

Slowly getting himself up onto shaky legs, he made his way out of the hotel to see if he could find a taxi. As usual, even at this late hour, the streets of Bristol were packed with tourists and the roads were busy with cars and cyclists.

Unable to flag down a taxi right away, he decided the night air may actually be better for him. He left the hotel and headed behind it, under the bridge, towards the art gallery. Rosie should have been finishing work soon, so he decided to sober himself up with a short walk and then explain to her he had had to go back to the office for a few hours as one of his cases was looking suspicious and his boss needed him to make some overseas calls. He'd get Rosie to call him a taxi from the gallery.

He waited at the crossing for the lights to change.

A few seconds later, he was walking down the road towards the gallery, avoiding the idiots on their bikes and the stupid kids on their electric scooters. "They shouldn't let them on the pavement, for Christ's sake, especially not at this hour," he said to no one in particular, but loudly enough for them to hear.

From behind the glass wall at the entrance to the gallery, he saw her. He stopped mid-stride, his breath taken away as it always was when he saw his wife. Even from that distance, he could make out the pear-shaped figure of a classic English lady and he would swear in any court of law that the blue of her eyes were so vivid that they lit up the road in front of her. As soon as she spotted him, her face lit up. He loved the fact that she had this ability to somehow smile from her toes to her head; it was as if her whole body smiled at once. He'd see the lady tonight, get the rest of his money and then make his excuses and leave. He'd even stop on the way home and pick up a bottle of Rosie's favourite Merlot and a bottle of his favourite Johnnie Walker whisky and then tell her about his unusual win at the races.

"Michael, what are you doing here?" Rosie called from over the road. "Didn't you get to the gym after work?" she said, using the same joke she always used when she saw he was unsteady on his feet.

"Funny lady!" he shouted back over the noise, giving her the guilty look he always reserved for this very conversation.

"You haven't drunk too much, have you?" she called loudly over the traffic.

He couldn't quite hear what she said, but it didn't matter, she'd be in his arms soon enough.

As the last cyclist shot past him, he crossed with his usual impatience, not bothering to even turn to see the red sports car screeching around the corner.

He might have been overweight and not as fit as he used to be, but he was still nimble enough on his feet to make it across the road onto the square just in the nick of time.

"Bloody lunatic!" he shouted to the car as it sped off down the road.

"Michael," Rosie whispered, realising her husband had been inches away from a fatal accident.

As he walked towards her, his legs unsteady from the alcohol still in his system, Rosie noticed something strange out of the corner of her eye. The red sports car had turned around and was coming back towards them. Before she had time to react, the car had left the narrow road and had mounted the kerb onto the square, its front bumper ripping off as it made the small jump off the road. It drove directly at him at an incredible speed.

"Michael...!" Rosie's scream was lost as the car tossed her husband in the air before screeching off back down onto the road, gone before anyone could do anything about it.

CHAPTER 9

Seico Brighton Office

Kiara got to the Brighton office later than usual. Tuesdays were always a rush in the morning at the Fox house as the twins had to be up extra early for netball practice at school before the actual school day properly began.

The girls went to Hurstpierpoint College, a private school nestled in the rural village of Hurstpierpoint just outside Brighton. The fees were a struggle for Ash and Kiara, but the twin discount they got helped, plus the teacher discount they received from Asher being on the staff also lessoned the blow each month. At first, Asher hadn't been keen on the girls being privately educated, as he had gone to a local state school and had done well enough for himself, but having got a job at Hurst College himself, it was hard to resist sending the girls there when he saw the facilities the other children enjoyed. Not to mention the other teachers, who all seemed to want the kids under their care to flourish in any way they could. So, they both made sure they did all they could do to keep up with the fees, even if it meant Asher doing private maths tutoring at weekends and Kiara working harder than anyone else at Seico to do it.

It was also the reason she was running late for the office today. One of the claims in her backlog was for a member of staff at the school. Usually, she would not be given a case so close to home, but this one just needed someone to establish a couple of simple facts and then sign it off and, as she was there every day, she was the obvious person to do it.

After saying goodbye to Mia and Jasmin at the school gate, Kiara quickly ran around to the chapel where she had arranged to meet the headmaster.

"Thank you for meeting with me today, sir." Kiara felt it was appropriate to address the headmaster of such an important establishment formally.

"It is a pleasure, Mrs Fox. How can I help you?"

"I just needed to ask about Mr Saunders, and the accident that happened last month."

"Terribly sad indeed. Yes, well, he was not on school premises, as you are aware."

"Absolutely."

Kiara had read the file just two days before, when it had landed in her pile. Mr Saunders, one of the long-term drivers that the school employed, had died at the wheel whilst heading back to the college, having dropped off the girls under-fifteen netball team to Brighton college for an away game. The only fortunate thing in the whole tragedy was that the bus was empty. It would have been a completely different thing if it had happened on the way to Brighton rather than the way back. When Kiara had first read the file, all she could think of was the fact that Mia or Jasmin could have been on that bus. Life was so random that way. One thing her job had shown her over the years was that when you leave the house in the morning so much of what went on was down to chance, and sometimes in a terrifying way.

"I just need to ask you if he had looked unwell when he collected the bus in the morning?" she asked the headmaster.

"From what I understand, he was in fine order. I was actually the last person to see him. As was quite usual, he stopped for a quick chat before he left. He was taking the bus to drop the girls at their match and, from what I have been led to believe, he had a heart attack and died on the way back. The bus itself was hardly damaged, to be honest, just a scratch where it hit the tree at the end of School Lane, so he can't have been driving fast, can he?"

"I agree, all the evidence shows that he was driving within the speed limit. It was perhaps just his time, if you believe that."

"God works in mysterious ways," he replied.

Kiara added a few notes onto the paperwork to confirm that she had spoken to the last person the deceased had spoken to and then handed the headmaster the document and a pen.

"If I could kindly ask you to just sign your statement here, and here, then I can close the file and release the funds to his widow."

"Yes, of course. And thank you for coming all this way to see me, it is most kind. Please do send our very best to Mrs Saunders if you speak with her."

"Of course."

"And Mia and Jasmin, wonderful girls, are they enjoying this term?"

"Yes, thank you, they really love it here." She was always surprised that he could remember all the pupils names at such a large school.

"Good," he said as he waved her goodbye.

Kiara watched him walk away and then gathered up the paperwork ready to head back to Brighton.

"Hey you."

She smiled at hearing his voice. She turned around to see Asher walking across the inner quad towards her.

"Hey lover boy. Shouldn't you be in your class?"

Before grabbing her around the waist and pulling her into a kiss, he checked no one was looking.

"They are on a quick break. I just put them through a test on quadratic equations and I think I blew their minds."

"If I had any idea what you just said to me I might have some sympathy for them."

"It's a polynomial equation of a second degree where x is an unknown variable and a, b and c are numerical coefficients."

"Ooh, I love it when you talk dirty," Kiara replied, pulling him in closely.

"Ha. I should get back to them," he said. "I just saw you from the window and had to come over and give you a kiss."

"We really need a break, don't we?" she replied, longing to spend the rest of the day in his arms. "It feels like ages since we got away from it all."

"I know. I feel the same. Why is it that when the girls were babies we seemed to somehow have more time; how does that work?"

"I've no idea."

"Tell you what, at the weekend, let's plan something for the next half term. Somewhere, just us, where we can just be us for a few days and plan all the holidays and trips we can do when the girls go to university."

"University is years away!" Kiara said, throwing him a sulky face.

"True, but you've got to have a dream," he said, giving her his best smile. "Tell you what, why not look up Lake Garda tonight. You've been wanting to go to the Garda Bike Hotel for ages now. I can lay by the pool and you can spend the morning cycling the mountains and then I can spend the afternoons massaging your legs better."

"Crazy man!" she replied, her heart bursting with the love she felt for him in that moment. "Sounds like the perfect break. This weekend, okay, let's book it."

"Absolutely."

"Promise?"

"Promise," he said before winking at her and jogging back to his classroom.

Kiara walked back to the car, the thoughts of a weekend at Lake Garda now swimming around in her head.

She pulled out of the car park and headed back to Brighton,

making sure she drove slowly around the last corner in School Lane, more out of respect for poor Mr Saunders than anything else. She felt bad that it had taken over a month to clear this case as it had been so cut and dry. She decided on the drive back that she would file the Powers' case once and for all, forget about the Bristol case and just get back to working on any new cases that were passed over to her. Somehow, seeing Asher had once again put her in a good frame of mind, giving her the clarity she needed to tidy her desk. He always had that effect on her.

As soon as she was back at the office, she headed straight for her desk and logged onto the system. She marked the Saunders case as agreed and made the transfer of funds to Mrs Saunders' solicitor. She then dropped Gemma a quick email to confirm that the case was paid, and she only had another three to do now, all of which had only been passed to her a couple of days ago and which she would get done by the end of the week for sure.

Once she had emailed Gemma, she wrote an email to Michael Hall explaining that she was going to close down her own case after all and did not need to meet up. She wished him well, thanked him for his earlier reply and hit send.

Almost instantly, her inbox received a reply. She was surprised he could reply that quickly.

She opened the mail and saw that it was an automated reply:

From: *The office of Michael J Hall*
Sent: *28 March 2022 10:52*
To: *Kiara Fox*
Subject: *Our Cases!*
This email is being monitored and you will receive a reply shortly from our human resources dept.

We apologise for not responding immediately at this very difficult time.

Seico Life Insurance Co LLP, Bristol Office

Kiara read it through twice, trying to understand what was meant by *this very difficult time*. It was an odd reply as an out of office message.

"Paul?" Kiara called out to her assistant.

He popped his head around the office door, a smile on his face as always. "Yes, boss?"

"Can you do me a favour please and call the Bristol office and see if you can speak with a Michael J Hall for me? He's one of our investigators in the West Country. I just emailed him, and the reply was a bit odd. See if you can get him and patch him through?"

"Will do, I should be able to find his number on the system."

Whilst waiting, Kiara pulled up the Powers case to check it was marked as paid, so she could officially close it down. The linked case for Martin Davenport was still there and, whilst she desperately wanted to ignore it, her fingers took a life of their own and clicked on the link opening up the file.

She started to read the notes that Michael had made and was once again perplexed by the similarities to her Powers case. It still bothered her as to why he would link their two cases together on the system rather than just phone her. She also checked the dates, and like her own case it had taken a long time to settle, so it was obviously also more complicated than at first glance. She scrolled down more to see the date he had actually paid it. It had been settled a week before it had been linked to hers. She couldn't understand that. Once cases were paid they were instantly moved out of pending, but he had not done that, instead he had attached it to hers. It really made no sense at all. She scrolled down the file further to the bottom and was shocked to see that he had not been the one to pay the claim. It had MJ's signature next to it.

MJ took the case off him and settled it herself, why the hell would she do that, since when does she involve herself with cases down in the West Country?

This was nuts, she thought. Just half an hour before, she was ready to leave this case behind, and yet here she was again, about to reopen that can of worms. She closed her eyes and took a deep breath. This was not right. She had promised everyone, including herself, that she would let this go. Despite the sick feeling settling in her gut, she opened her eyes with a determination that she was going to just look the other way, close her case and not look back at it ever again.

She reached for the mouse to add her digital signature and then move the file to settled when her screen went blank for a second, before coming back to life and taking her right back to the main login page. She hated computers, they always seemed to glitch on her. She typed in her password to log back in and then put in the reference to the Powers case. But it now showed as no client record. With a sigh of annoyance, she retyped the Powers case number into the search box. It came back once again with no client found.

"Paul?" she called out to her assistant once again.

"Yes?" Paul said, coming back into the office.

"My case, Martin Powers, did you change the login code?"

"Nope. Maybe you put it in wrong, do you want me to have a go?"

"I definitely got it right, I know it by heart."

She tried to log in again, even slower this time and calling out the client reference, letter by letter, as she typed it in.

The screen still returned as no client found. It made no sense at all. So, she typed in the reference for the Martin Davenport case instead, both the one she had seen on the screen and then the correct one as it should have been. They also came back instantly with 'no client found' messages.

"What the hell's going on?" The butterflies in her stomach were suddenly awake and getting busy.

"Let me try," Paul said, stepping forwards to her computer. "What are the codes?"

Kiara wrote them down on her notepad for him and he typed them all into the login box one at a time. The same 'no client found' messages returned.

"Do we have any hard files for them?" Kiara asked, knowing the answer before she was given it.

"Sorry, but everything is shredded as soon as it's loaded." The phone on Paul's desk rang. "Let me just get that and then I can call IT for you to see if there's a way of recovering files."

Kiara tried to calm her mind as her instincts went onto full alert. No one had the access to delete client records completely. Maybe the directors did, but no one else could and even the directors had backups that they couldn't tamper with. That was the point of the system, it was why no paper needed to be kept.

But someone had just this second deleted the files; she had seen them vanish before her own eyes.

Paul came back into the room. His face had lost all its colour.

"What's wrong?" Kiara asked.

"That was the Bristol office. Your guy there, Michael Hall, he's dead."

Kiara stood up and leant across her desk. "Excuse me?"

"He's dead. He was killed after work last night. They didn't give me any details, other than he was involved in a car accident."

"I was only in contact with him yesterday."

She sat back down at her desk, shocked by the news.

"Could you get me his office address please, and maybe his wife's name if that's allowed? I think we should send a card or something. I might have been one of the last people to have contacted him. And could you close my door on your way out, please? I need some quiet time to think."

"Of course. If there's anything else…" Paul said, not sure exactly how he should reply.

After he had pulled her door closed, Kiara tried to let it all sink in. Something was way off here. First the files linking up together, the unusual pressure she was getting to settle her case, MJ's signature on both files, the papers vanishing from the system and now this, Michael Hall dead. She knew his death probably was a pure coincidence, car accidents happen all the time. But really, did she actually believe that?

She picked up her phone and dialled an internal number.

Gemma picked up on the first ring.

"Hey, K. Thanks for sorting the Saunders case. Just three more to go. Which one are you on now? The Bradbury case, I hope. It should be a quick one and I'm getting pressure to close it from the solicitor. It would be great to get two done today."

"You got a moment to pop into my office? I just need to run something by you."

"Sure, no worries, give me a second."

Gemma was there under a minute later.

"Shut the door, could you?"

"That sounds ominous. What's going on?"

"I don't want anyone else to hear this. I think we've got a problem."

Gemma took a chair and pulled it as close to the desk as she could. "Go on."

"It's the Powers case."

Gemma's face instantly showed her anger at the mention of that name. "Oh, for Christ's sake, I thought we were done with that. You're bloody killing me, here."

"No, it's not like that. Please, just listen."

"I'm not getting fired with you over this."

"Let me finish!"

She told Gemma everything she knew.

"But no one can delete client records, it's illegal, and I'm not sure it's even possible. Can head office even do that? Let me have a look myself."

Gemma moved to Kiara's computer. She typed in the

references Kiara had written down earlier for Paul.

"Are you sure you've got them right?" Gemma said, confusion on her face as nothing came up.

"Check it yourself. Put in their full names and the offices handling them. Try the amounts being paid. Try the dates of birth. I've tried all the search options, but nothing comes up."

"I don't understand, it's not possible," Gemma said as she sat on the edge of the desk, as close to Kiara as she felt was acceptable.

Gemma lowered her voice. "We need to tell MJ."

"Not yet."

"If something's going on where someone can access our records and then delete them, she needs to know. What if it's a hacker or something? Every case could be hit, it could close us down."

"That doesn't explain the accident in Bristol, does it?" Kiara added.

"That's just a coincidence, surely? You can't think it has something to do with this?"

"Oh, do me a favour, Gemma. They're clearly connected."

"I don't know, it's all a bit movie-like, isn't it?"

"Movies and real life are not always so far apart."

"So, what do you suggest we do?"

"I need to think it through, but telling MJ at the moment just feels wrong. She's been pushing way too hard to get me to do this. And then the file just vanishes; it's all too odd."

"You can't think MJ is involved in this, she's as straight as they come."

"I'm not suggesting anything. But her name was definitely on both these cases, I saw them both. I just need a little time to see if I can find the cases on the system somewhere. I can always get Callum in IT to help, he's a wizard. If I can't find anything in the next twenty-four hours, then we can meet MJ together and, if she's not involved, she'll take it to the board. Okay?"

"I'm sorry, but I don't believe MJ would do anything wrong."

"I never would have thought that either. But look at everything. I mean, she's not been herself lately, has she?"

"We need to tell her right away."

Kiara had been aware of Gemma's crush on her for months. Up until now it had been something Kiara had largely ignored. However, she decided this would be a good time to test if it was something she could use to her advantage.

She put her hand on Gemma's knee and squeezed it. "Please, Gemma, just this once. I'm scared something is off here and I don't know who else I can trust." She reached Gemma's hand and held it tightly, her little finger catching hold of Gemma's and curling around it. "Please, I wouldn't ask if it wasn't important to me."

Gemma's heartbeat jumped a notch and her face turned a shade of red.

"Okay, I guess. But what if someone can actually get into the system? It could happen again quickly and then what...?"

"I'll look into it right now, this minute, I promise. Just give me a day before we talk to MJ, okay? Just don't say anything yet to anyone. Please, Gem, just trust me on this."

"Okay, but please do it quickly, it's really scaring me now."

Gemma got up and Kiara did as well, giving her a hug.

"Thanks, you're a lifesaver."

"Well, you know me, I can't resist a pretty face, can I?" she said, trying to hide her embarrassment.

Gemma left the office and shut the door behind her, still slightly flushed at the intimacy between them.

Kiara pulled up the number for Callum in IT. She wasn't sure she should bring anyone else into this yet, but without his help, she knew she'd get nowhere.

Gemma walked past her own desk, went into the meeting room and closed the blinds before picking up the phone. She really didn't want to betray Kiara's trust, but she couldn't sit and do nothing. This was for Kiara's protection as much as it was for her own. And MJ wasn't just their boss, she was their friend as well. She'd always have their back.

"MJ, something odd happened today and I think you should know…"

CHAPTER 10

Seico Insurance London Office

MJ didn't want to call Sophia again so soon, but she had no choice. What Gemma had told her was a risk to them all.

As usual, once the security protocols had been cleared, the phone was answered quickly.

"MJ, twice in a week, that's unusual."

MJ took a deep breath before she started. "I think we still have a problem."

"Your investigator, Kiara?"

"Yes."

"*Sì*. My friend saw her bring Jane's file back up on the system. I had hoped that once her husband was buried we could leave Jane in peace, at least for a few months. But it seems your Kiara is like a *cane con un osso* and won't let it go."

"She's good at her job. It's why the company gives her so much latitude."

"So it seems. But we promised Jane that once her husband was gone, she could have the same life we have given them all. Now it's all at risk, isn't it? And it's not just a risk to Jane, it's a threat to all of us. She needs to be stopped."

"I'm trying."

"MJ, she has to be dealt with." This time Sophia said it with much more force.

"She's just doing her job. You always said innocents would never be a target." With silence on the other end of the phone, MJ carried on fighting for her friend. "And she's got a family, twin girls and a husband." MJ heard the deep breath on the end of the phone when she mentioned a husband and pressed on. "Asher isn't like yours or Jane's husbands, or my..." She still found it hard to speak about her own history, even after so many years. "Asher's really kind. If something happened to Kiara, it would kill him. And the twins, they are only fifteen..."

Sophia couldn't believe what she was hearing. "Why would you say that to me, MJ? When have I ever ordered an innocent's death? We only do that with the abusers. I'm shocked you think I would do that. How long have we known each other, do you really think I'm capable of that?"

"I'm sorry." MJ truly was. "I'm just worried. And after Bristol..."

"Bristol was an accident; it was never meant to go down like that. But Kiara needs to stop. She needs to be warned off. We need to make her think twice about pursuing this any further. I'll call my friend and tell her to make a visit."

"You don't know Kiara like I do. She's not one to scare easily."

"What are you suggesting I do, then? We can't just leave her. If she's as good at her job as you suggest then it won't be long until she works it all out. You know the consequences if we're discovered. So, what do you suggest I do to protect us all?"

Sophia waited for MJ to answer.

"I've already had the files deleted," MJ said. "So, I'm not sure there is even anything left for Kiara to follow up on. Maybe she'll have nowhere to turn now."

"Then why have you called me? If it's all been taken care of and we are not in any danger, then why have you called me again? Let me ask you a very simple – and perhaps direct – question. Are we in danger?"

MJ hesitated. She wanted to say no, absolutely not. She

desperately wanted to keep Kiara safe, to put this behind them and just carry on as they had been. But deep down, she couldn't. She knew Kiara wouldn't just walk away. She knew her too well. She would keep digging and digging, until she found the bones.

"Yes, I think we are in danger," MJ had no choice but to admit.

"Okay. Please don't worry yourself. I'll take care of the problem. I'll never let any harm come to our *famiglia*, never. We are sisters, all of us, and family is everything. You just carry on as usual and don't worry about a thing. None of this is your fault. These things happen and, when they do, it's my job to take care of them."

"What will you do?"

Sophia ended the call without answering the question.

MJ managed to make it to the bathroom just in time to reach the toilet bowl before both her breakfast and her lunch came flying back up.

★★★

Just twenty-two miles away from Seico's head office near London Bridge was Her Majesty's Prison Bronzefield. It was nestled in the heart of Middlesex and was home to the largest number of female prisoners in Europe.

Her cell was on the fifth floor, third from the left at the top of the last metal staircase and nestled into the corner. It was the biggest of the prison cells, which was fitting for one of their longest serving inmates.

She pulled the heavy metal door closed, sat down at the small corner table next to her bed and took out the second mobile phone she kept hidden within the cushion on the small wooden chair. It was no secret to the officers that she had a phone; in fact, they made sure she received a fresh pay-as-you-go sim card at the start of each month. It was the least they could do considering the money each of them received weekly from her. But they didn't know about this second phone or about the only person it was used to call.

She dialled the number that only she knew existed and waited until the seventh ring, knowing it would only be picked up on number seven. It was The Lady's lucky number.

"Sophia." The Lady's voice was soft and warm. It masked the true nature of the woman hiding beneath the veneer.

Even after all these years, Sophia was still the only person that The Lady would consider taking orders from, and The Lady was the only person Sophia truly feared. Their relationship was both complicated and simple in equal measure.

They had met in prison ten years earlier. The Lady was only a few years older than Sophia, but no one could ever actually say for sure what her age was from looking at her. She was, by all accounts, an unremarkable-looking woman, who one minute could look twenty years younger than she was and in another moment twenty years older, simply by the way she would position herself. If she wanted to, she could dominate a room by simply standing at the edge of it, or if she chose to, she could place herself right in the middle and somehow fade into the background and remain unnoticed all night.

And she loved no one, she never had; not her abusive father, not her alcoholic mother, not the foster parents she had murdered on her eighteenth birthday to just stop their constant bullying, and not even herself. That was until the day she had come face-to-face with Sophia. On that day, without being able to explain to herself why, she had felt a deep love for someone, and it was the first time in her life that she had felt vulnerable.

Sophia had felt nothing back for her, except perhaps fear. She would watch her with fascination, envious of the way everyone around her took a voluntary step back. It had nothing to do with size or strength, neither of which she had been blessed with. It was simply her aura. By being near to her, the other inmates just knew they were in the presence of someone unpredictable, someone who quite simply did not care about consequences.

It was during The Lady's second month in prison, during exercise break, that she first came to Sophia's aid, and their friendship began.

As she had done ever since being sent to prison, Sophia did her best to keep herself to herself, which was not always easy or even possible. When it was time for the daily exercise, she preferred to walk the yard on her own and avoid the gazes of the other women. Most of the inmates were happy to stay within their own small circles, avoiding clashes with other groups and trying to stay out of trouble in the hope that come parole day they had a chance of early freedom. But for some, the small minority who knew that they would likely never be allowed an early parole, women like Sophia were considered sport. They would leave the obviously stronger women alone, there was no great value in starting a fight that would inevitably leave one of them in the infirmary. Equally, they would leave the truly fragile and weak ones alone, as there was absolutely no sport in hunting down and stepping on helpless mice. Sophia had become an obvious target for them. She was beautiful, despite the scarring, she was prepared to fight back, despite her being one against their ten and she had no one else looking out for her. For years, she had found herself a target in their games. Sometimes it meant she had to take the verbal abuse thrown at her and just turn the other cheek. Other times it would become physical, leaving her with no choice but to defend herself, which out of necessity she had quickly learned how to do. And then there were those times when she was cornered in the yard and threatened with sexual violence when the lights went out. At those moments, even if the violence never materialised, she wished she had died in that fire along with her husband.

Then one day, seemingly out of nowhere, The Lady stepped up to protect her, and everything changed.

It had been a normal exercise hour, as far as she was concerned. The abuse wasn't a daily occurrence, so she never knew when it was to come. The atmosphere in the yard than afternoon was more heightened than usual, she could feel it, but couldn't see it. And the guards, being easily distracted, where being kept busy at the other end of the yard. As Sophia reached the halfway point on her walk, she came face-to-face with the most violent gang in the prison. She quickly tried to catch the attention of the guards, but she knew they were looking the other way on purpose. It was known in the prison that even the guards kept their distance from this gang if they were able to.

"You're in our corner now, matchstick."

She'd been called that the first time she had exposed her burnt skin to the other women; normally it was said almost ironically, but this day it was being delivered as a threat.

Sophia turned back to retrace her steps rather than take the bait.

"Where you going matchstick?" another one of them said, moving out of the group and standing in front of her, blocking her from walking back the way she had came.

She turned again to walk back, only to be blocked by another of them. Very quickly she found herself surrounded and in the middle of a pack of hyenas.

"Matchstick, you are going burn again."

"Want to play with us?"

"Can't wait to visit you tonight, matchstick."

"We are going to light the block up with you!"

The jibes came fast and furious, and each one was accompanied by a push or a shove.

"I don't want any trouble," Sophia said to them.

"You don't get to choose, matchstick."

"We got ourself a bonfire to have with you tonight."

Sophia has no idea why they had chosen her today, but she knew her life and her sanity were now in danger. She'd heard about this happening before, she'd been warned. When this gang got it into their head that it was time to party, they would choose a loner, someone without any backup, but someone they knew would fight back and give them at least the opportunity of sport.

No one saw The Lady step into the middle of the pack. Sophia had heard the other women talk about the new inmate with a sense of fear and awe, but until that moment, she had never seen her in the flesh. She looked at her now and was surprised by how ordinary she looked.

Before anyone had a chance to speak, The Lady put both her hands into her pockets and just as quickly drew them out, clutching a small razor in each. Without a moment's hesitation, and with the speed and grace of a bird, she drew them across the necks of the two women closest to her. As both women fell to their knees, blood pouring from their wounds, she dropped the razers on the floor and took Sophia's hand. She moved her away from the gang and back onto the path where she had been walking. They were gone in the blink of an eye. No one saw it happen.

"Keep walking, and never talk about this to anyone," The Lady said to her, before leaving Sophia back at the entrance into the yard.

In the time it took Sophia to understand what had happened, The Lady had seemingly vanished back into the crowds of other women.

The two women from the gang died there in the yard, surrounded by their friends. Despite the governor suspecting it had been The Lady who had killed them, she had no way of proving it. The murders were put down to internal fighting in the gang and no more action was taken. As far as the governor was concerned all that had happened was that two of her most troublesome inmates were gone and the gang, now leaderless, had become much less of a problem for her.

Exactly a week later, Sophia had a visit from the governor herself.

"You are no longer going to be living alone, we have a new

roommate for you. And we are moving you to the cell on the corner, the biggest cell."

Sophia said nothing, she knew better than to talk back.

"Your life in here is going to be a lot easier from now on, as long as you do this one thing for me."

Sophia still stayed silent, but gave the slightest of nods to say she was listening.

"I suspect you already know your new roommate. Not that we can prove it, but she was the one who saved your life."

Sophia's face showed the shock that she felt at that statement.

"You don't think we know everything that happens here? We knew that your life was in danger, but there was little action we could take without them first doing something. But then she stepped in and saved you. I have no idea why she did that, but it seems to me that she has taken a liking to you."

"What do you need me to do?" Sophia asked.

"I don't know why she helped you, or what hold you have over her. But she's only got five years and I need her to do that with no more incidents, I want her gone as soon as possible. I need you to control her. If you do that then I promise you you'll be protected long after she is released. If you don't, then once she is gone, you'll go back to your old cell and you'll be on your own. You understand what I am saying?"

Sophia didn't understand, not really, but she had no choice.

"Sorry to call you so late at night," Sophia replied to The Lady, "but I have another little job for you."

"It's never too late for you to call me, you know that."

"*Salute.* I hope we don't have to do this by phone much longer. But for now, I have another problem that is in need of your particular *abilità.*"

"So soon?"

"*Sì,* I'm afraid so. You know how these things are. Unless one cleans up properly, there will always be some spillage."

"What do you need?"

"There is a problem I need taken care of. It's a little job down by the coast. I'll send you the details. But we can't have another Bristol. We can't *ever* have another Bristol."

"Of course, I'm sorry. Bristol was difficult. It was not meant to happen like that, I was just planning on scaring him, but he stepped in front of the car, and…"

"He wasn't meant to die. I told you to pay him the money, and then warn him of the consequences of taking this further."

"He never would have stopped, you do know that, don't you? He had kept a copy of the file on the company's mainframe. He would have been a problem for ever."

"Innocents can never die. I've told you that. I'll never ask you to take innocent lives."

"He wasn't innocent, though, was he?"

Sophia took a deep breath. She knew The Lady was a killer, cold blooded and without remorse. It was always a danger bringing her in. But also she needed those skills. Who else would be able to take care of the husbands, who else would be able to keep her widows safe?

"I need you to be more careful this time. This woman is a danger to us, but she is innocent. She is just doing her job. She needs to be stopped, though, we can't have her finding us." Sophia had to think carefully as to how to say this. "Do whatever you need to do, but do not take her life. Do you understand me? Do not take her life."

"I understand. When do you want this done?" The lack of emotion in her voice was chilling.

Sophia let out the breath she hadn't realised she had been holding in. "Give it a few days, let everything settle down. But be careful… I don't need to tell you your job, do I?" Sophia said, trying to match her friend's tone exactly, but not quite getting it right.

"Of course not." She wasn't used to Sophia criticising her

work, it was something that had never happened before. She felt the hairs on her neck bristle at the tone of Sophia's voice. But she said nothing back, she would never speak back to her.

"Stay safe," Sophia said before ending the call abruptly. She put the phone back into the tiny pocket hidden in the cushion. In just a few weeks' time, she would finally be free of this place, and she couldn't let anyone get in the way of that happening. She had spent most of her adult life in prison for self-defence; over half of her life taken from her by her abusive husband. She would give up no more of her life for him.

But balancing out her desperation to leave prison was her need for revenge. As the years went by, it had consumed her almost as much as the fire had.

If all went as she'd planned, she would be out of prison before the summer. She closed her eyes and thought back to the beginning. She took herself back to the fire. She could still feel the heat as it seared her flesh, still taste the smoke in her mouth as the left side of her face succumbed to the flames along with the house that had become her first prison.

As much as the memory pained her, she never wanted to forget what had brought her here. It was as much a part of her today as it was the day it happened. It was the reason she still existed. She ran her hand over the right side of her face, the undamaged side. The skin was so smooth that it never gave away fifty-five years of living, and she marvelled at how, even after all those years of being locked away from the outside world, her beauty had hardly faded. She could see from the way the guards and the other prisoners still looked at her that she was as beautiful as she always had been, until they moved their gaze to the other side and saw the scars and wasted skin, and then turned away in disgust.

But she loved both sides of her face. To her, they represented who she had been and who she had become. They were literally the two different faces of her life.

CHAPTER 11

Bristol
– Bristol Police Station

Rosie had heard enough from the two policemen.

She knew what she had seen. The car had missed her husband the first time, then had completed a sudden turn on the narrow road, drove back towards him, mounted the pavement and then sped off after hitting him. She saw the murder firsthand and yet the police were still insisting it was a hit and run accident.

"Mrs Hall, we do not believe that this was a deliberate act towards your husband. There is no evidence to support that this was anything more than reckless driving. We will find the driver, I can assure you of that, and they will be charged with his death, but unless we find anything to the contrary we will be treating this as a manslaughter, not a murder."

"Until you find the person who was driving that car, you cannot know for sure that it wasn't deliberate."

"Mrs Hall, we do know that. Other witnesses saw the accident…"

"But I saw the driver!"

"What you said you saw and what you actually saw are perhaps not the same thing."

"You're saying I'm lying to you, why would I do that?!"

"I am not saying that at all. It was dark and the car was travelling at high speed. And you saw your husband… you witnessed your husband…" He struggled to find the right words without causing her more pain.

"Go on, say it! I saw my husband die right in front of my eyes."

He paused before answering, allowing both Rosie and himself time to catch a breath.

"Yes, you did." He said it slowly and calmly, but not unkindly. He could see the pain she was in, but still he was not willing to stoke the fire by helping her believe something that simply was not true.

"You saw something terrible, something no one should ever have to see."

"And because of that, you think I am making this up, is that what you are saying?"

"No, that is not what I am saying. You were distressed, Mrs Hall, as anyone would be, and you thought you saw something that in fact you did not."

"I know what I saw, the driver drove past him once, then deliberately turned back and drove into him!" Her voice rose again in frustration.

The policeman referred to the papers on his desk.

"Firstly, no one else saw the car turn around. The witnesses only saw it drive onto the pavement, which they said happened because it took the natural turning of the road too fast."

"I saw it."

The policeman continued reading his notes as if she hadn't replied. "And then you said you saw what appeared to be an elderly woman driving the sports car, at high speed. You said that she was perhaps in her seventies, but you could not be sure because she was driving so fast." He looked back up at her and continued. "And therefore, you are suggesting that after this elderly woman drove into your husband, on purpose, she crashed the car into a wall and sprinted off down the street so fast that she got away from everyone. That is correct, yes? So, you tell me, Mrs Hall, does that not sound a little far-fetched to you?"

"It sounds very far-fetched to me. Of course it does. More so when you read it back. But it's what I saw and what I know to be the truth. My husband was murdered, and you need to investigate it as a murder."

"Mrs Hall, it was an accident. A young driver, perhaps a woman, perhaps a man, lost control of a very powerful vehicle, and sadly your husband happened to be crossing the pavement at that exact moment. It was a terrible accident, but an accident nonetheless."

"Please stop calling it an accident, it was deliberate murder. My husband works as a fraud investigator for an insurance company, he is – was – working on fraud cases. Maybe he stumbled onto something, and someone needed to stop him. Whoever it was he was looking into did this to him."

"And they sent an elderly woman in a sports car to run him over. Do you really believe that? I mean, if you are going to deliberately kill someone would you risk doing it as a hit and run, which by no means is a guaranteed success"

"I don't know, I'm not a murderer. I mean, maybe it was not the way she had planned it, but she saw him crossing the road and just took the chance… and, oh I don't know, I just know what I saw."

He looked at her squarely in the eyes and dared her to keep talking. He could see that she had no way of answering him.

"Mrs Hall, I assure you that we will do everything in our power to find the person responsible for this terrible crime and not a stone will be left unturned, but please let us do our job. I will keep you informed if and when we find anything out."

Rosie had left the police station before the sergeant could finish talking.

It had been two days since her husband had been murdered and, apart from visits to the police station and one to the morgue, she had been all alone, simply walking around their small apartment, room to room, with nowhere to go and no one to talk to. With no family of her own and having never bonded with Michael's family, she had no one apart from her colleagues at the gallery, and at the moment they seemed unable to know what to say to her.

She wanted answers and walking around a lonely apartment was not going to deliver them to her.

The office of Seico was only a short walk from her office at the gallery, so once she left the police station, she headed straight there before going to work and facing everyone. Her husband was an investigator, and the fact it was for an insurance company rather than the police force didn't make it necessarily less risky. He had often come home from work and told her about cases he had been working on, some of them involving millions of pounds in fraudulent claims. His job clearly was not without risk. Maybe he had stopped a fraudulent claim being paid and this was a revenge attack, or maybe he was chasing up a suspect and someone wanted him stopped before he found them.

She knew it sounded crazy and too much like a movie, but until she found out why this had happened, she was prepared to look at every scenario, no matter how it looked.

"Rosie, I am so, so sorry." Michael's colleague came from around her desk and took Rosie into a close hug. "I can't tell you how upset we all are. Michael was so full of life, such a character, I can't believe…"

"Please," Rosie interrupted her, pulling out of the embrace. "I know it was a shock to you all, but let us not pretend my husband was popular. He was loud, rude and he bullied you. I know that. But I loved him, I can't explain why, but I did. He was kind to me, and he loved me so much. But he was no saint, and I am sure the office will be, perhaps, easier without him."

"Rosie, I, we…" Mary stumbled on her words, unprepared to have been caught out like this.

"Let's just be honest, shall we, I prefer that, really. I just want to collect a few personal pieces from his desk, photos and such, and then I will leave you all alone to talk about him as you no doubt have been. If you could just give me the key to his office and then I can be gone and out of your way."

She handed over the key before quickly moving out of the way as Rosie marched past her into Michael's office.

"I'm not sure she's allowed in there?"

Mary turned to see her office manager come over. "I wouldn't go there if I were you. I was telling her how we are going to miss him, and she almost took my head off. She told me that she knew how we all really felt about him and, well, I think it's best just to let her take his personal things and then go."

Patrick stood back, happy to have not been the one to have faced that. "Perhaps you're right," he replied. "But don't let her stay too long; if anyone in head office knows she's in there, we'll be in serious trouble." He walked away from her desk, pleased to be able to stay uninvolved.

Rosie hadn't been sure her approach would work, but she knew how the office used to speak about her husband behind his back, she had heard it herself at office parties. It seemed to her that the best way of getting what she wanted was to throw it back at them and embarrass them enough to just let her pass. It had clearly worked, but she was now so embarrassed by her performance that she had to be quick and get out of there before anyone else challenged her or realised the subterfuge.

She sat behind his desk and switched the computer on. Luckily, his desk was in the corner of the room and couldn't be seen from the open door, but still, she wasn't sure if anyone in the office would see his terminal suddenly appear on a network or something. However, she had no choice, she had to take the chance and hope she could get away with it.

The screen sprang to life and prompted her to put in a

password. She knew what it was. Michael was the most indiscreet person she had ever known. She had seen him type in his password a thousand times. Even in public spaces he seemed not to care who was listening in or watching him, and on more than one occasion, across a room, he had called to her to remind him what his password was as it changed each month and he'd give it to her for safekeeping.

She was momentarily surprised when the screen had come to life, as she'd assumed that his password would already have been changed since his death. Luckily, it hadn't yet been reset, and she was in and staring at his emails. She went straight into the inbox and looked at the latest ones, most of them still unopened. She scrolled through, just glancing at the subject lines to see if anything jumped out. None of them meant anything to her as they were mostly all internal from other people in the office. But there was one that stood out as it had been flagged by him as important and was a different colour to the others. She clicked on it and saw it had come in from the Brighton office. The mail was short, just asking for a meeting, an urgent face-to-face meeting.

Michael only ever dealt with local cases; he had told her a hundred times that, whilst the company had offices all over the country, he had no interest in travelling and would only deal with claims in and around Bristol. So, why was he in contact with an investigator from Brighton? She forwarded the email to her home address and then went into the sent files and deleted it as a sent item. Then, for extra safety, she cleared it out from his deleted box as well. She had seen enough spy movies to know that emails were easily traced, and this at least was something simple she could do to protect herself.

She turned the computer off, grabbed a few photos from his desk and headed out of his office, trying to maintain her initial attitude.

"Did you get everything you wanted?" Mary asked.

"Yes," she said, and dropped the keys on the desk. It felt uncomfortable to Rosie to be so curt with another human being, but she didn't want them to suddenly see a softer side to her and keep her here talking longer than she needed to be.

"Okay, well, I'm truly sorry, we all are."

"Thank you," she said, with little emotion in her voice.

They stood looking at each other for an uncomfortable few seconds, and then Rosie turned on her heels and left.

Mary turned to Patrick and gave him a look that said she was pleased that was over, and then she sat back down and carried on with her own work.

★★★

A few hundred miles away, in a prison cell in Middlesex, England, a mobile phone vibrated as a message came through.

Sophia pulled the phone out of the cushion where it had been hidden and read the screen.

I am taking care of Brighton this weekend, but have another problem. When can we talk?

She dialled the number from memory and waited for the seventh ring before it was picked up.

"Sorry to disturb you again," The Lady said as she picked up the phone on the other end. "But we have another problem in Bristol. It's his wife…"

CHAPTER 12

RAF Parachuting Centre

At six o'clock in the morning, the sun was not fully up and the grass at the side of the airfield in Oxford was still wet from the morning dew. Kiara, being an early riser, loved this time of the morning, but for Asher it felt like the middle of the night. Most mornings, Kiara would be out of the house by 5.30 so she could get an early morning run down Brighton seafront before work, enjoying the smell of the sea and the noise of the waves to get her day started. Sometimes she even took a small towel with her, tied around her waist and braved the sea to cool down after her run. Asher, on the other hand, always got up at 7.10 on the dot, just as the twins were crawling out of bed, giving them just enough time to get dressed, grab some breakfast and be at school by eight o'clock.

"Come on, Ash," Kiara said, "look at the sky, it's beautiful, there's not a cloud in sight."

"All my eyes want to see right now are the inside of my eyelids."

"Lucky I drove then, isn't it?"

"Dragging me and the girls out of our warm beds at – what was it – four o'clock is not how we like our Sundays to start. You're lucky we came at all. Me driving was never going to happen."

"Don't be a grump. You're going to love it. Trust me, by the end of the day, you'll be begging to jump again."

"You mean you will. I'll be safely waiting with the girls, fast asleep, thank you very much. Hold on, what do you mean *jump again?*"

"Well, actually, there was something I'd forgotten to mention to you," Kiara said as she pulled the car into a parking space at the airfield.

Asher suddenly realised where she was going with this. "If you think…"

"Come on, Ash, live a little. It'll be great, the two of us soaring through the sky, superman and superwoman, saving the world."

"No way!"

"Asher Fox, you will be doing this with me," she said, climbing out of the car.

"No way," he said, following her and the girls as they walked towards the main office block. "You might want to risk your life like some adrenalin junkie, but my feet are staying firmly on the ground, thank you very much. When you're finished, you'll find me and the girls in the café over there, unless of course, the girls get the urge to go shopping, and then, if you live through this nonsense, you can come to Oxford city centre and find us there."

"I don't mind a bit of shopping, Dad," Jasmin cut in.

"I'm not missing this, it's brilliant," Mia said to her sister.

"Oh come on, it'll be fun," Kiara said, taking his hand in hers.

"Not a chance," he said, laughing at her and pulling his hand away. "I married a crazy woman," he said to the twins.

Kiara just shrugged and gave them a smile as she turned around to see if any of her workmates had arrived yet.

Kiara looked at her family standing there and smiled to herself. She knew he'd end up jumping with her. Kiara was the adventurer in the family, the one always dashing about and getting into life, whilst Asher was by far the more sedentary of them. But one of the things she really loved about him was the fire in his belly that she was able to ignite when she wanted to. She knew if she pushed him in just the right way, he'd have no choice but to meet her challenge head on. Deep down, he hated walking away from things, his DNA simply wouldn't let him. He wasn't sporty like she was and had no real interest in competing against anyone else, but he was fiercely competitive against himself and he hated the thought that she might think he was weak and pathetic if he didn't step up to the plate. Of course he knew in his heart that she would never think that, she would love him no matter what he did, but there was still that old-fashioned part of him that felt the man should not be afraid.

"So are you going to do it, Dad?" Mia asked.

"Not a chance," he replied. "Anyway, I never did the paperwork or signed anything, did I, so it'll be too late even if I wanted to."

"It's okay, darling, I did your forms the same time I did mine," Kiara said.

"Of course you did," he replied, shaking his head knowingly.

"See, he's so going to do it," Jasmin said.

"I know," Mia replied, causing all of them to laugh.

"Of course I am," Asher replied.

"Hey, Kiara!"

"Kieran, how're you doing?"

Kieran was one of the admin assistants at the Brighton office. He had only been with the company a few months, but he was already the blue-eyed boy; far too handsome for his own good, bristling with confidence. Outside of work, he just happened to be one of the youngest trained skydiving instructors in the country. He was a bit too boyish good-looking for Kiara, but the other ladies in the office swooned every time he walked in.

"The team are already there, you guys are the last."

"How can we be the last, it's barely six-thirty?"

"Most of them stayed over. I always use a little B&B around the corner when I come here. I sent an email around the office about it. Didn't you get it?"

"I don't remember seeing it. I've been pretty busy, if I'm

honest. MJ needs me to clear up my cases, so I've only really been looking at work emails lately. Is MJ here yet?"

"I haven't seen her. She didn't stay over either. She knows it's a seven-thirty start, though, so she's probably already at the hangar with the others or in the café. I should go over to the office and get the health and safety forms together. You guys can have a look around the airfield if you want, it's quite cool here, and I'll get all your suits and helmets ready."

"Hey, K, why didn't you stay over last night?" Gemma came marching over to them. "Hey Asher. Hey girls."

"What time are we jumping?" Kiara asked Kieran.

He looked at his clipboard. "Asher, you're booked on the third flight, you're on the second one, Gem, and Kiara goes first with me and Bob. I'm doing them all, actually," he said with a smile in his voice. "I'm the one videoing it all. If the weather holds, we could do the first jump in about an hour or so. Come on, Gem, let's go and round the crew up and start getting everything ready," Kieran said as he linked arms with Gemma and steered her back towards the office in the green hangar.

"Do we have time to grab a very quick coffee?" Asher asked him as he was walking away.

"Sure, but be quick. I need you both in the hangar in about half an hour."

As the Fox family walked towards the café, they passed another small office that was seemingly locked up. None of them noticed two ladies at the window openly staring out at them.

"You need to get to the hangar," the older lady said to MJ as she continued to stare out of the window at Kiara and her family as she walked past.

"What are you going to do?" MJ said, a genuine pleading in her voice to not go too far.

MJ had never felt so sick about anything in her life. She knew that, despite everything that they had been through, Sophia still had limits as to what she would have The Lady do for them. No innocents should ever die. Sophia had told her that time and time again and she believed her. Sophia made the final decisions, it had to be that way. But The Lady frightened her. She knew she had gone rogue in the past and was capable of doing evil things. She had no idea what Sophia held over her to control her like she did, but she also knew that The Lady could be unpredictable, and even Sophia couldn't always stop her. Just being near her made MJ feel frightened out of her wits.

"I'm just going to send her a warning, that's all," she said as she watched Kiara walk past the window.

"You don't know Kiara like I do. Sophia isn't here, she's not on the ground like I am. I can get Kiara to back away without any need for violence."

The lady turned from the window to look at her. "I never said there was going to be violence. I'm just going to speak with her children when they're alone."

MJ looked horrified. "You can't, they are just kids!"

"Just a friendly chat. Kiara needs to know we are watching them, and they are vulnerable."

"Let me talk to her first, please," MJ pleaded.

The Lady rounded on MJ, making her take two steps back until she was leaning against a wall and couldn't go any further.

"I think it's clear you've already tried talking to her and she hasn't stopped, has she? If she exposes you then she exposes me, and Sophia, and then all of the widows. Do you really want that to happen? Do you want to be locked away like Sophia? How do you think you would cope being locked up in a small cell for twenty-three hours a day, caged like an animal? Are you really ready to face that yourself? Because if we are found out, then that is what will happen. I can tell you, I for one won't let that happen."

MJ found it hard to speak back to The Lady, but she had no choice, her friend's life was on the line. "Please, just leave her family out of this, surely there has to be another time you can do it, when the kids aren't there, when she's on her own." MJ knew that given a chance she could get Sophia to listen to her and call The Lady off. Sophia and her had been friends since university, they were practically sisters, she was sure she would listen to her.

The Lady wasn't taking the bait. "We are only weeks away from Sophia's release, she finally gets out and you want to risk taking that away from her? We don't have the time to wait, I will talk to them today and you had better do as I say."

The threat was clear. MJ could see the darkness in her eyes, and it scared the life out of her. She knew she had to fight harder for Kiara. The thought that this lady could hurt Kiara or her family made MJ feel sick to the stomach.

But she also knew The Lady was right, she couldn't risk them all being exposed. Not now, not ever.

"What are you going to say to them?" she asked in a resigned voice.

"You don't need the details. Just do as I tell you and go find your team. I've got everything in place. You just need to make sure nothing changes, the girls will be on their own when their parents are jumping. You understand me?"

"I understand."

MJ left the office by the back door and then traced it around to the front, careful to stay out of view of the café, and headed for the hangar where everyone else was waiting.

Back in the café, Asher had got his coffee and a croissant whilst the girls had a donut each. Kiara just grabbed a bottle of cold water, she was more nervous than she was letting on and couldn't even consider coffee or breakfast at that moment. *He's much braver than me*, she thought, looking at Asher.

"You sure you don't want anything?" he asked her.

"I'll have something after," she said.

Asher knew she was scared, but he loved her too much to say anything. Instead, he just gave her a wink and let it go.

"Come on, girls," he said to the twins, "Mum and I are about to jump out of a plane."

With that, Asher grabbed his coat. "You guys go ahead of me, I'll see you by the hangar, I just need to use the toilet before I get into that ridiculous jumpsuit."

"It's okay, we'll wait for you, we've plenty of time," she said.

"I won't be a minute."

Kiara watched him walk away. She always knew he would end up doing the jump with her. He would never have let her do it alone. She really had found her soulmate with him.

As soon as he was back, she followed him out of the café, with the twins either side of her, and they made their way over to the others at the hangar.

"I thought maybe you'd chickened out," MJ said to Kiara as soon as she joined them, trying to hide the fear she felt.

"Not a chance!" Kiara replied, ignoring the odd tone in her friend's voice. She put it down to the fact that they were probably all a bit anxious about the impending jump.

"Hi girls," MJ said to the twins. "Is your mum letting you two do it as well?"

MJ's eyes started to well up and she had to turn away before Kiara noticed.

"Yes, Mum, please, we'll do it as well," Jasmin and Mia said in unison.

"Absolutely not!" Kiara replied.

"I'm sorry, girls, but you're still a little young for this. Maybe in a couple of years' time, though," Kieran chipped in.

Both girls looked disappointed.

"Sorry, girls, not a chance, now or in the future," Asher joined in.

"Right, can everyone grab a jumpsuit please? I just need to

find Neil. I'll only be a minute." Kieran went off in the direction of the office, leaving everyone to rummage through the pile of jumpsuits to find the right size.

"This is so cool," Bob said, holding up an extra large.

"Bloody *Top Gun*," Raj added with a huge grin.

Kiara grabbed a medium and handed Asher a small.

"All right everyone, gather around," Kieran called to the group. "This is Captain Neil Laughton," he said, introducing an impressive fifty-something man dressed in full skydiving gear and sporting a head of pure grey hair. "Neil is a legend; he was my instructor and is the best in the business."

"I haven't dropped anyone yet," Neil said with a warming smile.

"Apart from that time..." Kieran added.

"Yes, apart from then. But we'd been married a long time..." Neil finished their usual joke and let Kieran carry on.

"Neil will go in the first plane along with Andy, our other instructor. That's him over there by the yellow plane. We've also got Ian who'll be taking over from Andy on the second flight." Kieran checked his clipboard again. "Kiara and Bob are first. I'll be going along as well on all the flights as I'll be solo jumping, taking video and still pics of you all. Then we'll land safely and the guys will take MJ and Gemma on the second flight." He checked his clipboard again, even though he knew the order by heart. "Then Asher, Raj and Jules will go on the third flight."

"Kieran, I think we need to adjust that first flight," Ian said as he wandered over from the plane to join them. Ian was dressed like Neil and Kieran in the yellow jumpsuit that marked out the instructors, whilst everyone else was dressed in blue. "Apart from the new arrivals, everyone else has already weighed in and, looking at them, I suspect that she weighs a bit more than him – sorry, I didn't get your names," he said, addressing Asher and Kiara.

"I'm Ash and this is Kiara," Asher jumped in first. "I don't mind going first and K can take my place on the third go if that solves the problem. I can then sit with the twins and we can watch her cry as she comes down. That all right with you, my darling?" Asher added, giving his wife a poke in the side.

"I don't mind either way. It's not a surprise I'm heavier than my husband, as muscle weighs much more than fat," she added, poking him back, drawing a smile from everyone, including Asher, but embarrassing Ian as he suddenly realised what he had said.

Neil carried on from where his colleague had left off. "When we jump, we have to calculate weight ratios as well as height differences. When we're strapped together and flying through the air, our heights and weights must complement each other."

Ian looked around the group and made some mental calculations in his head. It was definitely better to take the husband first.

"As long as we all come down safely, I couldn't much care when I go," Kiara replied, finally managing to get the zip up to where it should be.

"You'll all be just fine," Neil said. "We complete on average four tandem jumps a day, four to five days a week, and so far, we've not had so much as a broken finger, let alone a fatality. This is safer than driving a car, and you're in the safest hands in the business."

"That's good to know," said Jules nervously.

Ian left them and headed over to the hangar by the plane, leaving Neil to take the group through the basic training.

"When we go in the first plane, the rest of you, including you two young ladies," he said, addressing Jasmin and Mia, who had wormed their way to the front of the group, "would be best to sit over there," he said, pointing to the corner of the airfield. "We'll be landing over there by those crosses, so you'll get the best view as we come in, and you'll see their faces as they land, pretty as a picture, I promise."

"God, I hope I don't get sick," said Raj.

"You'll be fine, sugar," Gemma said, taking his arm in hers, catching Kiara's eye and giving her one of her flirtatious winks.

Kiara grabbed Ash by the arm and pulled him closer, kissing him firmly on the lips. "Not long now, superman," she said, sensing his sudden nervousness now that things were starting to get serious.

"Right then, everyone!" Neil had to shout above the noise of the plane engines as they started up. "There are a few simple rules I need you all to follow." He walked forward, grabbed Asher by the shoulders and pulled him in close. "There are some important things you need to know."

"Number one is don't let go of the instructor!" Mia shouted out to her dad, drawing a giggle from her sister.

"Right then," continued Neil, placing Asher in front of him and clipping the back of his safety harness to the front of his own jumpsuit, "hang from me, young man, and put your legs between mine," he said to Asher.

"Excuse me?!"

"Like this." Neil pulled Asher off his feet and dangled him in front of him as he bent over in a skydiving position. "There you go, as you can see, he is safely strapped onto me in the front and his feet are tucked up between my legs. When we jump from the plane, this is exactly the position we'll take, except instead of your feet being between mine, they will be directly under mine. As soon as we jump, you will put your hands in a cross over your chest and keep them there until I tap you on the shoulder. Go on then, let me see."

Trying to look as dignified as he could whilst hanging between Neil's legs, Asher crossed his arms over his chest in that typical *X Factor* pose that Mia and Jasmin had perfected over the years.

"Perfect. Right then, as soon as we jump, you'll take this position and hold it for around thirty-to-fifty seconds. Then I'll tap you on the shoulder again and I want you to uncross your arms and hold them in front of you like superman."

Asher did as he was told – to the great amusement of the twins.

"Perfect. As you can all see, so far very easy. We'll freefall like this for seven thousand feet, which will take less than a minute. During this time, Kieran, our daring film producer, will be freefalling with us and taking photos and a DVD of you, so feel free to give him the thumbs up and the happy smiles.

"Once we hit five thousand feet, I'll tap you on the shoulder again to tell you to pull your arms back onto your chest into the X position and I'll release the canopy. You'll feel the sensation of us shooting back up, but in truth we'll just be slowing down; Kieran, however, will leave his shoot for some time and fly ahead of us so that he can be landed and ready to film us coming down. The final five thousand feet will be a gentle drift downwards and a chance for you to enjoy the beautiful Oxford countryside for a few minutes.

"The next bit – the landing – is where I need you to relax back and really let me do all the work. All I need you to do is curl your legs up as high as you can go; knees to chin, if possible. As we come in, I will bring us down onto my legs and slowly bring us to a halt."

"What happens if I put my legs down first?" Asher asked nervously.

"Why would you do that?! He just told you not to, didn't he?" Jasmin jumped in, showing everyone that, even at fifteen years old, she was picking it all up.

"It's okay, young lady, it's a fair question your dad asked. It's best to let me take us down, but if I see your legs are too low then I'll simply bring us down onto my backside and slide us along. So, your legs will be fine, as long as you let me take control.

"Right then, everyone, any questions?" He waited a few seconds for a reply. Receiving none, he lowered Asher to the ground and undid his clip. "Excellent. See, I told you, all nice and simple, just do as I say, and it will be the best ride of your lives."

"Hiya, boss man, sorry I'm late, I was checking the chutes."

"No worries, Andy. Everyone, this is Andy, our third instructor. As he said, it's always best to check and double-check the chutes. We always do our own before every flight, and each have our own names stitched to the bags to avoid any mix-ups, but as a precautionary measure, as instructors, we also check each other's; you never can be too safe, can you? Right then, Andy, you're with that chap over there," he said, pointing to Asher, "and I'm with this big guy," he said, taking Bob by the shoulder. "When Ian is back, he'll take the rest of you to get some water and then you hang out and watch the fun. You two come with me and Andy," he said to Asher and Bob.

Ian was walking away from the hangar with his eyes down on his phone having checked the parachutes himself when he bumped into someone. "I'm sorry, that was my fault," he said, looking up.

"It's no problem, young man," The Lady said as she bent down to pick up a piece of paper that he had dropped.

Ian didn't really notice anything about the older lady as she handed him back the list of names and then turned and walked away. If he had bothered to look back, he would have seen her go directly into the hangar instead of going around it, but he never did look back, he had no reason to.

"There you are, mate, is everything all right?" Neil asked as Ian joined them.

"Yes, all good and ready to go. I've left Andy's and your first chutes by the hangar and mine and your next ones are in the back room. I've marked them one to three for you for each flight."

"Excellent, Ian, thanks. Okay everyone, follow Ian and he'll get you settled. You two come with us, it's time to fly."

Ian looked at the crowd and then back at Neil. "I thought you were taking the lady on the first one?"

"I didn't realise how big that other fellow was until we had them lined up," Neil said, gesturing over at Bob. "I think this is a better ratio, especially with that slight wind lift."

"Okay, no worries," Ian said, as he pulled his list from his pocket and started to change the order of names, "you're the boss."

Asher and Bob followed Neil and Andy back to the hangar to collect the parachutes, which were clearly marked with the instructors' names as promised, and then they headed to the small yellow plane that had finished its taxiing and was parked just to the side of the hangar with its propeller spinning around.

Neil had to raise his voice once again to be heard above the noise of the plane. "Bob, I think you should go with Andy and Asher can go with me. You okay with that, Andy?"

Andy sized the two men up, and whilst both were similar weight, Asher was the shorter of the two, which fitted better with Neil, and also he was clearly the more nervous. Andy nodded his agreement that the last-minute swap was a good idea; he certainly thought Neil would handle the nervous one better than he would.

Asher smiled. Flying with the lead instructor felt like winning the lottery at this point. Andy clipped Bob to the front of his own suit and gave it a big tug to make sure he was properly clipped in. Neil did the same with Asher. Kieran had joined them and was already wearing his helmet, with a GoPro strapped to the front. He was also holding a portable camera that was strapped to his wrist.

"You guys ready?" Kieran asked them above the noise, a huge smile on his face.

Asher and Bob looked at each other. "I guess so," Bob said.

"Sure," Asher replied nervously.

Kieran pulled back the plastic door of the plane and stood aside for the others to get in before him.

"Put these on, please." Neil had produced a hat and goggles from a bag he was holding. "Make sure that they fit tightly, especially the goggles, as it's not only cold up there but when we freefall the wind speed is massive."

Both pulled on their hats and placed the goggles over their eyes.

"We'll go on first and to the back," Neil explained, "then Andy and Bob will follow, then Kieran last. We exit the plane in reverse of this order, so Kieran will jump first, but he'll hold onto the side while Ian and Bob slide out and he'll stay there until you and I go as well. He'll be taking photos of us as we leave the plane and then he'll freefall down, faster than all of us, grabbing pictures on the way down and then he'll meet us all on the ground so he can capture photos and video for us all as we land. When we get on the plane I'll sit first and then Asher you need to really snuggle close to me, almost on my lap. Bob, you'll do the same with Andy. Other than that, just leave it all to us."

As the five of them climbed into the plane, Kiara, the twins and the rest of the Seico team were led by Ian over to the grassed area where the landing would likely take place. Rugs with bottles of water had been laid out for them already. Luckily, the sky was blue, the sun was already out and the day was perfect for sitting and watching the RAF airbase come to life.

Apart from the Seico team, there were a number of other groups being shown around preparing for their jumps and there were another nine small planes taxiing around the airfield.

"I'm scared now, Mum," Mia said to Kiara as they settled on the ground.

"Grow up, Mia!" Jasmin shot back, acting like the older sister she was, bearing in mind the minute she had between their births.

"Shut up, Jas, you're scared as well!"

"No I'm not," Jasmin replied.

"Chill, girls," Kiara said, putting her arm around them both. "Dad's a superman, isn't he? He could fly down all on his own. I'd be more worried about me, if I were you, you know how clumsy I can be."

MJ sat in the middle of the group feeling sick. She knew she had to draw the girls away from the group somehow, but every fibre in her body screamed at her not to. She couldn't let The Lady get near the girls. She suspected that, at some point, the girls would want to go to the toilet or to get a drink and she would be following them then. All she had to do was make sure she stayed with them the whole time. There was no way she would approach them with her there.

She could even get a lift back to Brighton with them and stay the night; that way, nothing could happen on the way home, either. She could tell them she fancied staying over and visiting the Brighton office the next day. They'd have no reason to question that, she'd stayed overnight with them many times before. And it would give her time to call Sophia and straighten it all out. She was absolutely sure she could get her friend to let her sort the issue out. There was no reason to scare the children, or even to warn Kiara off. She could find a way to stop her looking into the cases, she could just settle the claims herself and put Kiara onto other ones. She knew Kiara would put up a bit of a fight with her, but ultimately, she was her boss and she had the right to do that. *Bloody Kiara*, MJ thought, *that woman is so bloody stubborn.*

Having planned it all in her head, she suddenly felt herself relaxing and her shoulders became less tense. She settled herself back in the knowledge that all would be well and decided she should enjoy the rest of the morning with her friends.

Across the field, the yellow plane had started to roll down the small runway. It reached maximum speed quickly and Asher could feel the bumps as it sped down the field. The noise from the ground and the bumps dropped away as the plane floated into the sky. He could still hear the propellers as they span, but it was a distant hum and everything else around him was silent for a moment. As the plane climbed higher, he noticed the plastic door start to suck in and out, slowly at first and then more violently as a greater height was reached.

"It's normal," Neil said as he sensed Asher tensing up. "As soon as we reach our fifteen-thousand-feet target and level out, we'll slide the door back and the noise will stop."

"Is that meant to be comforting?" he shouted to Neil above the din of the flapping plastic door.

"I thought so," Neil said back sarcastically. He put his hands on Asher's shoulders. "I've done this a thousand times, my friend, you're in good hands."

At fifteen thousand feet, the plane levelled out and Kieran shuffled forward, pulling back the door, as promised.

"You ready, Andy, Bob?"

"We're good to go, mate," Andy shouted back, not giving Bob a chance to say no.

Kieran shuffled forward and, without a second's thought, slid himself out of the door. Asher gasped as he realised Kieran had left the plane.

"Relax," Neil whispered to him.

"Here we go, Bob, our turn," Andy said as he slid forward, making Bob shuffle ahead as he was in front of him. Andy went right to the end and forced Bob out of the door until he was dangling, feet down, into the open air and Andy himself was sitting comfortably on the edge of the doorframe, his own feet down and outside. Andy took Bob's head in his hands and forced his head left, facing the front of the plane. Bob couldn't believe what he saw.

"Smile, my man!" Kieran shouted to him above the deafening noise.

Kieran was hanging off the wing, holding his camera in one hand and waving at Bob.

"Smile for the camera!" Andy said a second before he shuffled the last few inches and he and Bob fell forward out of the plane.

Neil by now had shuffled himself and Ash forward and, before Ash knew it, he was also hanging feet down in the middle of the sky attached to Neil, and having his head forced left to face a beaming Kieran.

"Asher, give the biggest smile for your girls!" Kieran screamed before he let go of the wing and darted downwards, diving towards Andy and Bob at an incredible speed.

"Hold on," Neil said as they tumbled forward into the open air.

Asher's scream couldn't be heard above the rush of the wind.

Seven thousand feet below them, Andy had opened his parachute and Bob experienced what he would later describe as the brakes coming on. It felt like they had come to a complete stop, when in fact they were still heading down, but at a much-reduced speed.

Bob's face said it all.

"You okay?" Andy said as he tapped Bob's shoulder and brought his arms back from a superman pose to the *X Factor* cross.

"Oh my God, oh my God!" Bob screamed. "It's bloody amazing!"

Kieran had his arms out in a flat position that slowed him down so he could take a few pictures before he then pulled off left and waited for Neil to let out his parachute and stop Asher just in time for him to take a few snaps.

Before he had time to react, Neil and Asher shot past him, the turbulence they caused knocking him sideways, forcing him to correct his position and not fly off course.

Neil should have had their chute up by now. Kieran looked down and saw them falling fast, spinning out of control. He quickly adjusted his pose and pulled his own arms in by his side and dived downwards in an attempt to catch them before they reached an altitude where all help was futile. He reached his own final safe height before he reached them, and he had no choice but to pull the chord on his own parachute or else face certain death.

As he was jolted to a sudden stop, he saw them continue downwards in a death spin.

Back on the ground, the twins had their eyes fixed on their dad.

"Mum, what's happening?" Mia said.

"Mum!" screamed Jasmin. "Why is Dad spinning like that?!"

"Mum!" both girls screamed as they saw their dad was in trouble.

Kiara couldn't answer them. She was frozen in place, not willing to believe what she was seeing.

Asher had already passed out by the time he and Neil hit the ground. Neil hadn't been so lucky. His experience as a skydiver and ex-special forces gave him the mental capacity not to panic and to stay alert. For the briefest of seconds, he envied Asher.

Kieran, Andy and Bob landed safely under a minute later. By then, a crowd had already formed around the crushed bodies, and the sound of the emergency services was ringing in the air.

Kiara sat back down on the rug, the twins tucked in next to her, all three of them in a state of shock. The rest of the Seico team, along with Ian, had jumped up on their feet the moment they'd realised what was happening, but there had been nothing they or anyone could have done to save them.

MJ didn't know where to look, she only knew that she couldn't face looking at Jasmin and Mia after they had watched their dad crashing into the ground from fifteen thousand feet. And she knew that if she caught Kiara's eyes then she would know without a doubt, that she would see it written all over her face, that she had been the cause of the death of her husband.

MJ turned away from them and looked towards the exit of the RAF airfield, towards the road that led out of the airbase. There was a single lone car going in the opposite direction to the emergency vehicles that streamed in through both the entrance and the exit. The car waited at the side for all the vehicles to pass it before pulling back out on to the main road. It was a small, white hatchback, a most ordinary vehicle, and it was being driven by the most unremarkable-looking Lady.

As it pulled into the distance, MJ knew what she had to do.

CHAPTER 13

2 Greyfriars Close, Hove

11ᵗʰ May 2010
(Twelve Years Earlier)

*H*e was going crazy, more than ever before. *After years of abuse, Sophia instinctively knew that this time it was heading to a whole new level of pain. Her memories took her back to the A&E hospital ward she worked on before she was married and to the many broken bones and damaged organs she'd witnessed from the domestic violence cases that were brought in. At that time, she never for a second expected that she would end up being just another one of those statistics. And she could not have known at that moment just how badly this night would end.*

As usual, it had come from nowhere. She had been in their bedroom putting away the ironing when she heard the front door slam and felt the footsteps reverberate in the floorboards as her husband pounded up the stairs like a raging bull. She knew she should hide, she looked around in desperation, but it was their bedroom, there was nowhere to go where he wouldn't find her. The door flew open with such force that the inside handle struck the wall behind, causing a deep gouge that would still have been there today if not for the fire.

"Where the fuck were you?!" he screamed at her as he marched into the room.

"What d-d-do y-y-you m-m-mean?" she stammered. Her stammer was always accentuated when she was scared.

"What d-d-do y-y-you m-m-mean?" he copied her, giving his voice

100

an almost cartoon-like quality. He was always patronising when he was starting to lose control.

It had been the same when she was a child growing up. When she was frightened, which was most days when her drunken father poured into the house at the end of the day, her voice would tremble, and the words would barely come out. She was forced to speak slowly in front of him, and her father would tease her nastily about it before hitting her mother and blaming Sophia for giving him a daughter who couldn't even speak properly. She realised that she had let history repeat itself.

"Well, where were you?!" *her husband screamed.*

What did I forget? Where was I meant to be? *Sophia racked her brains trying to remember.*

He stepped forwards and punched her so hard in the face that her head span and she fell to her knees. She could feel the blood start to flow from the tear in her lip.

"Get up and answer me. Get up!" *he bellowed.*

She got unsteadily to her feet. She breathed deeply to make sure the words came out clearly, so not to rile him any more than she had to.

"I'm sorry. I forgot." *She said the words slowly, trying to remove her stammer and her accent, as she knew that they would rile him even more; both were traits that when they'd first met he had found so sweet and alluring.*

"You don't even know, do you?"

"I'm sorry," *she said, lowering her eyes to the floor. She could see the blood drip from her mouth onto the cream carpet and she briefly wondered if she would ever be able to get the stain out.*

"The fucking hospital! You were meant to pick me up from the fucking hospital. But I suppose since you quit your job there you've forgotten it even exists."

"I never quit. You made me stop working."

"I never quit, you made me stop," *he copied her once again.*

Suddenly she remembered. He was presenting his thesis on bowel cancer and the ways in which his early alert system had proved such a success in the local study. He was now ready to apply for major funding to expand it into the national arena before finally going worldwide. Today was his big meeting.

He had told her a month ago that this study would prove his theory beyond a doubt and that if today's presentation went well then the hospital board would add their weight to his application for the next tranche of money needed for him to at last stand on the world stage along with all the other professors in the hospital, the professors who looked down on him because of his age. She remembered clearly the venom in his voice when he talked about them.

"Your presentation. Oh my God it was today. I'm so sorry." She tried to keep the fear out of her voice.

"For Christ, speak properly," he said, shaking his head, but with less force in his voice.

Maybe he wasn't going to go nuclear after all. She took a tentative step towards him, hoping he would remember the amazing work he was doing and focus on that rather than her.

"Did they give you their backing?" she asked as sweetly as she could, despite the swelling in her bottom lip.

"Of course they did!" he roared, the anger coming back like a bursting volcano.

He stepped up so close to her that she could feel the heat rising from his body.

"It was all great until I was left standing at the entrance to the hospital waiting for a lift home, looking like a fucking prick in front of everyone. That's how it fucking went."

She had no time to react. The punch hit her so hard in the stomach that she doubled over in pain. The second punch was as hard as the first and was followed by a third delivered so quickly that her nose shattered before she crashed onto her back almost out cold.

"I knew you'd forget!" The kick in the ribs was given before the sentence was finished.

"Everyone else's wives were there waiting." He bent down and grabbed her hair, pulling her to standing.

"*Everyone else's wives had their car doors open.*" He punched her so hard with his right hand that, as she fell onto the bed, he was left standing with a clump of her hair in his left hand. "*That's how it fucking went, you bitch!*" His spittle sprayed over the bed and hit her in the face. She desperately wished she would pass out and no longer be present. But she just lay there, still conscious, the pain so bad her face was starting to go numb. Her left eye was already swollen shut, but her right eye could see everything. She could no longer hear his words, but she could see his mouth screaming at her and she could see the pictures crash one at a time as he grabbed handfuls of her perfume bottles and her hairbrushes and anything else he could find and flung them at the walls all around the bed.

Then she was up again on her feet. He had leant onto the bed and grabbed her once again by her long, red hair and lifted her up to standing. She could feel the strength in his arms and had no way of defending herself.

Her husband was not the usual professor type. He was the youngest at the hospital by two decades and was built more like an American football player than a doctor. Even in the best of times, she was no match for him physically. He flung her across the room like a rag doll. She crashed sideways into her dressing table, breaking at least two of her ribs and fracturing her ankle as her foot twisted backwards.

"*And if you had bothered to show up on time, you would have seen them all congratulating me on the fantastic presentation I gave.*"

Surely, she heard wrong. It went well? They gave him the money? Then why was he so angry? It made no sense. She tried to speak, to ask him why he was so angry with her, but her mouth was so swollen that the words would not form, and no coherent sound would come out. But he could read her lips all the same.

"*What?!*" he screamed into her face. "*You want to know what's made me angry?*" He laughed at her. "*You have no idea, do you? We've been married what, ten years, and you still don't know me. Why am I angry?*" He got so close to her again that his spittle washed into her face. "*After all I am doing to save lives. After all I am doing for everyone out there dying of cancer. And you not only don't come and pick me up afterwards to congratulate me, but I have to tell you again what I was doing today. Do I really deserve so much disrespect from you? Do I?!" he screamed.*

He took in a deep breath. He looked down at her lying in a heap on the floor and shook his head sadly. He stared at her once beautiful face and sighed to himself as the blood around her face caused her remaining good eye to blink rapidly. Her mouth was turned down in pain as she clutched at her broken ribs.

He walked backwards and sat on the edge of the bed. He stared at her and shook his head in pity.

He lowered his voice, the edge still there, but he became much more controlled. "This can't go on, can it? Everything I am doing to make other people's lives so much better and then I have to come home and face this." He looked around the room as if she had caused the mess rather than him. "It's just not right, I don't deserve to be treated like this. I think it's time we put an end to this, don't you?"

She tried to focus her mind over the pain. She couldn't work out what he meant. Was he going to divorce her at last? Was he really going to set her free from all these beatings? She had tried to divorce him after just the first few months of marriage when he had started to hit her. But he wouldn't let her. And no one ever believed her when she tried to tell them what he was like. Until today, he had never hit her in the face, he had never left any visible signs of the abuse he made her suffer. So, no one had believed her. And no one would listen when she told them the professor, the kindest and most thoughtful man they knew, could possibly do such things to a woman. They branded her sick. Deranged. So, eventually, just like her mother before her, she took the abuse and never spoke about it to anyone.

But today was different. Today he had hit her so hard, and in the face, that there was no way he could get away with it. Not unless...

"It's time to end this." He was still talking, more to himself than to her, and he pulled the door shut as he walked out of the room. She heard his footsteps as they skipped down the first set of stairs. Then she heard the next door open and his footsteps down on the second short flight of stairs to the garage.

She realised this was not like the other times. She understood with a sudden clarity that she had to get away before he came back. At last, she now had the proof of what he did to her. This was her chance of exposing him for the monster he was.

She tried to get herself up, but the pain was suffocating. He must have damaged her lungs when he broke her ribs.

His footsteps on the lower stairs were her signal to put the pain aside and move, it was literally now or never.

With strength she never knew she possessed, she reached up to the middle drawer on her dressing table and pulled herself to standing.

His footsteps were now on the main staircase. The way he was skipping and humming to himself made it sound like he didn't have a care in the world.

She staggered towards the door and stood behind it, hiding herself from the entrance.

The handle turned and the door swung open. It hit her foot and stopped it moving further. He didn't acknowledge the fact that they don't have a doorstop and that the door seemed to swing back at him, he was enjoying himself too much to care about the little things.

Without stepping fully into the room, he threw an open bottle of a hundred proof cooking brandy from the doorway onto the bed. It splashed all over the duvet and spilled onto the carpet.

He calmly pulled a cheap lighter from his trouser pocket and lit a cigarette.

"How devastating it will be when they call me at the hospital to tell me my wife was drunk and burnt our house down. Luckily, I have just renewed the insurance policy."

He threw the cigarette onto the bed and, in an instant, the feather duvet was alight.

"Now, my darling, I think it's time you went to bed," he said as he walked further into the room, expecting to see her on the floor curled up into a ball.

Before he could register that she was no longer on the floor where he had left her, he was given a sharp push in his back, which set him off balance. A second, more desperate, shove pushed him down onto the bed.

His hair caught alight as he fell face first into the brandy soaked duvet. The fire spread quickly to his eyes and then to the rest of his face. He pushed himself off the bed, screaming in pain, but by now his whole head was ablaze.

The next thing to catch fire was his white work shirt and tie and then finally his black crease-free chinos. In a matter of seconds, he was fully ablaze, stumbling blindly around the room and howling like a wounded animal. She stood there, rooted to the spot, fascinated, just watching as her husband of ten years was cremated alive.

The fire had spread to the curtains and the carpet as quickly as it had to her husband, and it felt like she was standing inside an oven. Her husband, the learned professor of medicine, the wife beater, stumbled into her, forcing them both out of the bedroom door, into the hallway and then tumbling down the stairs. He was dead by the time they reached the bottom. The fire spread fast as it followed them out of the bedroom and touched everything as it went. By now, she had managed to crawl to the front door, her body in agony from the beating she had taken and her head sizzling as the fire had managed to grab hold of her red hair and was now creeping down the right side of her face. With a last desperate effort, she reached up and twisted the door handle.

Outside, a crowd had gathered as black smoke was escaping through the cracks in the window and the flames licked behind the glass higher and higher. The door suddenly was open, and two pairs of hands took hold of her wrists and dragged her out on to the grass. She felt the heat die down on her face as a blanket was used to put out the flame. Then there was a voice she recognised from somewhere in the crowd. MJ, is that MJ she could hear?

A man's voice took over asking her questions.

She couldn't make out his words. Something about someone else? About her husband? Was he asking her if her husband was still in there?

She managed to mouth a reply, not sure if the words had come out. Her body no longer hurt and the fire on her face was oddly warming. He had to be dead, she felt sure he was. His days of tormenting her were over. She no longer cared if she lived or died, she only cared that he couldn't hurt her any more. She managed a weak smile before her eyes closed and everything went dark.

CHAPTER 14

Prison Cell

*F*or the first few years of her sentence, Sophia had had a prison cell all to herself and had spent every waking moment of it in fear for her life. She'd suffered endless taunts by the other prisoners about her disfigured face and had fought off repeated attempts by sexual predators, both fellow prisoners and guards. She knew that, one day, her strength would give out and they would get what they wanted from her, but until then, she would fight back with every bit of energy she had left.

And then The Lady was shown into her cell.

The guards slammed the cell door shut the second they could, leaving Sophia to whatever fate had in store for her. But fate is a very odd thing and sometimes its designs are much more complex than you could imagine. In front of her eyes, she witnessed a change in her new cellmate; it was minute, but it was palpable. Gone were the threatening charcoal eyes that had forced the guards to fear for their lives and that had made the other inmates unwilling to challenge her. Instead, they were replaced by almost bluey grey eyes that were both soft and kind that they seemed to reach directly into Sophia's heart looking for a friend. And gone was the feeling of death that The Lady had worn over her shoulders like a shroud when the guards had led her into the small room a moment before, and in its place was almost nothing, as if The Lady had breathed out her personality and what was left was something almost gentle. In fact, Sophia had to look hard into The Lady's face to make sure that it was still the same person facing her that had just come in and that there hadn't been a magic trick that swapped out one person for another. She seemed so different that Sophia had to really look at her closely to make sure her eyes weren't playing tricks on her.

The Lady reached out a hand and took Sophia's in hers. "It looks like we are going to be sharing this cell until I can find a way to escape this place," she said, so gently that Sophia had to lean in to catch the words. "Just so you know, I am in here for manslaughter. I was given five years. In truth, it was murder, but they couldn't make that stick, so I was given the lesser charge. I was sloppy. It'll never happen again. I believe we'll be sharing this cell for the remainder of my stay, and I don't want there to be any secrets between us, I'd really like us to be friends. Now you know my secret, it means we can be honest with each other, doesn't it? So, tell me why you are being held here?"

She waited for Sophia to respond. "Um, well, um, I'm Sophia. I am in here for murdering my husband. I was given a life sentence for killing him. He died in a horrible way, in a fire," Sophia said easily. There was something about The Lady that made Sophia feel completely at ease saying this.

"Did you murder him?" The Lady asked.

"No. Well, not exactly. It was self-defence."

"Were you pleased he died?"

"Yes."

"Did he abuse you?"

"Yes."

"Then he deserved it." She said it with no more affliction in her voice than if she was asking for a cup of tea or a piece of cake.

"Why did you save me," Sophia asked her, "in the yard, from those women?"

"I don't know," The Lady said honestly.

"They were going to hurt me."

"They won't be hurting you now."

Sophia felt a weight leave her shoulders. "I won't let anyone hurt me again, not ever."

"Good, and I'll make sure they don't," The Lady replied.

"And I am going to get my revenge, on all of the abusers. I am being treated like a murderer, so will do my best to live up to it and make all of them pay for what happened to me. I am going to make every abuser pay for what they are doing."

Sophia had at last put into the open what she had been planning all those years since the judge sent her to prison for simply saving herself.

"Now we know each other's secrets, we can't betray each other, can we?" The Lady said, still holding tightly onto Sophia's hand. "So, now we can be friends."

From that day on, life in prison took a dramatic turn for Sophia. Not a single inmate or guard tormented or threatened her any more. In fact, it was quite the opposite. Everyone could see that The Lady was not only Sophia's friend, but also her protector.

Over the weeks that followed, the power in their cell seemed to change as well. The Lady, who everyone seemed to fear, had fallen under a spell that Sophia had not meant to cast. Neither of them truly understood what had happened, but The Lady would do anything for Sophia and had made it her sole mission to make sure her cellmate's plan became reality. The Lady had become the Luca Brassy to Sophias's Don Corleone. Everyone in the prison feared The Lady and The Lady seemed to fear Sophia.

The guards allowed them to eat first. They allowed them extra exercise time. And they even allowed Sophia to keep a secret phone stashed in her cell, so that she had access to the outside world. As long as Sophia kept The Lady away from them, they would give her anything.

Life in prison settled into its routine. Sophia and her new cellmate kept themselves to themselves and everyone around them was happier for it. The days were repetitive, boring, but at least they now had each other for company. And with Sophia allowed to have access to her phone, it meant she could stay in contact with her closest friend on the outside, MJ. They had been friends since university, living together while they completed their nursing degrees and being almost inseparable until Sophia had married. From then on, they hardly saw each other. Things got gradually worse as MJ would question the bruises that Sophia would try to hide and would try to get her friend to talk. Things came to a head when one day Sophia turned up to their monthly lunch date with straps around her body to still the pain of her broken ribs. MJ couldn't sit there any longer and do nothing.

"If you don't call the police then I will," she had said to Sophia. "I just don't understand how you can let him do that to you."

"You don't understand. He is under so much pressure. Every day he has to go to that hospital and save someone else's life. Can you imagine what that must do to you?"

"So, he saves someone's life and then takes it out on you! Listen to yourself. Listen to what you're saying! One day he'll come home in a rage and then what? What if he totally loses it? Are you prepared to die to keep this monster happy?!"

"He's not a monster. He doesn't mean to hurt me. He loves me."

"I can't sit by and just watch as he kills you. I can't. I won't do it."

As MJ walked away from her, Sophia knew that their friendship was changed. 'He doesn't mean to hurt me'. It was something she had said to MJ so many times that she had come to truly believe it.

She didn't see MJ again until the day when the fire took her husband's life and half her face away. She had never known that her friend had always kept a watchful eye on her, always there in the background in case she needed her.

MJ was the first there when she was taken to court for his murder and she was the first and only one who visited her in prison; and had done every month since she was locked away. It was MJ who inadvertently was the catalyst for what came next.

It was a normal morning at the start of another month when MJ came for her monthly visit to the prison. Sophia noticed, for the first time, a change in her friend. "Why are you holding your side like that? And your make-up, under your eye, it's covering a bruise."

"It's nothing. I had an accident, it's fine."

"Who is he?"

"Please. It's nothing."

"Who is he?" Sophia pressed her friend.

"We've been going out for about eighteen months now. He's my boss at the hospital. I didn't want to tell you. Not with you stuck in here. I couldn't tell you I had met someone and fallen in love. It would have been too cruel."

"How long has he been hitting you?"

"Sophia, please don't..."

"How long?"

"He hasn't done it a lot. It's just he works so hard, the shifts are so long. And there's so much pressure these days..."

"How long?"

MJ took a deep breath before she continued.

"Since I moved in with him. Since he asked me to marry him. About a year."

"You're engaged to this... animal?"

"Sophia, you don't know him."

"He'll not stop, you do know that, don't you?" She pulled her hood down to reveal her damaged skin. "Is this what you want? To end up looking like me? To end up in a place like this?"

"You don't understand. He doesn't mean to do it. He loves me, he really does."

"You need to leave him."

MJ looked down. She knew her friend was right. She had always known, even from the first time he had hit her. But like most women in an abusive relationship, she felt at first that he never meant it, and with time and her help she could change him. But, over the year, the abuse had got worse and he had made her feel like it was all her fault, that somehow she was the cause of it.

She had lived through Sophia's abuse, never understanding how Sophia had let it happen, and now she found herself in the same position.

MJ looked up, the tears streaming down her face. "I don't know how to leave him," she said. "I did try once, just a month after I moved in, but he begged me to stay. He looked so sorry. And then the next time I even packed my bags. But that time he locked the doors and forced me to stay. He really hurt me. I couldn't go to work for nearly two weeks. I'm scared. If I try to leave again, he said he'd make sure I'll lose my job. He's already taken my money, so I'll have nothing. Where would I go? What would I do without him?"

"Why didn't you tell me?"

"How could I? What could you have done from in here?"

"I'll help you. It's time we stopped this."

Sophia had to save her friend. She knew this was the time she had to put into action her plan for revenge.

The first thing was to deal with MJ's fiancé. But she needed MJ's help to do that. She needed her friend to no longer be a victim. This was part of her plan. The only way she could stop women being the victims was to do what she did. To take back control of their lives. To understand that they no longer had to be the abused, that they could end it, that they had the power to end it forever.

Over the following months, visit by visit, Sophia convinced MJ that not only did she not deserve to suffer like she had, that she needed to take back her life and that there was a way she could do it that would also give her the financial freedom to never need a man ever again.

MJ's agreement to her plan coincided with The Lady's release from prison.

***

It didn't take The Lady long to reacquaint herself with the outside world. After her release, she blended back into society seamlessly. Over the years before her arrest, she had established numerous identities and had kept a number of properties around the country. No one had ever really known who she was. She was the neighbour you only noticed once or twice, but never really saw. She was the old woman walking her dog who you thought looked like all the other old women in the park. She was no one. She had made her money over the years by working in secret for wealthy families who needed her special skills to help them keep their wealth. If it meant breaking into someone else's house or business and finding their secrets, then she was

The Lady for the job. If it meant frightening a competitor into pulling out of a bidding war, then she was The Lady for the job. If it meant killing someone, anyone, then she was The Lady for the job. Her skills had become stories of legend in certain circles.

Being arrested and convicted of manslaughter had been a shock. She had been sloppy. She had pushed a woman off a train platform at London Bridge station just as the London to Portsmouth train was rushing in, killing her instantly in the most graphic way. The job had paid The Lady a cool half a million pounds and had removed the woman as head of a global company, giving her second-in-command the only chance he would ever have of taking the top spot. It had been an easy job by all accounts. Follow the woman from her home to the station and then push her at the right time. She had done it before, it was not hard to make it look like a suicide or an accident. But this time, The Lady had waited just a fraction too late. By the time the train was up to speed and The Lady was in position, a guard had been walking past. At the last millisecond, The Lady spotted him and she managed to twist her body slightly to make it look like she had slipped into the woman rather than push her. Usually, she would then manage to blend into the crowd and not be noticed, but her error of judgement had shocked her enough to make her pause a moment too long. And that was all that was needed for the guard to see and hold her. And for the CCTV to capture the moment.

It was her first time in prison, and also meant the waste of one of her identities. The loss of an identity was something that really upset her as they took so long to put together, but it was ultimately worth the sacrifice to stop the authorities finding out her real name.

She knew that the prison time itself, whilst an annoyance, would not be hard for her, and that it would teach her a valuable lesson in not being distracted on a job. What she never foresaw was meeting Sophia, or the profound change it would have on her life.

As soon as she saw her she knew life would never be the same again. She had fallen in love with her the moment she had first seen her in the prison yard. It wasn't a love of the heart, because her heart was not capable of love, this love was so much stronger. This was more like the way a mother loves a daughter. She couldn't explain where this feeling came from, but whatever the reason, it meant she would protect her with her life.

When they were alone in the cell for the first time and Sophia had told her about her need for revenge, she knew that her entire focus from that moment on would be on making that happen.

Her first job when she was released was to assume one of her other identities and become invisible again. She did this within hours and left the authorities blind as to where and how this lady had vanished.

The next thing was to make contact with MJ and tell her of Sophia's plans to remove her fiancé, in the most final way possible.

"I can't do it," MJ had pleaded as she sat across from The Lady on the park bench where they had been meeting every Sunday morning for the last few weeks.

"It's time," The Lady said. "But it has to be you. That is Sophia's one condition. For you to take back control of your life, you have to be the one who does it."

MJ understood she had to go through with it. The beatings had got steadily worse, and she knew in her heart that it wouldn't be long before he could go too far and either permanently disable her or worse, kill her.

"How will I do it?" she asked her teacher.

The Lady took a vial out of her handbag.

"One drop of this in his morning coffee every day for a month. Bit by bit, his body will start to break down until eventually his heart will stop."

"Will it be painful?" she asked. Her voice betrayed the fact that she did not want him to suffer.

"At the end, yes. As it should be, he should suffer as you have suffered," The Lady replied. "But it is untraceable, so no one will ever know you caused it to happen. And then the life insurance policy will have to pay out to you. You'll have over a million pounds in the bank, you'll never need to work at the hospital again. You did put the policy in place, didn't you? Exactly as I instructed?"

"Yes. I did it in joint names. He didn't push back because if anything *happened to me then he would get the money. He seemed to like the idea,"* MJ *said, with irony in her voice.*

"And you insured it with Seico? That's important."

The Lady had chosen Seico as the company for Sophia's plans as she had been instrumental in helping the current owner take control of the business some years before, and she knew he would not be able to refuse her now.

She had told him that he was to make sure the policies that she helped set up were fully re-insured. That way, he could continue to run his company legitimately whilst giving her the platform she needed for Sophia's widows. As long as all their life policies were re-insured, Seico would not have to suffer any losses. They were the perfect partner for Sophia's widows.

"Yes, I did. We are both healthy, so there were no medicals needed or anything. We simply had to fill in some forms and they gave us the cover."

"Good."

"So, once it's done, I'll get the policy money?"

"Yes, you'll no longer be in danger. And you'll be rich. You'll be able to live a good life, unafraid any more. This is the gift Sophia is giving to you."

"And how much of the payout does Sophia need me to hold for her?"

"This isn't about money for her! Surely you know that. This is your friend making sure you don't have to go through all the years of pain she went through."

MJ *did know that; she always knew that. But she knew* The Lady *as well and she was sure that her role in this was not going to end as easily as that.*

"So, if I'm not giving any of it to Sophia, what about you? What price do you want me to pay?"

"You're smarter than I give you credit for," The Lady *replied.*

"How much?" MJ *asked.*

"I don't need your money either," The Lady *said contemptuously.*

"Then what?"

"Once it is done, naturally, after a few months have passed, you will take up a position of head of medical underwriting at the insurance company.

116

You are the first one we are helping. But there are many more we can save. Sophia wants you to help her find other victims and then you will pass them to me. I'll help them the way I helped you. You will work for Seico. You'll handle their business in the usual way and will be paid well as a senior manager there. But, every case we put through, every abused woman we help will apply for cover. They will all go through your team for medical underwriting and you will personally sign off on every single one of them."

MJ thought about it for a moment. She knew she had no choice but to agree. She tried to work out who the victims in this crime would be, apart from the abusers, but were they really victims? She thought not. The insurance and re-insurance companies would lose millions, of course, in fraudulent claims. She thought about that for a minute. Did she care? No, she decided, she really didn't. She couldn't care less if they lost money, they certainly made enough from their customers over the years. She came to the conclusion that actually it was brilliant. They could help all these abused women, give them a chance in life after their husbands were dead and the only losers were the men who deserved it, men like her fiancé, and big businesses like the insurance companies, and no one really worried about them.

The Lady looked MJ deeply in the eyes as she sat there thinking. She could see MJ getting it, she saw the smile as it appeared on her face. MJ wanted to help Sophia, and she knew that there were women out there who needed their help as well. But she also knew that she had no choice in the matter, The Lady now controlled her life as well.

"Remember," The Lady continued, "that we are doing this for Sophia and for all the women like you and her who have suffered at the hands of their husbands."

"I get it," she said.

MJ knew the plan and loved it. They would use MJ's medical contacts at the hospital to find women like them and then they would help them. And never would any innocents be hurt. Sophia had stressed that. Only the abusers would die, no innocent person would ever lose their lives or ever suffer like they had.

The phone vibrated from across Sophia's cell and brought her back to the present.

She looked at the clock by the bed. It was just turning nine o'clock in the morning. She always stayed in bed later on a Monday, until just after nine. It cost a little extra to be left alone to sleep in, but she had the money for the bribes, and the officers were always happy to earn some extra cash. She counted the rings and got up on the fourth. She lifted the cushion from the chair, unzipped it and pressed the answer key just after the seventh ring had finished.

She waited until the caller spoke first.

"I'm so sorry, Sophia," The Lady said down the phone. Sophia could hear her voice waver, exposing a vulnerability she never knew her friend possessed.

Sophia paused before replying. She sat down on the chair and pulled the red cloak over her shoulders, making sure that the hood covered the burns on her face, as she always did when she felt exposed, which she did the moment she heard the fear in her friend's voice. "It sounds like we have another problem," she replied. "Did you not take care of Brighton?"

"Maybe," she answered.

"Maybe?"

"I'm not sure how it happened like it did. It was the perfect place. They were on a charity skydive. I had the order of flights earlier that morning and I was assured that they are fixed once they're set. But at the last moment, they changed the flight order. I had no idea until afterwards, by which time there was nothing I could do."

"What have you done?" she asked, her voice a mixture of fear and anger.

"Her husband died instead of her. And she watched it happen."

"Oh my God. She was not meant to die! No one was meant to die, you knew that. I told you, no more innocent people could die."

"I was protecting you. It had to go down like that. I couldn't risk her exposing us."

Sophia's other phone vibrated. She picked it up and saw it was MJ calling.

The Lady carried on speaking. "It might be enough to stop her, though. You never know how people are going to react when something like this happens," she continued. "It may be enough to make her walk away now."

"I need to go," Sophia said, the anger in her voice clear for her friend to hear. "Call me tomorrow, at seven pm. We need to contain this."

"Of course."

Sophia put the phone down and wiped away the tears that were now running down her face, following the contours of her damaged skin. *Another innocent person dead, and I caused it,* she thought bitterly to herself. Her phone started ringing. She pressed the answer button, knowing that the conversation was going to be extremely painful for them both. She could feel the cell walls closing in around her. For years, all she had thought about was surviving this place and making those men pay for what they do, and now, with just a few weeks until her release date, life was crashing down around her once again.

CHAPTER 15

Seico London Office

MJ was alone in the boardroom. She pulled the blinds down so no one would see her. She was in no fit state to be seen this morning. Her hands shook uncontrollably as she dialled the number.

Sophia picked up after what seemed like an eternity.

"MJ," she said. Her voice gave away her inner turmoil.

"She killed Asher," MJ blurted out. "She tried to kill Kiara. But she killed Asher instead. You promised me. You said no one innocent would ever die. I can't do this anymore." MJ blurted out, "It happened right in front of me, it was terrible. And Kiara, and the girls, they were sitting next to me. They saw their dad die, how will they ever get over that…?"

Sophia interrupted her mid-sentence. "I know. I have just been told. It was never meant to be like this. But accidents can happen, we can only control the controllables, you know that, you've lived this life long enough to understand that."

"Accident? That wasn't an accident. She promised me she was just going to talk to them, but that was never her plan. You had her kill him. You said you'd never do that. You lied to me, your only real friend in the world." MJ could barely keep control of herself. "And to actually see it happen, to be there…" MJ was shaking so much that the words were barely audible, "and it was all my fault, I could have stopped her doing it…"

"It was a terrible accident, nothing more. You can't blame yourself."

"It wasn't an accident!" MJ screamed down the phone. "She did it on purpose. And you ordered it. It was meant to be Kiara, wasn't it? Kiara was meant to die like that, in front of her children. And you told her to do it like that. How could you do that?"

The pain was clear in Sophia's voice as she spoke. "You know I never wanted that to happen. I told her to speak with Kiara, to threaten her, yes, but not to harm her."

"So, why did she do it then?!"

"She had to take care of the problem that was in front of her. She was trying to protect me, all of us. Kiara wouldn't let it go. She was becoming too much of a risk to all of us, you included. But I never meant to hurt her, or her husband, or their children. They're innocents in all this. I am – was – we were nurses. We trained to save lives, not take them. We don't do that, we're not monsters."

"Aren't we? Isn't she? You didn't see her; she didn't care at all. She doesn't care about anyone. She's doing this now to protect herself. She's scared she'll be found out again and go back to prison. She'll kill anyone to stop that, even me. Even you!"

"MJ, enough!"

For the first time in a long time, Sophia saw the situation starting to get out of her control.

"I told you I could warn her off, but you wouldn't listen, would you? No one had to die over this, I could have stopped her. You could have stopped it if you had wanted to."

Sophia leant back in her chair, taking in the accusing words being thrown at her. She knew MJ was right. *No one had to die.* It was true. She had been clear to her friend that no one could die, not any more. She never wanted it to go like this. She never wanted Michael Hall to die. And she never wanted Kiara or her husband to die.

Or did she?

She knew her friend was a killer. She always knew that. Did she order their deaths to protect herself? Had she turned a blind eye to the truth for so long just so she could protect herself? Had she become so immune to the horror of murder that it no longer held real consequence to her?

When her friend had managed to install MJ into Seico as the chief medical officer, she knew that they would be able to set her plan in motion. It had been easy for them to have MJ insure her fiancé's life and even simpler to kill him. That murder, the first one, had gone so smoothly, and it seemed at the time that it had had to happen. But she had never truly thought about the emotional effect it would have on them. For the next year, MJ had stopped visiting her and it had been a relief to not have to face her. But The Lady was always there. Desperate to continue the plan. Always pushing her to do more, to save more abused women. The second murder didn't have the same effect as the first. The third even less. By the time they had hit double digits, it was all business.

However, Asher being killed took her right back to the first. Sophia had never intended for him to lose his life, nothing could have been further from her mind than that. Of course, she knew that The Lady had a very dark side that she never fully understood, but going against her orders once again and killing a completely innocent man was too much.

So many men had died to satisfy her need for revenge – evil men, abusive men – but how did that square the circle when even one innocent person had died? It didn't; it couldn't. She knew she had to stop. They couldn't kill another innocent person, not one more. It needed to stop. But she couldn't face staying in prison any longer. She had to end this killing, but she had to be released. And she had to protect her widows from ever being found out.

"I could have saved him. Asher didn't have to die." MJ's voice brought her back to the moment.

122

"Kiara wouldn't have stopped. Not until she found out who we were, and then what? I can't spend another twenty years locked in here, I would rather die today than face that. And what about you? Can you really give up your life for a ten-by-ten cell? And then what about the other widows? After all their suffering, do they really deserve to end up in here, like me, treated like criminals, murderers?"

"But what about Asher?! He didn't deserve to die!" MJ shouted down the phone.

Sophia couldn't argue any more. "It wasn't meant to happen that way. I never ordered her to kill anyone. But I can't control her from in here. She'll do anything to protect me, you know that. I need to get out. That's the only way we can stop her now. What's done is done, there's no way we can change it. I told you years ago that when I get out of prison, you can be allowed to walk away. You're a rich lady now, you can go anywhere you want. It's just for a few more weeks and then it can all be over, for all of us."

There was silence on the other end of the phone. Sophia could just about hear the deep intakes of breath as the tears rolled down MJ's face.

"Maybe you're right, maybe it's time for you to stop. You've led this campaign for me for so long now. You've done so much for the widows, so much for me. It's time I let you go."

"But what about Kiara and the twins?" The tears were starting to run freely down her face, making her words come out in sobs. "Please, I couldn't bear anything to happen to them, I couldn't live with myself if she did anything to them now."

"Do you really think I want to see any more innocent people die? Kiara's children need their mother. Kiara needs to mourn her husband now and then be a mother to her children. Her days at Seico need to end, and then she'll have no reason, or way to follow this up. And then we are safe, all of us. There'll be no need for my friend to ever see them again."

"Really? Can you honestly stop her?" MJ said, the hope in her voice palpable over the phone.

"There's no evidence anything untoward happened at the airfield. And we've no more widows in the making. You should go back to the office and make sure Kiara's files are clean. And check that Jane Powers' case is deleted from the system, for good this time. And the same with the Bristol case, there must be no trace of it anywhere. And then you can resign from your position. Leave the company and move away from all of this, from me."

"And you promise me, Kiara and the girls will be fine."

"All she has to do is look after her children now. If she does that then it's over. You make sure she takes the next few months off. As her boss, you can force her to take time away. So do that one last thing and use the next few weeks to clean everything up. And then your time with the widows can be over. I'll deal with my friend. Okay?"

"Okay," MJ replied weakly, the fight already having left her.

After the call ended, Sophia lay back down on her bed. She couldn't hold her tears back any longer. She buried her face into her pillow and cried. She had no more than a few weeks left of this place and then she would be free. As the tears flowed freely down her damaged face, she vowed that there would be no more. No more deaths. No more threats. No more widows.

CHAPTER 16

Seico Brighton Office

A Week After the Skydive

"We just think it's too soon. It's been barely a week since we lost Asher..." Kiara's mother-in-law had to stop in between words to take a breath before continuing. "I'm sorry, it just feels unreal to say that still."

"I know, I'm the same. Every time I think of what happened it's like I'm suffocating all over again," Kiara agreed. "But I have to go in. I need to tell everyone at work about the funeral and I need to just clear my desk of the outstanding cases. People still need me to settle their claims, I can't just let them down."

"But surely someone else can do your work for a few more weeks? And you can just message your secretary about the funeral. The girls need you here, surely, it's just too soon to leave them."

"It'll just be for the morning, I promise. And they have you and Peter here."

"Did someone just take my name in vain?" Peter said as he lumbered into the lounge and dropped into his favourite chair. Unlike his son, who had been relatively fit, Peter was morbidly obese and was never happier than when he was snuggled into his favourite chair and allowed to nod off.

"Kiara wants to go back to work, and I was just saying I think she should take more time off," Judy replied.

"I just said it was for the morning, not the whole day."

"It'll do her good to get out of the house. We can look after the girls. You go, darling, don't worry about a thing."

"Thanks, Peter, and I won't be long, I promise," Kiara replied, giving Peter and Judy a kiss each on the cheek and leaving the room before her mother-in-law could reply.

"Poor love," Peter said to Judy, "she is far too young to be a widow."

"I'm sorry," Judy said to her husband as she started to cry again. She left the lounge, tears streaming down her face, just as the twins came into the room.

"Is Granny all right, Pops?" Mia asked Peter as she and Jasmin perched on the edge of his chair.

"I don't think any of us are, my darlings, I don't think any of us are."

In the week following the skydive, Kiara's life had been a wave of emotions. It had never occurred to her that she would have to live her life without Asher, it had been a given that they would grow old together, yet here she was suddenly a single mother of twins facing a future that was totally alien to her. Not only had she lost the love of her life, but whenever she tried to picture him in her mind, all she could see was him crashing into the airfield in front of her. If it wasn't for Mia and Jasmin, she had no idea if she would be strong enough to get up each morning, let alone survive a full day, but they needed her more now than ever and she had to find the strength to keep going for them.

She pulled the car into the parking spot outside the office and turned off the engine. She thought coming to work would be good for her. Sitting in the house day in, day out with her in-laws, as much as she loved them, was suffocating her. And every time her and the girls looked at each other, they would well up and fight back the floods of tears that were threatening to drown them all. It had only been a week since the accident, but sometimes it already felt like years since she last saw Asher. They had never spent more than a couple of days apart since they first started dating, and now she couldn't even think about him for a moment without feeling like she was dying inside. She couldn't go into the office and face everyone yet. She thought she could, but suddenly it all felt too overwhelming.

She turned the car back on and was just about to reverse out of the space when there was a knock on the passenger side window. It was Gemma. She made a sign for Kiara to lower the window. "What are you doing here? We didn't think we'd see you for…" Gemma's voice broke. She couldn't get the words out.

"I just needed to come in, I had to get out of the house. And I need to talk to MJ. She was sitting with me when… it happened."

"I'm so sorry. We are all so devastated. I wish I knew what to say."

"It's okay. It's affected everyone, not just me. I can't imagine what you are all going through, having seen it happen." Kiara found herself flipping from the crying widow into the mother hen. It was a natural way of protecting herself by protecting others. She climbed out of the car and walked around to give Gemma a comforting hug. "Come on, let's go inside."

Kiara led the way, holding Gemma's hand in her own as she helped her friend up the stairs to their floor.

"What are you doing here?" MJ blurted the words out in shock as she saw the two women coming through the door.

"Charming!" replied Kiara sarcastically.

"Oh my God, I didn't mean it to sound like that. I'm just surprised to see you, that's all. Come here." MJ came forward and threw her arms around Kiara's neck, pushing Gemma to the side. After a quick hug, she pulled away and placed her arms on Kiara's shoulders like an older sister would and looked into her eyes. "You should be at home with the twins, not here. It's too soon, you need to…" MJ stopped talking, not sure how much or what she should say.

"To what?" interrupted Kiara. "To sit at home with Asher's parents and listen to them go on about losing a son? Or sit with my girls for hours on end and try to explain why there can't be a God or else their father wouldn't have died like that right in front of them?"

"I'm sorry, I don't mean to sound like everyone else. It's hard to know what to say to you. We're all a bit lost to be honest."

"I know. I know. You didn't mean it. No one means it. Everyone is just looking out for me. If everyone wants to help then just let me come back to work for a few hours and try to be just that little bit normal"

"I'm sorry, I get it. I mean, I don't, I can't... you know what I mean. Look, just don't stay long, okay? I told the board I would make sure your work was sorted, so I've been doing that myself. Everything's getting sorted, okay?"

"I'm sorry as well. I just keep shouting at everyone. I don't mean to. I know you all care about me, honestly I do. Please just let me get a coffee and do a little work, it'll help me, and I promise I'll not stay long or do too much."

"We are all still shell-shocked. I've been shouting at everyone as well. Of course, though, do whatever helps, please, whatever you need."

"Thanks, I appreciate it. Gemma, I'd love a coffee and maybe a little update on my cases, if that's okay?"

"Sure thing, K. Give me a moment."

Kiara went into her office, pulling the door closed behind her, and sat down at her desk. She powered up her computer and watched as the screensaver sprang to life, throwing up a picture of her and Asher at the finish line of the Eastbourne Ironman event that she'd completed the year before. The screensaver showed her coming across the finish line in just under thirteen hours as the photographer caught Asher and the girls rushing to meet her. The tears instantly started pouring again just as Gemma came into the office carrying a coffee.

"Oh, K," Gemma said, putting the coffee down and rushing around the desk.

Kiara wiped her eyes and stopped Gemma coming in for a hug. "Please, Gem, don't. I need to just deal with this." Gemma stepped back awkwardly, not sure what to say or do. "Just update me on my cases, okay?"

"Sure, no problem. MJ settled the Brompton case and also the Riley case yesterday. And she has passed the Khan and McIntyre cases to Peter to handle, and the Simpson and Bollingbrook cases to Shirley. I think that was all you had outstanding."

"Yes, that was it. They are all okay, I think, nothing stood out, so I'm sure they'll all just be easy to settle. And the Powers case?"

Gemma was taken aback a little at hearing about that case once again. And Kiara could see that she'd said something that had caused Gemma a problem.

"What's going on?" Kiara asked.

"MJ didn't want me to talk to you about that case."

"Why?" Kiara leant forward, looking directly into Gem's eyes.

"Look, she didn't want you to know. But she settled the case herself."

"So, you found it back on the system, then? Where had it gone? Did you find out why it had vanished? And did the Bristol case come back as well?"

"No, we couldn't trace either. I still can't."

"Then how did MJ settle it? Surely she would have had to find it first."

"I asked her that. But she just told me to mind my own business. She said she was going to go into the accounts and just send a payment and if the files stay lost then so be it."

"But that makes no sense," Kiara said as she turned her focus to her computer screen and tried to bring up the Powers case. As Gemma had said to her, the case was still not coming up. So, she quickly logged out of the client database and logged directly into the accounts page, which as a senior person she had access to. She scrolled down until she saw the name Powers and found the payment MJ had made. The first thing she noticed was that under the client claim number the field was left blank, which meant it could not be traced to a case. The second thing she saw took her breath away. "What the hell?" she said as much to herself as to Gemma.

"What is it?" Gemma said, walking around to the terminal.

"The date she paid the claim."

"What about it?" Gemma could see the date at the top right of the screen. "That's odd, why would she come in on a weekend to pay a claim?"

"Not just any weekend, is it? It was Saturday the 3rd of April. She came into the office the same day that my husband died right in front of her and settled a fucking claim! What the hell's that about?"

Gemma turned around to check the door was closed before turning back to Kiara and spoke to her quietly. "I have no idea," she whispered. "But keep your voice down, she might hear you. I thought it was strange that she just ignored my worries about the cases vanishing from the system. I thought she'd go apeshit and would start calling in IT. But she just swept it aside and told me not to talk about it to anyone, especially not to you. And the way she said that, it kinda spooked me, to be honest. I've never seen her talk like that. Then the next thing I heard was that she had handed in her notice."

"What?"

"She handed in her notice. She said after the accident that she just couldn't work here any more."

"So, my husband is killed, and on the same day, she comes in, pays a claim and then hands in her notice for the job she loves? This is not right, something is going on here."

It took Gemma a second to catch up with what Kiara had said.

"What do you mean Asher was killed? It was an accident. We all saw it."

"Was it, though? What did we really see? Doesn't it all sound a bit odd to you? Think about it. I am pressured to settle a claim that I don't want to settle. And then days later, after I push back, the files vanish, my husband dies and then MJ resigns. I have no idea what it all means, but something is not right here."

Gemma didn't know what to say. She just stood there looking at Kiara, lost for words.

"Just trust me, something isn't right. Look, I need to get to Edinburgh and see Jane Powers. Maybe she knows something. I need you to book me a flight. But don't tell MJ, okay? Not a word."

Gemma stood in silence, not sure if she could, or should do what Kiara was asking of her.

"I need you to do this for me."

"I don't know. I mean, MJ is our friend, isn't she? She wouldn't do anything to hurt you, or Ash, she just wouldn't."

"Please. I never ask you for anything, do I? Please, just this once, I need your help. After this, I'll never ask for anything ever again, I promise."

Gemma knew she had to help. She had also started to feel that something was amiss here, and aside from that she found it almost impossible to turn Kiara down.

"Okay, I'll do it. But please be careful. If you're right, I'm scared something will happen to you as well."

Kiara came around the desk and pulled Gemma into a hug, and whispered in her ear, "I'll be fine, I have to do this. I love you, Gemma, you're the best, I just couldn't do this without you. But keep it between us, okay? Don't tell anyone, not until I know more." She felt Gemma nod her head. "Book me a ticket for the morning." She felt Gemma nod again.

Kiara left her office, stopping briefly at MJ's desk on the way out. "Thanks for letting me come in, MJ, but you were right, it's too soon. I'll leave you to it, if that's okay? I know my cases are in good hands."

"Take all the time you need. And call anytime. I'll always be here if you need me."

MJ took Kiara into a hug and kissed her on the cheek. Kiara felt as if her face was on fire.

"Of course, MJ, thanks, I can't tell you how much that means to me," she said as she slowly turned and walked out of the office and down the stairs to her car.

"Gemma," MJ called out.

"Yes?" Gemma answered, trying to keep the fear from her voice.

"I'm popping out for a couple of hours, you can hold the fort while I'm gone. Just take messages for me, okay?"

"Sure, MJ, no problem."

As soon as MJ had left the office, Gemma booked the flight and emailed the tickets to Kiara's private email address rather than her work one. She never considered, though, the fact that her own work email and the office credit card were also being monitored.

CHAPTER 17

Bristol – The Gallery

A Week Since Michael Hall's Death

At midday, the sun was shining brightly through Rosie's window in the small office at the top of the art gallery. In happier times, she loved it when the sun bounced off the glass walls that circled the gallery as it painted her offices in a rainbow of colours that would make her feel relaxed, almost restful. But now, much like everything else in her life, it simply annoyed her.

"Damn it, the bloody sun, I can't see what I'm doing."

"Are you sure you should be working today, Rosie? You're clearly not ready to be back yet," Rosie's manager asked, not hiding the impatience in her voice. Rosie's mood was starting to have a negative effect on everyone, and office morale was seriously being affected.

"How are we meant to work with the blinds up?" Rosie replied. "I can barely see my screen. I'm trying to reorganise the Italian masters for the show, but I can't see one from another like this. Why can't we just close the bloody blinds?"

"Rosie, please take an early break, will you? I've got too much to do myself and I can't concentrate with you constantly complaining about everything."

"I've got to plan the floor before the end of the week…"

"It was not a suggestion, Rosie," she cut her off mid-sentence.

Without another word, Rosie logged off, grabbed her iPad and stormed off to the lifts, pressing the button to take her to the lower floor where the public café was located. It had much better lighting there as it led straight onto the main viewing floor. Since coming back to work, Rosie spent more time in the café than in her office. Her colleagues quietly wished they could move her desk there permanently.

"I know she's lost her husband, and only a few weeks ago, but still…" her manager said more to herself than the other people crammed into the small room. They all nevertheless grunted in agreement.

Rosie heard them as she climbed into the lift and almost climbed back out to tell them what she really thought about them. But she knew that would be the end of her job. And having only recently lost the one true love of her life, she couldn't bear to then lose the only other thing that she'd ever loved. Since Michael's death, it was only her job at the gallery that kept her from going totally insane. In fact, even before his death, it was always a toss-up as to which she loved more, her husband or the artwork that she was surrounded by every day.

The café was unusually quiet that afternoon, so she easily found an empty table in the corner far away from prying eyes and opened her iPad. She clicked on the email application and brought up her home account that contained the emails she had forwarded to herself from Michael's office computer. She read each one of them through a final time and knew she had to respond, although she wasn't sure exactly how to say what she wanted to say without making herself sound like a crazy person. She decided to just go for it and be damned. She tried to tell Kiara everything, from the moment the car had turned and headed towards her husband to when she stormed out of the police station in fury. She read the email back to herself and was ready to hit send. But something was stopping her. As much as she wanted to vent and as much as she desperately wanted to talk to this lady, her instincts screamed at her to be careful. What if she was right, and this was not a hit and run, but a premeditated murder? Should she really send an email to someone she didn't know telling them everything she was thinking? What if this Kiara Fox was somehow part of it, wouldn't she just be putting herself in danger as well? Rosie sat back and took a breath. She knew she had to do something, and Kiara was perhaps now her only link to what happened. With a quick swipe, Rosie deleted the entire email she had written and composed something much simpler.

Dear Kiara,

Many thanks for writing to my husband. I am sad to tell you that he recently died in a car accident.

I know that this may sound odd, but I do not know many people from my husband's company and it sounds like you may have known him? It would really be so helpful to me if you would maybe take some time to call me (my number is below), as I think it would really help in my grieving if I could just talk to someone who may have known him.

I hope you are able to call me.

Thank you,

Rosie Hall

Without overthinking it any more, she hit send and closed her iPad. She had no idea if she would get a reply, or if a reply would even be helpful. Or maybe, she thought, she had just thrust a burning branch into a hornets' nest. She sat back in her chair and contemplated what she had just done. She concluded that whatever happened next, at least she had done something; it was better than just accepting his death was an accident, when she would always know deep down it was not.

As Rosie shut her iPad, the email she sent pinged into two

different inboxes, one a computer in Brighton and the other to a phone in a prison cell in Middlesex.

Rosie felt suddenly desperate. What was she doing sending an email like that? And making it so cryptic. If this Kiara was part of the problem, then sending the email had already put her life in danger. But what if she was like Rosie herself, what if something similar had happened to her? Would that not make them allies? She had to speak to her and find out what she knew. Maybe she could even warn her before something bad happened to her or her family. She owed it to her. She was a colleague of her husband and she needed to tell her what she knew, or at least thought she knew. She opened her iPad again and pulled up the emails that contained Kiara's phone number. Without hesitating further, she made the call.

CHAPTER 18

Edinburgh – The Powers Estate

Explaining to her in-laws that she had to go to Edinburgh for a few days for work had not been easy. Having to explain it to the twins had been even harder. None of them could understand how, a week after Asher's death, she could go back to work, especially jumping on a plane and leaving them all. Kiara was desperate to explain to them that this was more than just work, that leaving them was the single hardest thing she would ever do, apart from burying her husband. But how could she tell them that she was investigating the murder of their son, of their father, of her husband? She couldn't. She knew that if she tried to explain it to them they would tell her to let the police handle it and that she should be with her family and nothing else at this time. But she had been in the investigation business long enough to know that, unlike her, the police don't rely on their instinct, they understandably need hard proof before they take action. She felt certain that if she didn't do this now then whoever was behind Asher's death would walk away scot-free.

She had to leave the house before the sun was rising, knowing that, as she was already in their bad books, it was easier to just go than try to explain her reasons once again. She would have to be honest with them all when she got back, but just not yet. She was keeping her family in the dark to protect them and they'd understand that once all this was over.

The flight that Gemma booked her onto was due to leave Gatwick Airport at 8.55am and would land in Edinburgh just over an hour later. She got to Gatwick with enough time to have breakfast and plan her trip. Sitting in the airport waiting for her flight to be called, she logged on to Quality Hire Car using her mobile phone and booked a car to be waiting for her at Edinburgh Airport.

She thought back to the first time she had driven there, to the funeral of Martin Powers. It felt to Kiara like a whole other lifetime. She couldn't quite believe how much her life had changed in such a short time, and that it could never be the same again.

Once she had landed and was in the hire car, she needed time to take stock. She had been running on adrenalin since she had been back at the office and only now did she stop and think about what she was going to do.

Do I really believe Jane Powers is mixed up with Asher's death?" she asked herself. *What am I going to do, just roll up to her house and accuse her of murdering my husband? And what are the chances that she'll even be at home when I get there? For fuck's sake, this whole thing is such a bad idea.*

Her phone rang, bringing her out of her thoughts. She didn't recognise the number. She hadn't been expecting any calls, perhaps apart from Mia or Jasmin, so she let it ring out rather than answering it. After putting the address for the Powers' home into the car's satnav, she checked her phone to see if the caller had left a message. They had.

"Ms Fox, Kiara, this is Rosie Hall, Michael's wife, from Bristol. I recently sent you an email, but it never really said what I wanted it to say. I believe Michael was killed. They say it was a hit and run accident, but I don't believe them. I really need to talk to you. I think he was murdered, but I don't know why, and you were maybe one of the last people to speak to him. Please call me back."

Kiara's heart was beating fast listening to Rosie's message. She played it a second time to make sure she hadn't missed anything.

Two murders. Both connected to Seico; one an employee and one the husband of an employee. Kiara's resolve returned as a red mist surrounded her. She would definitely call Rosie back, but not before speaking with Jane Powers. She put the car into drive and followed the satnav's instructions to leave the airport on the M6 and drive straight for the first thirty miles before taking a sharp left and moving into the maze of country lanes that would eventually lead her to Jane Powers' estate. On the drive, she ran through the meeting in her head. She would calmly and professionally approach Jane and firstly apologise for bothering her again. She would explain that as the claim was settled that she just needed to have Jane agree that the file could be closed and that no more action would be needed. She would do this on the pretext that it was a normality, just part of the process. She was doubtful it would be questioned. During the short chat, she would probe just a little into how Jane was coping emotionally and then ask if Seico, and particularly MJ, were helpful and supportive over the whole period. Her aim was to establish a link between Jane Powers and MJ that should not be there. It was a simple plan, but one she needed to do face-to-face. The truth was always in the eyes not in the voice.

But the best laid plans are often not as simple as they should be.

She drove up to the main gate, which was already open, but now sported a 'For Sale' sign. As she sat in her car about to drive in, another car came down the drive and pulled up almost alongside her. A shortish girl and a young muscly man climbed out. She watched the man take a sign and a short ladder out of the car boot and carry it over to the gate. Kiara left her car and walked over to speak with the girl as the man went about his business replacing the 'For Sale' sign with a new sign which simply said 'Spoken For'.

"Excuse me," Kiara said. The girl turned to her in surprise, having not noticed her getting out of the car. "I didn't know the Powers estate was up for sale."

"Actually, we've already sold it," she replied. "It's unusual to have a grand house like this come on the market, so it went almost overnight for the full asking. We've other places, not as palatial, but still beautiful, if you're interested?"

"Oh no, sorry, I'm not looking at the moment. I'm an old friend of Jane's. I heard about her husband Martin and, as I was in the area, I just wanted to drop by on the off chance she was in. I assume she's home?"

"Yes, I just delivered the good news to her about the house."

"It certainly sold quickly. Martin only passed away a few weeks back. Jane must have put the house up for sale right away, then."

"Actually, Mrs Powers and I have been talking about it for nearly a year now. She wanted me to be ready for when she gave me the nod. I think she wanted to scale down, they didn't need something this big. So, I already had a few exceptional people lined up. I always like to over deliver for my clients. So, if you ever have a house to sell, I'd love to have a look. I have a bank of people asking me to find them their perfect home, so I could get you a quick and high price, I'm sure. Do you live nearby?"

"So, you knew Martin as well, then?" Kiara said, trying to keep the sales girl on topic.

"Mr Powers? No, I never met him. Jane always saw me here when he was working away or would meet me at my office. I think she wanted to surprise him, or maybe he just wasn't as keen on selling as she was. Anyway, I think we're done now," she said as the young man took the ladder away, leaving the new sign up and opening the car boot again. "Here's my business card," she said, handing Kiara a laminated gold-lined card. "Remember to call me if you ever decide to move home, and as a friend of Jane's, I'll even give you a discount on my fee."

"Okay, I will, I promise," Kiara said as the woman joined the young man in the car and waved at Kiara from the window as they continued on their journey, heading towards the main road.

Kiara stood for a moment staring at the sign and pondering on the words that the estate agent had said to her. Jane had been planning on selling the house long before Martin's death, and he knew nothing about it. He had never even wanted to sell. But Jane had been so convinced that she could sell that she had an estate agent lined up in the wings ready to jump. There was clearly a lot more to Jane Powers than the grieving widow she had met at the funeral.

Kiara climbed back in the car and carried on up the long, winding driveway until she came to the main house. She parked in the nearest designated space, about twenty feet from the steps that led up to the front door, directly next to a brand-new Mercedes sports car that carried the registration number JP1. A new toy for the sad widow, Kiara thought. Definitely a car that was not suited to a county home with small country lanes that no doubt were hard to navigate in the wintertime. This was a car that was destined for a swanky city penthouse. She locked the small hire car and walked up the sweeping stairway that could have come straight out of an old eighteenth-century novel and came face-to-face with an imposing wooden door with a huge circular doorknocker.

Without hesitation, Kiara lifted the knocker and rapped on the door twice. Within a few seconds, she could hear footsteps in the background. The door was pushed open, making Kiara step back slightly. The familiar elegant outline of Jane Powers appeared before her.

"Oh, I thought you were the agent coming back," she said with her slight Scottish lilt. "I know you, don't I?" she said, looking deeply at Kiara.

"Yes, I am – was – the investigator on your late husband's life policy. I also came to the funeral."

141

Jane was clearly taken aback by this and instinctively moved backwards into the house, not as an invitation to Kiara, but more as a protection for herself. Kiara quickly stepped forward across the threshold as if an invitation had been given.

"I'm so sorry to surprise you like this," Kiara said, as she pushed the door closed behind her.

"No, I'm sorry, I didn't mean to come across like that. I just never expected to see a stranger at the door. I don't have many visitors this far out. And then when you said who you were I was a little taken aback. Do forgive me. Please, come in."

"Thank you." Kiara was equally taken aback. She had built Jane Powers up in her mind to be a cold-blooded killer. Someone who not only killed her own husband but also was responsible in some part for Asher's death. She had transferred all her fears and emotions into this one woman, and yet standing here in front of her, looking into her eyes, she saw nothing but sadness and loneliness, and perhaps even fear. Certainly, there was nothing evil or hard in those beautiful eyes. "I'm so sorry to have startled you and to have turned up uninvited."

"It's fine. Really. Please, let me take your coat. And come in, let me get you a drink."

She led Kiara through the hall to a small lounge at the bottom of the staircase. "What can I get you? A hot drink, tea or coffee? Or maybe a small whisky?"

"Um, actually, I think I'm fine, to be honest."

"Okay, well, sit down, please." Jane led them to two small armchairs that were by the window. "And tell me why you are here. If I recall, you have to come a long way to see me, so this must be important."

Kiara wanted to launch into her prepared speech. Question the suspect but give nothing away. Draw her out. Find out about her secret relationship with MJ. But sitting there looking at Jane Powers, she simply couldn't imagine she was caught up in anything other than the very sad loss of her husband. She had no right to be there, or to accuse this poor woman of anything.

Kiara got up out of the chair. "I'm so sorry, I shouldn't have come here. I shouldn't stay."

Jane stood up as well and gently took Kiara's arm. "Please don't go. You want to ask me something, I can see that. Please, I have nothing to hide." She led Kiara to sit back down and took her own chair opposite once again. "Please," she asked.

Kiara could feel the tears welling up in her own eyes. She wasn't sure exactly what to say, but the words simply came tumbling out.

"I think your husband was murdered," she blurted out. "I always knew there was something wrong with the claim. I couldn't work out what, but my instinct was constantly going wild. So, I had to find out why. But something happened. I must have said the wrong thing to the wrong person and now my own husband's been killed." Her tears started to flow as she felt the words pour out. "And the only link I have to his murder is you and your husband. And there's another lady as well, in Bristol. Her husband's been killed too, and I think that they are all connected, I just don't know how."

Jane Powers stood up quickly, unsteady on her feet.

"My husband died, he was not killed!" she said, raising her voice at Kiara. "How dare you, how dare you…" she fell back into her chair, struggling to catch her breath.

"Oh my God, I didn't mean it to come out like that," Kiara said, as she rushed to Jane's side.

"My inhaler, I need my inhaler." Jane could hardly speak. "It's in my room." She tried to get herself up, but her arms and legs suddenly lost all their strength.

Kiara helped her to stand, taking the taller woman's weight into her own.

"Where's your room, I'll help you get there," she said.

"Upstairs. First room on the right." She barely got the words out in between trying to snatch a breath.

Kiara, taking all the weight she could, helped Jane up the stairs to the top and then led her into the first room on the right. The bedroom was huge, almost as big as Kiara's whole downstairs at home. She could feel Jane pulling to her left towards another closed door within the room, which she realised went into the bathroom. She helped Jane into the room and over to the marble sink. Jane leant on the sink and pushed Kiara away. "Just go," she said, pushing Kiara away.

"Let me help find your inhaler," Kiara said.

"Just leave me alone!" Jane shouted at her, suddenly with enough strength in her voice to startle Kiara, to force her to back out of the bathroom into the main bedroom. Kiara turned to leave the room, but noticed a large balcony running almost the full length of the opposite wall. The door was open. She walked over and went outside, taking in a lungful of air.

She couldn't believe she had done that. She had turned up out of the blue and then just told her that her husband's death was a murder, and, in fact, part of a triple murder. How did she think she would react? What a fool she was.

"I'm so sorry, Jane, I don't know what came over me, it was insensitive to just blurt all that out…" Kiara said, as she turned around back into the room. What she saw froze her to the spot.

Jane Powers was no longer in the bathroom. She was standing in the middle of the room. She had a gun in her hand, a small handgun. It was pointing at the floor, but Kiara backed up into the wall of the balcony nevertheless.

"You're not meant to be here, they said no one would ever find out," Jane said.

The gun was shaking so violently it could go off at any moment. Kiara found herself shrinking down to the floor, trying to keep out of the line of sight.

"You don't want to do this, Jane," Kiara said, trying to keep her voice steady and unthreatening.

"They promised it would be better once he was gone."

Kiara needed to calm her down. But more than that, she needed to know who Jane was talking about. She had to know who was doing this to them, who had killed Asher.

"I'm sure it wasn't your fault, Jane. It was them, not you. But who are they, who made you do this?" she asked gently, just one friend asking another friend an almost innocuous question.

But Jane wasn't listening to her, her hands and voice were shaking so much that she looked as if she might break down at any moment. Kiara watched nervously as the finger on the trigger twitched backwards and forwards.

"Only Martin was meant to die, no one else. They said no one ever dies apart from the men who deserve it."

"Please put the gun down, Jane, you don't want to hurt me, do you?"

"He deserved it, you know, he was a monster."

Kiara tried to keep her talking, to keep her mind focused on her rather than the gun.

"Is that why you killed him? Because they told you that you had to? Did they make you kill him, Jane?"

Jane looked up, her own eyes glazing over as she stared directly into Kiara's eyes.

★★★

In her own mind, she was back two years ago. It was their wedding anniversary. And it was the night Martin had stolen from her the one thing that she was unable to ever forgive him for.

"I told you I don't want children!" he screamed down at Jane, towering over her as she sat at the dining room table having just finished the anniversary meal she had spent the day preparing for them. The thunder of his words was so strong that the flames from the candles on the table flickered aggressively, throwing spikes of shadows around the walls. Jane desperately wanted to get up and turn the lights on to shake off the darkening atmosphere in the room, but she was too frightened to even move an inch. She knew that Martin's temper could go one of two ways. Either it would burn out with exhaustion, as it often did, sending his obese body back into his chair gasping for breath as he verbally abused her, or the adrenalin would start coursing around his body, giving him a burst of energy that he seemingly could only expel through physical violence. She lived in a lottery with just two numbers, and neither were ones where she could win. She closed her eyes and lowered her head, hoping beyond hope that it would be the first as, over the years, his words had become less painful to her than his fists.

"Don't you dare look away from me!" he screamed down at her, his left hand grabbing the top of her head, bringing her face up to his as he drew his right hand back to slap her hard.

Martin Powers was a large man and Jane could do nothing to stop the viciousness of the strike. She flew from the chair as it toppled over and landed on her back near the door, her head hitting the floor hard whilst her hands instinctively went to her tummy as protection to what was growing inside.

She felt the kick before she even saw it. She knew instantly that this was going to be one of those nights when the adrenalin would win over the fatigue and the fists would win over the words.

"Martin, the baby, please…" she shouted after the first kick hit the inside of her thigh.

"It's not my baby, is it, is it?!" he screamed down at her, the spittle showering her.

"Of course it is!" she screamed back as another kick landed, this time only inches from her stomach.

"It's his, isn't it, your fucking personal trainer? That bald fuck!"

"Ross is more man than you'll ever be," she shot back with

venom, seemingly no longer afraid of his reaction. "But no, it's not his. It's yours. Don't you remember the night? Surely you do! It was when you raped me after smashing my face into the door. It was the only thing that could get you excited, wasn't it, taking me like that...?"

He never let her finish the sentence as he landed a punch full on her nose, breaking it for the second time in their marriage.

"Whore!" he screamed at her. "Fucking whore! I should never have married you. You'll get nothing from me. I'll throw you back where I found you, I'll leave you with nothing."

The final kick landed directly in the middle of her stomach. As she lost consciousness, she knew what he had done, that he had taken from her the only thing she had ever truly wanted.

***

Jane started to walk forwards, the gun still levelled at her own feet as the memory of that night started to fade. Kiara sank back further into the wall, sliding along into the corner as Jane came and stood over her, the gun so close that Kiara could almost see into the barrel.

"They didn't make me kill him, they helped me. They showed me what I could do. He had to die. He was a monster. I lost our baby because of him, he kicked me until our baby was gone. And then he blamed me for losing him a son. Every day he hurt me, every day since we were married." She looked down at Kiara as if she was seeing her there for the first time. "And he would have killed me as well, eventually. Men like that always end up killing their wives. And they always get away with it. She told me that herself. It happened to her, you know. She's still in prison, nearly twenty years of her life and all she was doing was protecting herself. But I'm not as strong as she is. I can't go to prison. I can't. I'd rather have let him kill me than have that."

Jane suddenly steeled herself. The shaking stopped. The tears stopped. She'd made her choice; she was ready to do what she had to do. She looked Kiara directly in the eye. "I won't go to prison like her," she said with sadness in her voice.

"You don't have to, Jane. It doesn't have to go down like that."

"How do you know? Who even are you?!" she screamed at her.

"Please. I'm a mother as well, I have twin daughters. Mia and Jasmin, they are so beautiful. They've already had their dad taken from them. They can't lose me as well. Please, Jane, don't leave them without a mother as well."

Jane stepped back slightly, looking around her as if she suddenly realised where she was. "He deserved what we did to him, for everything he had done to me, to my baby."

"But I haven't done anything, have I? And my own husband, Asher. My children's father. He didn't deserve to die, did he?"

"She wouldn't kill your husband. No innocents ever get hurt. Only men like Martin. She promised me that."

"Who is *she*, Jane?"

Jane stepped to the side of Kiara and backed herself into the opposite corner. "She promised me," she said, looking deeply at Kiara.

Kiara watched, almost as in slow motion, as Jane raised the gun up and turned it to face herself. "Jane, no, don't!" she screamed and jumped up to try to reach Jane before she could pull the trigger.

"I'm so sorry…" the words barely left Jane's mouth as she pulled the trigger, sending a bullet into her own brain. The force of the shot thrust her body backwards into the wall and then over the balcony.

Kiara reached her a millisecond too late. The spray of Jane's blood hit her face as the momentum of running forwards forced Kiara right into the corner where Jane had been standing. She braced herself to avoid following Jane over the wall. She couldn't help but look down and see Jane's body spread twenty feet below by the front door, blood seeping from the hole the bullet had left in her temple. Kiara stumbled back into the bedroom, running into the bathroom, only just making it to the sink in time before being sick.

She looked into the mirror above the sink. Her face was covered with blood and fragments of bone. She was almost sick again but managed to hold it down. She turned on the hot tap and wiped herself clean, taking long, deep breaths to calm her heartbeat down. She couldn't help Jane now, she knew that, but she couldn't leave her body just lying there. She had to go down and face her. She had to take a sheet and cover the body and then call the police.

She left the bathroom and walked over to the bed and pulled the heavy duvet onto the floor. The fitted sheet underneath came away easily and she dragged it behind her as she started back down the stairs. As she neared the bottom, she heard a key turning in the front door lock. Startled, she found herself pulling the sheet with her as she dashed behind a full suit of armour that guarded the lowest stair in the hallway. The front door opened, and she watched as an older lady stepped into the hall, a gun in her hand, this one pointing upwards. She held her breath as she watched her pull a long tube from her pocket. Kiara assumed it was a silencer, the kind of thing she had seen numerous times in spy films. Whoever she was, she had now stepped slowly into the hallway, screwing the barrel onto the end of the gun as she turned her head left and right, before looking upwards, focusing on the floor above.

The Lady, gun in hand, slowly walked forwards, so quietly that her feet made almost no sound at all. Kiara drew in a deep breath, trying to silence the beating noise her heart was making in her head. The Lady stopped suddenly and turned towards the suit of armour that was now directly to her left. She raised the gun in one action, ready to shoot. Kiara, purely on instinct, pushed forward with all her strength, forcing the heavy suit of armour to fall sideways, straight into her, forcing the gun to slip from her hand and making her sprawl on the floor. Kiara leapt forwards as she screamed in anger, the bedsheet seemingly following her for a few steps as it initially caught on her shoe before it came loose. Kiara grabbed the door handle and ran down the outside steps towards her car.

Just as she reached for the driver's door, a bullet hit the side window door, covering Kiara in shards of glass. Without even turning around to see what was happening behind her, Kiara sprinted off away from the car and ran down the drive towards the front gate. Her muscles twitched in recognition as if the gun had been a starting pistol and she hit her maximum speed within seconds. With clarity of mind, she knew that there was no way the older lady could catch her before she reached the road; she wasn't sure the same could be said for a bullet.

She made it through the gates in under a minute and had started running down the centre of the road just as a car was turning the corner, heading directly at her. The driver slammed on his brakes and came to an emergency stop as Kiara slid up onto his bonnet and then back down onto the road, landing on her backside. The driver jumped out of the car and ran around to her.

"Oh my God, I didn't see you. You came out of nowhere! Are you okay?" he said as he reached down to pull Kiara up. "Oh my God, you're bleeding!" he blurted out, noticing the scratches where the shattered glass had left its mark on her face.

"We've got to go!" Kiara screamed at him. "She's got a gun!"

"What? Who's got a gun?" the man said in surprise as he leant forward and pulled Kiara to the side of his car out of the road.

Kiara felt the man fall backwards almost in slow motion as a blood red river burst from his face. For the second time in a matter of moments, Kiara's face was covered in someone else's blood and bone. Another bullet followed quickly, this time striking the car door, so close to her that a spark flew back and hit her in the cheek. The shock woke her up out of the trance she was falling into. She turned and saw The Lady at the gate. The gun was in her hand, taking aim, this time levelled perfectly at Kiara. In the split second it took the bullet to leave the gun, Kiara's incredibly quick reactions took hold and she dived through the open car door as the bullet ripped into it, in the exact spot she had been standing. The car's key was still in the ignition. The driver must have leapt out without thinking about the key when he had driven into Kiara. She turned it and threw the car into reverse, driving backwards at such a speed that she could hardly keep the car in a straight line. She reversed into the corner of the drive, lucky that the road remained empty, and then pulled the steering wheel hard to the left, making the car spin on its axis until it was facing the other way. Thrusting the gears into first, she slammed her foot on the accelerator and sped off down the road before The Lady had a chance to take another shot at her.

The Lady lowered the gun before turning around and nonchalantly walked back up the drive. Before she reached the body of Jane Powers, she took her mobile phone from her bag and took a deep breath before making the call she would rather have avoided.

Five miles down the road, Kiara pulled into a layby. Her heart was still beating furiously in her chest, but her hands had at last stopped shaking. Her fear was once again quickly turning to rage. She couldn't believe that in the space of under an hour she had witnessed a suicide, a murder and had been shot at numerous times, and she was sure by the same people who had murdered Asher. She pulled down the visor and looked at her bloodied face in the mirror.

"Enough!" she said to herself in the mirror. "It ends now. Whoever the hell you are, you are not going to kill anyone else."

She leant forward and opened the glove compartment, taking

out a packet of wet wipes that she found. She took a few out and cleaned her face. It struck her once again that the driver, another completely innocent person, had also just been murdered. And he had wet wipes in his car. The investigator in her put it together in her mind and saw the man at his home with a family of his own. A young child in his arms and a wife by his side. The sad picture that had formed in her mind brought tears to her eyes.

She knew she had to get to the airport first before doing anything, but once she was through security and safe from whoever was doing this, she would phone the police anonymously and tell them that a man and a woman had been killed and point them towards the Powers' mansion. She wanted to do more, but she had to get out of Edinburgh safely and get home to her own children first. Her stomach tightened as she thought about her twins, Mia and Jasmin. If whoever they are could do what she had just seen, then there was no guarantee her daughters would be safe. She once again put the car into gear and screeched out of the layby, at the same time pulling her phone from her pocket. Keeping one hand on the steering wheel, she dialled her own home number with the other. The phone connected right away, but all she heard was the old message on the answerphone that she and Asher had recorded when they first moved into Brittany Road.

"... Sorry, but please leave a number and one of the little Foxes might just call you back."

"Call me, immediately. One of you, I don't care who, just call me. And don't go outside. Lock the doors and stay in. Just trust me on this, okay? And call me right back."

She dropped the phone onto the passenger seat and put her hand back onto the steering wheel as she pushed her right foot as deep onto the accelerator as it allowed.

CHAPTER 19

Edinburgh Airport

Kiara pulled into the outside car park at Edinburgh Airport and found an empty space in between two other similar sized cars. She pulled in tightly to them with the hope of being able to hide what was ostensibly a stolen vehicle splattered with the dead owner's blood and a string of bullet holes. She could barely think about it without feeling like she was about to throw up. But she had no choice, she had to get back home to her daughters and if she phoned the police now and reported everything then she had no doubt she would be retained at least for the evening, which would leave the girls and her in-laws vulnerable to whoever these people were. Walking away from the stolen car, she realised that she would have to call the hire car company as well and tell them that their car was sitting outside a stately home in Edinburgh with bullet marks down one side and its passenger window blown through. She almost laughed out loud as to what they would say to that. Her emotions were clearly running wildly from despair to hysteria. She had to get a grip on them right away, as without a clear mind, she'd never make it safely onto the plane and back home to Brighton.

Having parked the car, she went into the main terminal building and headed for the toilets. She needed to make sure that all the blood and mess was off her and that she'd not draw the attention of the border police. She was surprised looking at herself that she looked remarkably fine. Most of the blood was already off from the wet wipes she'd found, and her hair had not moved an inch from the moment she'd left the house that morning. She rubbed some water onto the small red stain on her sleeve and then rolled down the cuffs on both arms to cover the marks left from the glass that had sprayed onto her from both cars.

Once she felt ready to face everyone, she left the bathroom and headed over to the EasyJet desk.

"Good afternoon, madam, how may I help you?" The young girl's accent was so strong that it took Kiara a second to understand what she had said.

"I have a flight booked for later tonight, but I would like to see if I can get onto an earlier one, maybe something going soon…"

After some to-ing and fro-ing, with Kiara happily agreeing to pay the full amount once again – she would have paid anything at that point – she was put on the next direct flight, which was due to leave within the hour. She took the new boarding pass and rushed straight to security, knowing that once she was off the main floor and over the security line that she would be safe from whoever might have followed her there. She looked closely at every older woman that she saw, but the problem was, even though she had been up close and personal with her, she somehow couldn't recall exactly what the woman had looked like; all she remembered was thinking it odd that an old woman was pointing a gun at her.

Once she was through security, she felt the threat drop slightly. She was still worried for her girls, but she doubted the woman could get to her home before her. Thinking about her girls made her remember that no one had answered the phone earlier and no one had called her back. The tension instantly came back to her. She took out her phone and placed a call to her home number. This time it was answered after one ring.

"Kiara, where are you? We've been so worried since you left that message. What's going on?"

"Are the girls with you?"

"The girls? No, they are at school. You're scaring me, what's happened, and what did you mean lock the doors?"

"I'm sorry, Judy, I can't explain right now. I'm on my way back, my flight is about to leave. Can you do me a favour and just get to the school early? I need you to pick up the twins as soon as they leave the building and take them straight home. And just don't answer the door to anyone, okay? No one."

"What's happened? What's this all about?"

"Just trust me, please. As soon as I get home, I'll explain, but for now, just do this. Okay?"

"Okay, but you're really scaring me."

"I'll be home as soon as I can. Just lock the doors and wait for me."

Kiara cut off the call, checked the boarding pass on her phone and willed the time to go just that bit faster. She could feel her heart beating like a hammer in her chest. She kept a constant look around the boarding area in case somehow she had been followed there.

The Lady watched Kiara clear security and head for the safety of the lounge. There was no way for anyone to tell from the outside the anger that she felt in that moment. She couldn't even for a second consider that she was losing her touch, but she knew that Sophia would soon start to doubt her. Firstly, there was the mess in Bristol where she had killed Michael Hall rather than simply threatening him, which had been a last-minute decision on her part, but she still felt it had been the right one. Then there was the mix-up at the airfield, which was definitely an error and down to her. And now she'd not only let Jane Powers die, but another innocent man had been murdered and Kiara had managed to get away. She personally had no feelings about all the so-called innocent people she had killed, but she knew that Sophia could never fully come to terms with what sometimes had to be done.

And she was starting to wonder if she was getting too old for this job. Never before, in all her years, had she missed a target, yet suddenly here she was, unable to stop one woman from exposing them all. She needed to finish her once and for all.

She checked the departure screen. She had made it to the airport in the nick of time. After Kiara had driven off, she had walked back up to the main house and taken a set of car keys that had been lying in an ashtray near the front door. It took her less than a minute to find the black Range Rover. She assumed it had once belonged to Martin Powers by the disgusting smell that still lingered in the seats. She drove to the airport just a few miles behind Kiara, briefly stopping on the way to hide the gun in the forest where she had left it hidden over a year before when she had first driven up to meet Jane Powers on MJ's recommendation that they could help the women. She had liked Jane Powers and was not happy that, because of Kiara Fox, she was now lying dead on her driveway. She would make her pay for that.

After she saw Kiara head to the gate, she slowly walked over to the check-in desk and bought herself a ticket for the same flight to Gatwick. The only seat left was right at the back of the plane, but that suited her perfectly, as it meant she could hide away, although she knew Kiara would likely not recognise her even if she had been seated right across from her.

She took her boarding pass and walked straight to the lounge. She knew that she should update Sophia right away, but she didn't want to tell her just yet what had happened. She would have to tell her soon enough, she knew that, but she wanted to do it at the same time as telling her that she had taken care of Kiara Fox once and for all and that her prison release was secured.

CHAPTER 20

Gatwick Airport

The plane journey was without incident and landed exactly on time. Kiara disembarked and headed straight for the short-term car park where she had left her car only a few hours before. Her mobile rang as soon as she was settled into the driver's seat, making her jump. She had to take a deep breath and calm herself down once again. She looked at the phone but didn't recognise the number. She wasn't sure she should take it in case it was MJ or perhaps even the police, both she would rather have avoided at that exact moment. But on the third ring, she couldn't help herself and swiped the phone to answer it.

"Hello," she said faintly into the handset.

"Hello, is that Mrs Fox?" came the reply.

"Who is this?" Kiara asked softly, scared of what the answer would be.

"I'm sorry, the line is faint, I can hardly hear you. This is Simone from Quality Hire Car, in Edinburgh. I need to speak with a Kiara Fox urgently."

Kiara cut the phone off without answering. She had no idea how she could possibly explain everything that had happened to their car. And just now, she had more important things to worry about. She dialled her home number. The phone rang five times before cutting to the answerphone. She hung up before the machine had time to make its pitch. She redialled her mother-

157

in-law's mobile number. It also rang five times before going to answerphone. Again, Kiara cut off without leaving a message.

"Oh, for Christ's sake, answer the bloody phone, Judy," she said to her empty car as she started the engine.

Her mobile rang back almost at the same time as she put the car into drive. She answered it without looking at the caller's number.

"Judy," she blurted into the phone.

"Er no, sorry, it's Rosie. Rosie Hall, from Bristol? I was hoping you would have called me back by now."

"Oh God, I'm so sorry. I was going to, but… I'm not sure where to start…"

"Do you know what happened to my husband? That would be a good starting point," Rosie said accusingly. "Did you have something to do with it?"

All bets were off now, and Rosie wanted answers.

"No, I didn't." Kiara replied, taken aback by the accusation being levelled at her.

"My husband was murdered," Rosie replied. "I know he was, and maybe calling you just puts me in danger as well, assuming you're part of this. But I've no one else to try. And no one is listening to me…" Rosie started to cry down the line.

"I do believe you. I really do. And I'm not part of this, I can promise you that."

"You believe me?" Rosie said hopefully, desperation pouring out in her voice.

"They killed my husband as well."

The line went quiet whilst Rosie tried to take in what Kiara had just blurted down the phone.

"Rosie, are you still there?" Kiara asked into the silence of the phone.

"Yes, I'm here. They killed your husband as well? Oh my God, I'm so sorry."

"And just this morning, I was shot at. So yes, I believe you. But I can't talk now. I've got to get home. I've left my children with my in-laws and I need to get them all somewhere safe. And then I'm going after them. I'm going to take these bastards down."

"Who are they?"

"Once I've got my girls safely away, I'll come to you. You might know more that you think you do. You're in Bristol, right?"

"Yes."

"I'll call you as soon as I can. You can trust me, Rosie, I'm not one of them. Just please keep your head down, okay? These are serious people. And stay by your phone. I'll call as soon as I can." With that, Kiara cut off the phone and sped out of the car park, heading straight onto the M23 back home to Brighton.

Kiara broke every speed limit along the way, so desperate to get home that she didn't care about the consequences. She pulled into the small driveway in front of her house, almost knocking over the potted plant near the front door and rushed into the house.

"Mia, Jasmin?"

"Kiara, is that you?" The voice came from the lounge.

She rushed in. Peter was sitting in his usual chair near the conservatory.

"What's going on with you today? You've left Judy scared out of her wits."

"Where is she? Does she have the girls?"

"She went to the school as you asked her to. I have to say, I wasn't happy with the way she drove off. She could kill herself, or someone else at that speed."

Before Kiara had a chance to reply, the front door opened. Kiara span around.

"Mummy!" the girls cried in unison, running into her arms.

"Gran got us out of school early. I managed to miss chemistry!" Mia said with a delighted edge to her voice.

"And I missed maths, result!" Jasmin joined in.

Kiara held them so close as tears ran down her face.

"Mum, you're squashing us," Mia said, trying to break away from the tight grip.

"I can't breathe," Jasmin said as she and Mia pushed Kiara away.

Judy came forward and took Kiara in her arms as Kiara broke down in tears.

"What's happened, darling?" Judy asked. "What on earth's going on?"

"I don't know where to start. I'm not even sure I believe it all myself."

"Try me, my darling."

Kiara sent the girls upstairs to their room and then told Judy and Peter everything, from finding the Bristol case attached to her own Powers case, to Asher's murder, Jane Powers' death and the attempt on her own life. Even though it all sounded so outlandish as she told them, it somehow once again brought her the strength she needed to do what she had to do.

Judy and Peter sat there and listened to the whole story.

"Have you called the police?"

"Not yet. I needed to get here first."

"So, we'd better call them now," Peter said.

"You believe me then? You're not going to tell me I'm having a breakdown or something?"

"Of course we believe you," Peter replied. "As bonkers as it all sounds, we know you well enough to never doubt you."

"Thank you, both of you. I don't think I'd have the strength to go on if I didn't have you two supporting me."

"What do you need us to do?" Judy repeated Peter's question. "I think you should call the police right now and tell them everything. I mean, people have been murdered, haven't they?"

"I know that. But I need to get you all to safety first."

"I'm sorry, Kiara, but I think you need to call the police first," Judy said. "I honestly don't understand why you haven't already called them, you could have done that when you were driving back."

"I will, I promise, I just need to be careful who we speak with. I don't want to put anyone else in danger. And I want to get you all to safety before I do anything else at all."

"Where do you want us to go?" Peter asked.

"Do you remember my friend from university, Nick Taylor? He and his wife spent the last bank holiday with us. He's the lawyer I went to university with. He lives in Worthing, just up the road. No one would think of looking for you there. And he's a criminal lawyer now and might know someone in the local police who we can call."

"And you really think he'll help? It's a big ask," Peter said.

"He'll help for sure. I want us all to be out of here within ten minutes."

"How long do we pack for?" Judy asked with a wobble as the fear crept into her voice.

Kiara took her mother-in-law's hands in hers. "It won't be long, I promise you. I have a plan that'll draw them out. Just a few days, and then it'll be over, I hope."

"What are you going to do?" her mother-in-law asked.

"I'd rather not say. Just trust me, I know what I'm doing. But I need you all to be safely tucked away first." Kiara called up the stairs, "Girls, throw some clothes together, you're going away with Gran and Gramps for a few days. And bring your iPads and your schoolwork."

"Cool!" the girls shouted in unison.

"Do we have to bring schoolwork?" Mia asked.

"Yes, you bloody do, it's a not a holiday."

They were out of the house and in the car within minutes and Kiara called Nick Taylor as she pulled out of the driveway.

"Hello, darling, long time no speak," Nick said.

"Are you at home?" she asked him.

"Yes. But just about to pop out to the office. Why?"

"Stay there. I can't explain over the phone, but I need to see you."

"Sounds a bit urgent, is everything okay?"

"No, it's not," Kiara said before cutting off.

"Don't you think you should have told him you have a car full on its way over and maybe someone's trying to kill you?" Peter asked.

Kiara looked over at her father-in-law and gave him a look that simply said, 'Would you have done that?' Peter smiled and nodded in silent agreement.

CHAPTER 21

The Lady – Gatwick Airport

The Lady smiled to the flight attendants as she left the plane and slowly made her way with the other passengers towards the exit sign.

Without any luggage to collect and not needing to go through passport control, she was out of the airport and heading to the car park in a matter of minutes. Her phone rang in her bag. She took a deep sigh. Only one person knew her number. She considered not answering, which was totally out of character, but thought better of it.

"So, did you take care of our business?" Sophia said, skipping the usual niceties that would start a conversation between them.

It was clear to The Lady that her friend was more anxious than ever, no doubt because she was almost at the end of her prison sentence and so close to being released. Also, it hadn't escaped her own attention that their last few conversations all included the fact that she had been unable to take care of the Kiara problem. She was not used to missing her target, and certainly not multiple times.

"No. There were problems." She couldn't lie to Sophia.

"Problems?"

"I arrived too late. By the time I got to the house, Jane was dead and Kiara was on her way out."

"You killed Jane?! One of our widows! Why would you do that? After everything I promised her. I told her I'd keep her safe…"

"I never said I killed her."

It took a moment for that to sink in before Sophia could answer again. "If not you, then who did? I can't believe Kiara killed her. MJ would have told me if she was a danger. I can't believe she went there to kill her."

"Sophia, please, calm down."

"Calm down! One of my girls has been killed and I should calm down? What is happening with you? You never made mistakes before. You would never have let any harm come to one of our widows."

"I never said the investigator killed her. And I never said I did. When I got there Jane was already dead. She may have fallen. She may have even taken her own life. But I don't think the investigator did it and I certainly didn't."

The Lady could hear Sophia taking a deep breath. She let her friend settle herself. She had known her long enough to know when to keep quiet and let her find her voice.

"And Kiara, I assume you spoke to her and warned her off, without harming her?"

It was now The Lady's turn to take a long, deep breath. "She got away from me before I had a chance to talk to her."

"Again?"

"Yes, again. And there's something else."

"Go on."

"I tried to stop her. But there was a man. A stranger. He got between us, and he was shot. I couldn't avoid it."

"Another innocent person. I told you no more deaths, why did you even have a gun, you were only meant to warn her. We have to stop this now. We can't go on like this any more."

"I have to stop Kiara first. She knows too much now. If she

pieces everything together then you might never get out of that place. You have to be released before you die in that hellhole, we need to stop her before she gets to the police."

"I don't care about my freedom, not any more. We were never meant to hurt any innocent people. We find them. We kill their husbands. Their abusers. We settle them into a new life. That's all. No one else should ever die."

"You ordered me to take care of Kiara, to stop her."

"I never said to kill her."

"You know what I do, and you know what had to be done. Did you really think all I would do is talk to her? She is a direct threat to everything we are doing and to both you and me personally. You know what needed to be done. You can pretend otherwise, you've always known. I did what I had to do to protect you. You can't survive another twenty years in there."

The Lady could almost hear Sophia's brain fighting itself to come to terms with what she had started.

"It needs to stop now. No one else can die because of me. And no more widows will be made. You understand me? It stops today."

"No."

She knew that Sophia would never allow her to keep going, not any more. But she was not going to abandon her now. She was going to see her friend a free woman, even if she had to kill a hundred people to make it happen.

"No! This is not up to you! You work for me. I created the widows and I say when it ends, not you. And it ends now."

The Lady had already made up her mind. She knew what she had to do. She cut off the call and stripped her phone of its SIM card, breaking it into small pieces and throwing it into the gutter. She climbed into her car, drove out of the airport and headed south onto the M23 towards Brighton.

★★★

Back in her prison cell, Sophia stared at the phone in her hand. She knew she had lost control of her. Up until that point, The Lady had only ever followed her orders, she would never have gone against her wishes. Sophia also knew that her friend was both deadly and unpredictable and could at any time become a liability. But she really believed as the years went by that there was a genuine understanding between them, that she would never betray Sophia's trust and that she would never take an innocent life to further the cause of the Widow Project, or even to protect Sophia, for that matter. This was the line Sophia had drawn and she felt secure in that. She also knew that The Lady was somehow under her spell, she had known it from the beginning and she had used it to manipulate her to do what she needed her to do.

She had to ask herself if she was really surprised that a time would come when her friend would do anything to protect her, even take a life for that. Deep down, she always knew that the risk was there. And she wondered if, in reality, she'd revelled in the power she held over her.

She dialled the only other number that was stored in her secret phone. It only had to ring twice before it was answered.

"MJ, I need to see you."

When MJ heard the ringtone her stomach had lurched. She had thought it was all over for her, that she would be able to finish the month out at work and then fade away from this life forever.

She felt physically sick having to give an answer.

"MJ. Did you hear me?"

"Yes, I heard you. Please, don't ask me to come there."

"We can't do this over the phone."

"You said this was over for me now."

"I can't call her off, I've tried, but she won't listen to me any more. We need to talk about your colleague." Sophia couldn't name Kiara on the phone in case someone was listening, but she knew that MJ would understand what she meant.

"You said you would leave her alone. You said that; you promised me…"

"It's not me any more…" she had to pause to find the right words… "She just wants to protect me, and she believes that is the only way to do that."

"Oh my God. We have to stop her."

"Come and visit me, tonight."

"They won't let me in that quickly. I need to register first and that can take days."

"I'm texting you the governor's number now. She'll let you in for the last visit of the day."

The phone went dead.

MJ didn't know what to do. Should she phone Kiara and warn her? But what could she say? She should phone the police. But then what? Kiara could still be in danger and MJ herself would be arrested, possibly even for murder.

She knew what she had to do. As much as it made her sick, she knew.

She called the number Sophia has just sent her.

"I've been told you can help me with an emergency visit," MJ said as soon as the phone was answered.

"You are already on the list," came the reply, before the phone abruptly cut off.

CHAPTER 22

Prison

MJ waited along with all the other visitors alongside her. She was exhausted. The drive from the London office to the prison was only an hour, but she felt like she had been on a roller coaster ride since the skydive and had barely managed a couple of hours' sleep in the days that followed. So by the time she arrived, she was almost dead on her feet.

She looked around the room, but no one made eye contact or seemed to care who else was there. They all simply sat on the small three-legged stools and kept their eyes either down into their own laps or fixed ahead. MJ knew if she closed her own eyes that she would probably not open them again. She took a long sip of the bitter coffee she had grabbed from the machine near the entrance and hoped that the caffeine would do its intended job. She hadn't seen Sophia in person for over ten years. Being back now reminded her of what they had done all those years ago and how she could have so easily ended up in prison for his murder just like Sophia. If not for Sophia, her own life would have been so different. She found her mind taking her back to those days.

★★★

She was back at the flat with Ivan, on the kitchen floor, lying on her side, trying to protect her kidneys as the kicks rained down.

"Why do you think you can talk to me like that?"

"What did I say?!"

His next kick was higher, much higher, directly at her head.

"You know what you said. And how you said it…"

After that, she remembered nothing apart from waking up in bed an hour later, a cup of tea on her bedside table and her fiancé sitting next to her with a sorrowful look on his face.

★★★

MJ wiped the memory from her mind as she sensed the people around her tense up as the doors on the other side of the window opened and the inmates were let through. She looked up and saw Sophia walk into the room. No matter how unsettled she felt being there, she was still excited at seeing her best friend. It was Sophia who had saved MJ from Ivan. It was Sophia who had made sure he would never hurt her, or anyone else ever again. And it was Sophia who had made sure she had enough money of her own to never have to rely on anyone again. She owed her everything.

Sophia sat down and picked up the handset that connected the two of them. "I never wanted it to come to this," she said to MJ down the phone.

"It's been so long since I saw you. I should've come before now," MJ replied, tears in her eyes at seeing her friend locked up whilst she was free to walk around and go wherever she wanted to.

"It's okay, I understand."

"You taught me how to fight back." MJ realised she had said too much. The prison listened to everything. "I'm sorry," she said.

"It's okay. I'm happy to see you now. I'm so pleased you received my message to come in. I heard about your sister, I heard she's unwell. Very unwell," Sophia looked MJ in the eye as she spoke. MJ understood that Sophia was talking about Kiara and not her non-existent sister. "She's been unwell for a while now, hasn't she?" Sophia continued. "I asked my doctor friend to see her."

MJ nodded.

"I know my friend wants to help, but I think she may have the wrong medication. She doesn't know your sister's medical history and I'm scared she's going to give her something that hurts her instead of helps her, could even cause a fatality." MJ listened intently as Sophia spoke so slowly so as to make each word count. "You need to tell your sister to be careful. Really, she should avoid seeing the doctor if she can. Maybe she could take a holiday, somewhere in the sun, where her and her children can relax and forget about everything for a while."

Kiara's life was in danger and Sophia was telling her to get her and the girls away from here, as far away as possible.

"Can't you just call your friend and say that my sister is feeling okay now and won't be bothering anyone any more?" MJ asked, keeping up the pretence and trying to phrase it in a way that would not alert anyone listening to what they were talking about.

"I tried, but you know how stubborn my friend can be when she wants to be. I am sure your sister will be fine, but just in case, do as I say and speak with her. Encourage her to get better somewhere in the sun, somewhere far away from our weather. And maybe you can go with her. I think it will be good for you to get away. I would hate you to catch anything as well, this illness can be deadly, and you are as susceptible to it as your sister."

Sophia leant in close to the window and looked deeply into MJ's eyes. *Be careful*, her eyes screamed at MJ. *Both of you need to be careful*. She wasn't allowed to say anything without talking through the handset and she dared not mouth anything with the cameras all around them. All she had was the fact that MJ knew her so well and could understand what that stare meant.

MJ put her hand onto the window that separated them and

Sophia did the same. Then both women turned away, one walking back through the door towards the cold cell that awaited her and the other heading out into the dangerous streets, worried not only for her friend's life but also for her own.

Despite her exhaustion, MJ had to get to Kiara before The Lady did. She pointed her car to the Sussex coast, to Kiara's hometown.

CHAPTER 23

Nick Taylor's House – Worthing

"Don't you think that maybe you're being a bit dramatic, darling? It's a little bit fantastic, don't you think?"

"Everything I've told you is true."

"Asher's death was recorded as accidental, there was nothing untoward about it. It was tragic, of course, but it's a dangerous sport and these things can, and do happen."

"They killed him. And they tried to kill me. Look, if you won't believe me then fine, but please, just look after my girls and in-laws, just until I can find a way out of this."

"Of course I will." He paused. "You're really serious about all this, aren't you?"

"It's all true, I promise you. Soon enough, the murders will be in the news. Jane Powers killed herself, but then that man who tried to help me…" She had to take a moment before she carried on. "I think MJ, my boss at work, is involved. Whoever she is working for has killed all these people and now they know I am coming after them my girls could be in danger. I need to do this, I have to find whoever killed Ash, and get some evidence so that the police will do something. But I can't do that and protect my girls at the same time."

"Don't worry about the girls, they're safe here. But if what you're saying is true then we need to call the police. I can't just let you do this on your own."

She took Nick's shoulders in her hands and looked deeply at him. "We will call them, I promise. But give me a little time to get some evidence, or at least find out who they are."

"I'm sorry, but you can't ask me to do that, not if you really think Asher was actually killed by whoever they are."

"I know it's a lot to ask, but I just need you to trust me on this. I need to get to Bristol and see Rosie, I can't let them hurt her, and she might know something that really can help me. And I need to confront MJ, she might be the key to me finding whoever these people are."

"If what you've told me is true then surely confronting MJ could be just as dangerous?"

"I don't believe she'd hurt me. Since Asher's death she's changed. She didn't know that they were going to do that. Whoever they are, and whatever they have planned, she wouldn't have agreed to them hurting me or the girls."

She could see that Nick wasn't sure how much of this to believe, or what he should be doing about it.

"Someone killed my husband. I wouldn't make this shit up."

"Okay, okay," he said.

"You know my job puts me in the firing line all the time. I find criminals and expose them. And I'm bloody good at it."

"Too good maybe."

Kiara took in his words. *Too good.* Was Asher's death her fault? Had she pushed too hard? MJ told her to pay the Powers claim. She'd begged her to. Threatened her with losing her job, even. MJ knew something could happen. She had been trying to warn her off, but she wouldn't listen. She never listened.

"It wasn't your fault. You were just doing your job, you couldn't have known." Nick could read her like a book. He knew she was blaming herself for Asher's death. "Go and do what you need to, and I'll look after the girls, I promise. Just be careful. But you know I need to call the police, right? I'll let you go, but I'm calling my friend Bruce the moment you drive away."

"Knowing the girls are safe is all I need from you right now."

Kiara pulled him into a hug and kissed him on the cheek.

"What's going on here then? I turn my back for just one moment…"

Kiara turned to see Nick's wife standing there, a huge smile on her face.

"Nah, he's too ugly for me. And nowhere near smart enough," Kiara said, taking a hug from Jennie.

"How are you, darling? You know, since… Sorry, I have no idea how to phrase this."

"It's fine, Jen, who does? I'm doing okay."

"Aunty Jen!" Mia and Jasmin screamed as they also came into the room.

"Hi Jennie," Peter and Judy echoed as they joined them.

"Wow, a Fox family party. Hi everyone. What a lovely surprise," Jennie said, taking in the group of people now around her.

"I think you should get going, Kiara," Nick said to her above the noise.

"Yes. Sorry, Jen, hate to love you and leave you, but I've got to run. Nick will fill you in on everything," she said, throwing Nick a look, which he returned with an eyebrow raise.

"Jen, darling, let's, er, have a little chat, in the kitchen, maybe."

Kiara gave the kids a final hug and smiled at her in-laws before leaving them all in the safe hands of Nick and Jennie.

As soon as Nick saw Kiara pull away from the drive, he sat his wife down and explained everything to her. Peter and Judy cut in and filled in the missing details whilst the girls played on their iPads in the next room, completely oblivious to the drama unfolding.

"You need to call Bruce."

"I know," he sighed.

"Now."

"I know."

He picked up his mobile and made the call.

The phone rang only once before diverting to the local station.

"Sussex Police, how can I direct your call?"

"Chief Superintendant Bruce Simpson, please."

"Whom may I say is calling?"

"Tell him it's his brother-in-law."

CHAPTER 24

Bristol

Rosie picked up the phone on the third ring. "Hello?"

"It's me, Kiara."

Rosie took a breath before answering.

"Are you there, Rosie?"

"Yes."

"I'm on my way to Bristol. We need to talk. But I'm worried you're in danger, can you go somewhere safe, where they can't find you?"

"If they wanted to hurt me then they would have done that by now."

"It's moved on a bit since we spoke. I went to Edinburgh to see Jane Powers, the case I was working on, and I was attacked."

"Oh my God, what happened?"

"I'd rather tell you when I see you. But two more people have died. This is serious."

"You killed two people?"

"No. Of course I didn't! Look, just get yourself somewhere safe. I'm scared they'll start silencing anyone else who might know anything, and you've been asking questions, haven't you?"

"Well, I did shout at the police, more than once. And I've certainly made a bit of noise around Michael's office."

"Exactly."

"I'll be safe at the gallery. I can stay in the café, it's always really busy there. I can find a place where I'm surrounded by people. They can't do anything to me in a crowd. I'll message you the address."

"It'll take me a couple of hours to get there. But just stay safe, okay?"

CHAPTER 25

Worthing

"Mr Taylor, do you know exactly where she is now?"

"I really don't. She never told me where she was going, and she's switched off her 'find me' on her phone."

"Do I need to tell you how serious this is? This is now a murder investigation and obstructing the police is a serious matter."

"I am well acquainted with the law, officer," Nick replied to the young policeman who had accompanied him to the police station. "And I'll do everything I can to help, but all I can do is tell you what facts I do know, and at the moment Kiara's whereabouts is not one of them."

"Two bodies have been found today and your friend," he looked at his notes, "Mrs Fox is implicated in both. The Scottish police have passed everything to us, but they are keen to talk to her in person. They have a car she hired covered in bullet holes at a residential property, a car stolen from a victim also covered in bullet holes, which she left at the airport before catching a plane to Gatwick. We now have two seemingly unconnected bodies, both shot."

"I know all this. It was me who told you. One of the bodies, a Mrs Jane Powers, took her own life, and the other – I don't know his name – was a man who just tried to help and was in the wrong place at the wrong time. What I need you to tell me is who the hell is doing this? Because I can tell you for certain it is not Kiara Fox."

"Mr Taylor…"

"When if your chief super back?"

"Mr Taylor…"

"Now, officer. I came here to help my friend and right now all you're doing is making wild assumptions and seemingly doing nothing to track down who these people are. I've already pointed you to a company called Seico Insurance Group. I've already pointed you to a senior person there called Mary-Jayne King who is Kiara's boss. What I want to know is what you're going to do about it."

"What we are doing about it, Mr Nicholas Taylor, is *our* job, not yours," came a new voice from the doorway.

Nick turned around to see a man his own age and very familiar to him enter the room.

"Bruce, thank God, I've been trying to call you!"

"What the hell is going on, Nick?" he asked him as he took over the conversation from the the young officer. "I have dead bodies in Scotland that suddenly are my problem and the main suspect on the run, seemingly with help from my sister's husband. Do you care to elaborate?"

Nick quickly brought Bruce up to speed on everything he knew.

"And where is she now? And please don't give me that crap about not knowing, I can tell when you're lying, even before you've decided to. Help me, mate, let me keep your friend safe and catch these bastards, whoever they are."

Nick knew that if Kiara was going to get through this then he needed Bruce as much as Bruce now needed him.

"She's gone to Bristol to meet the other investigator's widow, a Rosie Hall. She's worried for her safety, and I suspect she also thinks she'll have an ally in her. She'll be there by now, I'm sure, she left a couple of hours ago."

"Okay. And then? What's she planning next?"

"I don't know everything, I'm not sure she's even got that far herself. But she said she was going to confront MJ, her boss."

"From what you've told me, she thinks this MJ character is part of it. Do you believe that?"

"If Kiara believes it then I do. She's a smart cookie, Bruce. You met her, actually, at my fiftieth. Tall, tanned, quite stunning, actually."

"Oh yes. The one with the husband who was clearly punching above his weight." Bruce realised what he had just said. "Sorry, that was crass, wasn't it?"

"Asher was a good guy."

"We'll get to the bottom of this, mate. Look, for now, you go home and stay with her girls. I'll put a couple of cars outside your house, just in case. Meanwhile, I'll get hold of this MJ character and will contact my Bristol counterparts and see if they can track down Kiara and Rosie and get them into safe custody."

"Thanks, Bruce. I couldn't bear anything happening to Kiara or the girls, especially not after Asher…"

CHAPTER 26

Bristol

Rosie was sitting in the gallery café space when Kiara entered. The moment she walked in, they knew who each other was. It was obvious from the way both of them seemed to be looking for someone.

The Lady knew who they both were even before Kiara sat down next to Rosie. She'd seen them both plenty of times, she could have picked each of them out amongst a festival crowd if she had needed to. Neither of them saw her sitting there, just a table away.

The Lady had arrived at Brittany Road as Kiara was pulling out of the drive and then had followed her to Worthing, to Nick Taylor's house. She was tempted to stay in Worthing and send Kiara a message and a photo of her parked there. That would have been the most effective way of controlling her, but something deep within her just couldn't let her get away again. And she needed to know what was so important to Kiara that would make her leave her family so soon after what had happened. So, for the next two hours, she had followed Kiara all the way to Bristol in a car that was almost as innocuous looking as she was.

Kiara sat down next to Rosie and both ladies took a second to size each other up.

"You're alone?" Kiara asked.

"Nope, I have the Bristol Symphony Orchestra sitting and ready to play at a minute's notice," Rosie replied.

Kiara laughed. "Sorry, that was a stupid question, I deserved that."

"And you weren't followed here?" Rosie asked in seriousness.

"Yes, I was followed by a troupe of travelling assassins, who are sitting right next to us at that table just waiting to pounce," Kiara replied, pointing to The Lady's table without realising just how close she was in her description.

"Touché," said Rosie.

The two ladies stared at each other for a moment longer, neither knowing exactly how to continue the conversation.

"You go first," they said in unison.

"Sorry, you go…" again in unison.

The Lady sat listening to them, wondering how either woman had had the ability to survive her attacks so far.

"Let me," Kiara replied quickly before Rosie could speak again. Rosie nodded. "Both of us have seen our husbands murdered in front of us. And I was almost killed yesterday as well. This must be all connected to the cases your husband and I were working on. And I need to know what you know so I can piece it together."

"I agree. But I'm not sure I know much. I was hoping you could fill in the blanks for me, to be honest. Tell me about yesterday, what exactly happened?"

"I went to Edinburgh, to visit the widow of one of my cases. I believe it all started with her and the life claim she put in when her husband died. I was never comfortable with the claim, not from day one. I don't know what it was exactly, maybe it was the fact that there was no explanation as to why he had been in so much pain before he died, or it might have been the way his widow spoke to me when I first called her, like she had something to hide, but whatever it was my instincts just kept telling me something was off. But each time I pushed back and started asking questions, MJ, that's my boss at Seico, kept fobbing me off and pushing me to settle it. I wish I had now, maybe if I had, Asher…" Kiara had to stop talking as the emotions of the last few weeks started to surface.

"Go on," Rosie prompted her. "Your boss wanted you to pay

the claim, but you didn't," she reminded her where they were in the conversation.

"Yes, sorry, that's right. MJ seemed to be fighting me all the way on it. We've been friends since I started at Seico, MJ and I. In fact, I joined Seico almost three years ago and she was the first person I knew there. Anyway, with this case, she just wouldn't listen to anything I said, she was just 'pay the bloody case or else'. I'd never seen her like that and part of me thought I should just settle it and move on, but that's just not me. If I see something wrong, I need to act on it. It's what I'm paid for, for Christ's sake! I just wanted MJ to let me do my job! But she wouldn't."

"Michael was never like that," Rosie interrupted Kiara's flow. "I wish he had been. I did love him. More than I can say. But I knew his faults as well. He was always looking for the quick wins, even if it meant cutting corners. I'm like you, the exact opposite to him, but he was what he was. I think he did it for me. You know, taking risks, by pushing through cases just to get them off the books and make himself look like he was busy all the time. I'm sure that's why the company rewarded him more, you know, for the number of cases he cleared each month rather than the fraud he found. I remember him talking about an MJ, I think she was his boss as well. I seem to remember something about her telling him to settle a big case a few years back and it really pissed him off."

"Did he pay it, though?"

"Oh God yes. He might have hated being spoken to like that, but he never would have had the balls, or even care too much, not to do it. And he knew if he settled his cases quickly and kept his caseload down that he'd get a little extra in his pay packet."

"It's crazy, isn't it?" Kiara said. "I was always being told to speed things up and stop missing my targets just because I wanted to do the right thing, whereas your husband got bonuses for just clearing his cases no matter if they were fraudulent or not. The whole insurance industry seems really fucked up sometimes."

"I always tried to tell him that doing the right thing was better than just doing the job, but anyway, like I say, he was what he was. So, why did you and Michael start talking?"

"I'm getting to that bit," Kiara said, trying to take back the narrative. "Eventually, I had no choice but to just pay the claim as I was being threatened with the sack. So, I visited Jane Powers, she's the widow I was talking about. I went up to her husband's funeral in Scotland. Long story short, I came back and was about to pay the claim when I realised I was in the wrong file. I almost sent millions of pounds to the wrong account. After I logged out and logged back in, that was when I found your husband's case. He had attached a file he was working on, which was almost identical to the Martin Powers case in the way they died and the claim amount, to my file. I have no idea how he managed to do that, but nevertheless he did. So, of course, instead of just paying my one I made contact with him right away. Anyway, from there on, it's all a bit of a blur. Your husband was killed in a hit and run at around the same time that my husband was killed at a charity skydive we were doing."

"Oh my God, that's awful. Did you actually see it happen?"

"Yes. My twin girls did as well."

"Oh my God!" Rosie put her hands to her mouth in shock.

"Looking back now, I know it wasn't Ash they had tried to kill. It was me. Clearly to stop me poking around any more. But something happened at the airfield that meant us having to swap places. And… anyway, he died, and it was just the worst thing. My girls won't ever forget seeing their dad die like that. Whoever did that to him, they are ruthless, what they did was evil."

"And after that, you still didn't pay the claim? And you went back to see her. I'm not sure I would have been as brave as you."

"It wasn't right away. I was off work a couple of weeks first. Then I went back in. You know, just to get out of the house and try to get a bit of normality back, whatever that is. Also, I just needed to know if I was missing something. I wasn't sure exactly what I would find, but I needed to just go back to the office."

"I was the same," Rosie said. "After I lost Michael, I went apeshit at the police. They were so convinced it was an accident that their investigation seemed limited to just finding the driver rather than looking at his work and seeing if it could be tied in to one of his cases like I was telling them. So, I went to his office to try to find something, anything, that could prove I was right. That was when I saw your email to him, and it just somehow gave me hope that there was someone I could talk to."

"So, I went back and pulled up the cases," Kiara continued. "And I found that not only had MJ paid my case, but she had done it on the very day that Asher died. I couldn't believe that, after everything she saw, she then went straight back to the office and paid my case out. Also, my case and your husband's case had both been deleted from the system."

"What?! Surely that just makes it look even more suspicious?"

"I know. Unbelievable, isn't it? I mean, talk about trying to cover your tracks and getting it wrong."

The Lady at the table next to them tried to keep herself calm, but just hearing what MJ had done made her blood boil. Such stupidity. She vowed to herself that she would deal with that girl as well, as soon as these two were taken care of.

"So, I jumped on a flight to Edinburgh. I needed to look Jane Powers in the eye. I needed to know if she and MJ were in on this together somehow. If maybe *they* were the ones doing all this. Then it all just went crazy. Jane killed herself right in front of me. I went back down the stairs to get out and ran right into this lady." Kiara tried to picture her, but there was just nothing she could recall. "I don't even know how to explain her. She was definitely older than me, but I can't say by how much exactly. It all happened so fast. We struggled and she shot at me as I ran away. And she killed this poor guy who had stopped to help me. I managed to get away and got back home. I took the girls and my in-laws to an old friend of mine, someone I really trust, and then I came here to see you. And that's it in a nutshell, I guess."

Rosie sat back in her chair and took a deep breath. "So, this all goes back to the two cases," she said. "I think maybe Michael was doing something he shouldn't have. I mean, he would usually have just paid his case without even thinking. But the fact he didn't and then attached it to your case? That's really not like him."

"What do you think he was doing?" Kiara asked.

"A few years back, maybe even six or seven years, he was working for a different company and had to leave. He had promised to pay a claim really quickly after a woman had died, but only if her husband would pay him on the side from the claim money. The husband reported him, and he was sacked. He had been lucky the company didn't prosecute him, but they didn't want the bad publicity. I almost walked out on him when I found out. But he promised me it was a one-off and he wouldn't do it again."

"So, you think he was blackmailing whoever these people were?"

"It makes sense, doesn't it? But this time it wasn't just a relative of someone who died, this time it really was fraud and he found himself blackmailing real criminals. Maybe he demanded money from them before he paid their claim."

"And maybe he was also threatening them with the fact that he had kept a copy of the claim in case they ever came back to him," Kiara added.

"It's certainly a motive for them killing him," Rosie agreed. "And by attaching his case to your case he pulled you into this. Oh my God, Kiara, this is all Michael's fault. I'm so sorry. It's all his fault." Rosie started to cry.

Kiara took her hand. "It's not his fault, Rosie. I mean, of course, what he was doing was wrong, but he didn't kill Asher, did he? And he didn't try to kill me. Whoever he was blackmailing did this. And I need to find them."

Without either noticing, The Lady on the table next to them

scribbled something down on a piece of paper before picking up her bag and heading for the exit. As she reached the door, she stopped briefly and spoke to a young boy who was clearing the tables. "Excuse me, young man."

He turned to face her with a huge smile on his face. "Hi," he said, all his attention focused on her.

"I don't suppose you would be kind enough to give this to those ladies at the table over there." She gestured to where Kiara and Rosie were sitting. "I saw one of them drop it when they came in."

"Sure, no problem," he replied.

"Thank you, my dear," she said, patting him fondly on the shoulder with one hand whilst deftly removing his mobile phone from the pocket of his trousers with the other. As he walked away from her, he hadn't noticed the difference in the weight of his pocket now that the 250-gram phone was no longer there.

As she left the café, she looked back and watched him take the note to Kiara. He didn't realise until after his shift that evening that he had lost his phone sometime during the day.

As soon as she left the café, she took a small pin from her pocket and used it to take the SIM card from out of his phone, before dropping the handset into the nearest dustbin. She put his SIM card into her own phone and sent a text.

We have a serious problem. It goes a lot deeper than you can imagine. I am taking care of it, but we must talk.

Her phone pinged back instantly.

Do nothing. No more deaths. I told you, it has to end now.

Sophia was wrong. It wouldn't end by doing nothing. That would just lead to it all falling apart, and maybe even a police hunt for her. The only way to end this was to close all the loose ends.

She deleted the texts and then walked around the corner, keeping the exit to the gallery in plain sight. She wasn't sure how this was going to play out, exactly, but she wouldn't be leaving Bristol without knowing exactly what else those two ladies knew.

Bristol

Back in the café, the young waiter had approached the ladies and put the note on the table.

"Who gave you this?" Kiara asked, looking around the café.

"That woman leaving now," the boy replied. He turned to the doorway, but there was no one there. "Wow, she was quick for an old lady," he said, "she's already gone."

"What exactly did she say?" Kiara asked him.

"She just said one of you dropped this when you came in."

As he was walking away, Kiara called him back. "What did she look like?"

The boy stood still. He couldn't quite remember. He looked back at the door to picture the conversation, but nothing came. "I don't know, really," he said. "She was just an old woman. Sorry."

While Kiara was talking to the boy, Rosie had picked up the note and read it. "You need to see this," she said, handing the note to Kiara as the boy walked away to another table to clear some plates.

Kiara took it off her.

Stop looking for us. If I can find you here, I can find the twins. You'll not be told again.

"What are you going to do?" Rosie asked her after Kiara put the note back on the table.

"I'm going to find them and stop them."

"But what about your children? That note is a direct threat to your family. They almost killed you in Scotland, and they've already killed both our husbands. Maybe we need to do what she says."

"She won't find my girls, they are hidden away. I need to stop them. They killed the only man I have ever loved. I won't let them get away with that. And they won't leave me wondering if one day they'll come back for me and the girls."

"Surely we should just call the police?"

"You tried that and where exactly did it get you?"

"I know. And I'm not sure I would trust the police to take care of my children if I had any."

"Exactly. Look, I will call the police, of course I will, but I just need to know who these people are so that when I call them I can make sure they know who they are after. But I don't want you to get involved. Not now, not after this," she said, holding up the note.

"I am involved, like it or not. They killed my husband as well. I'll do whatever you need me to do."

Kiara sat for a moment and considered their options. "We need to be careful, but we need to be quick. The twins are safe for now, but I don't know for how long. We need to find out who this lady works for and take the police straight to them. I'm just not sure you should get directly involved at this stage, though."

"If you don't want my help then why did you drive all the way here?!"

"I needed to meet you. I thought maybe you would know something that would help me find them."

"You could have called me again."

"Would you have told me anything over the phone?"

Rosie thought about that. Kiara was right, she wouldn't have trusted her just from a phone call.

"Fair enough. But you're here now and I want to help…"

Kiara was torn. She came to Bristol just to try to get some information, anything that could help her, but she never wanted to get Rosie to put herself into the line of fire. She knew from talking to her that whatever she said she would not stop her. She'd also lost someone she loved and she was not going to let that go even if Kiara begged her to.

"… I'm going to do a little poking around in the Seico system again, whether you think I should or not. There's something in there that I missed and I'm going to find it. So either you can tell me what you think I should be looking for or we can go our own way and just hope that we both find what we want."

Kiara had no choice but to tell her what she wanted to hear.

"If you can still get into Michael's computer then there is one thing you could look for. It was something that Jane Powers said to me. I can't remember her exact words, but she said something about how she couldn't go to prison like 'her'. That 'she' has been in prison just because she was protecting herself. She also said that 'she' promised Jane 'she' would never kill an innocent."

"Who is she talking about?"

"That's what I need you to find out. Whoever 'she' is could be the person we need to find to end this. Whoever she is, is probably the one pulling all the strings."

"So what am I looking for?"

"Whoever she is, she is in prison for murder, and she is somehow connected to Seico, maybe as an old life insurance claim that someone tried to put in, or somehow she's related in some way to my boss, MJ. Seico was only started about twenty-five years ago, so this should be right near the start of the company, and a murder, maybe a wife killing her husband or partner, well that's got to have been high profile enough in the company's early days to have been saved in their history. Maybe you can look at the old news section. Seico likes to document its history for all the staff to see. I looked at it when I first joined the company. It's just a link from the home page, I think it's up in the right corner if I remember. I'd do it myself, but I've got somewhere I need to go. Maybe you can search back to the company's first few years and see if anything comes up."

"Okay, I'll get access to his office, somehow. Last time I bullied my way in, maybe that'll work again."

"Just be careful. If you think you're being watched then get out of there smartish."

"I'll be fine."

"I mean it, these ladies are killers. I'd much prefer you to just go home and lock the doors and let me do this."

"It's not going to happen. Whilst I'm sneaking back into Michael's office, where will you be going?"

"I think it's time I found my own way into prison."

CHAPTER 28

Seico Office – Bristol

Rosie left the café and walked around the corner to Michael's office. She wasn't convinced that the information Kiara had asked for would be on the Seico system, but she needed to try. Also, she had to do something, she could no longer just sit around and play at the edges. The fact that they even had a slim chance of finding out who had killed her husband was enough for her to take whatever risks were necessary.

She had been standing outside the office door for what seemed like a lifetime, even though it was no more than a few minutes, trying to work out what she was going to say to get in. Given that the last time she was there, she was really rude to them, she now couldn't imagine getting a warm reception if she just strolled up to the reception desk. She needn't have worried. Just as she was about to press the buzzer, the door was pushed open, and Ellie came marching out.

"Rosie! Erm… er, how are you?"

"Oh, you know, Ellie. It's been hard, it's still so raw."

"Of course it is," Ellie replied, putting her hand on Rosie's shoulder. "What are you doing here, do you need something else?"

"Well, the last time I came, well it was all a bit fraught, wasn't it? And I left in such a state…"

"Did you forget something? Was there something personal in Michael's office you wanted?"

Rosie was happy to let Ellie take the lead as it had given her the excuse she needed.

"I still haven't cleared Michael's office yet," Ellie continued. "I know I should have by now, but we've been so busy, and well, I don't know, it just felt insensitive, somehow."

"Yes, there was something I wanted. Michael had a number of our holiday photos on his laptop. I know he was told never to put personal stuff on there, but you know Michael, he always did whatever he wanted. One night, I remember him showing me them and he promised to email them all over so I could have copies. But he never got around to it, and I'm scared someone will delete them all. I know it's not fair of me to ask but is there any way you'd let me take a quick look at his laptop and just forward them to myself? I can't tell you what it would mean to me."

Ellie was already late to meet her friend for lunch and she desperately wanted to get away from Rosie and avoid any more difficult conversations, so she agreed quickly.

"Just be careful to turn it off afterwards. Patrick's not in right now, but I'm sure he'd go nuts if he knew I was letting you into Michael's office again, especially his computer. The login is still his email, but the password, which you'll need to forget afterwards, has been changed, it's now 'Lockedterminal01'."

"Oh my God, that's amazing," Rosie said, giving Ellie the tightest hug. "Thank you so much."

"Just be quick, and make sure you put everything away afterwards. I'd be in so much trouble if Patrick finds out," Ellie repeated once again to make sure Rosie kept it between them.

"Absolutely," replied Rosie. "By the time you get back from lunch I'll be out of there and no one will be any wiser."

Ellie held open the door for Rosie and then let it shut as she walked away from the office, relieved that Rosie was no longer aggressive towards her. She felt bad for Rosie with all that she had lost, but ultimately all she wanted was a quiet life and, if it meant letting her copy a few photos, then what harm could that do?

Rosie climbed the stairs to the first floor and walked into the main office as if she was meant to be there. But there was no reason to have done that. Apart from a couple of temporary workers on desks in the corner that faced away from the entrance, the office was empty. Nevertheless, she needed to look like she belonged, just in case either one of them turned around and questioned who she was. Reaching Michael's office she was pleased to find its door unlocked.

She turned on the light and pushed the door closed before taking the seat behind his desk. With a deep breath of anticipation, she opened the laptop and typed in the new password that Ellie had told her. The laptop sprang to life. She clicked on the Seico History icon that was in the top right corner as Kiara had said it would be and she watched as the first page came on the screen. Even though she should not have been surprised to see her husband's face staring back at her, it still brought all the emotion back and her throat dried up as the tears began to form in her eyes. She didn't want to read the article that was splashed across the front page, but she had no choice, she couldn't look away. The article spoke about the dedication of Michael Hall. How he had been with the company almost ten years, he was a competent and dedicated member of the Seico family and his death had been a tragic accident. She wanted to scream into the room that he was murdered, that it was no accident. And that they never knew him, not really. That he had been a wonderful husband, giving her everything he could, that he was the one true love of her life and that no matter what platitudes they came up with there were no words that could describe the love that they had for each other. She wanted to scream, but all her energy was gone. She closed the lid of the laptop and sat back in the chair with a deep sigh, closing her eyes.

What she hadn't expected when she opened her eyes a minute later was to be looking upon the face of The Lady that had taken her husband's life.

Both women stared at each other. Rosie pushed herself up from the chair and was about to scream for help, but The Lady's deep stare somehow had the effect of taking the words away before they had left her mouth. There was something evidently evil in those eyes, something Rosie had never been in the presence of before.

"Sit down, Mrs Hall," The Lady said to her in a soft, almost bored way. Rosie did as she was told. "I wasn't sure who I should follow from the gallery, you or that very persistent friend of yours. The fact that she jumped straight into the only taxi that came by whilst you walked around the corner made you the lucky one this time. But I'll get to her soon enough."

"What do you want from me?" Rosie found her voice again, although this time her own words came out so hard that she didn't even recognise herself as the one saying them.

"Want? Nothing really. Well, not much, I just want to know how much you know."

"I know you killed my husband. And Kiara's husband."

"Amongst others, yes. But do you know why I did that?"

"Because you're a psychopath, that's why."

"Come now, Mrs Hall. Aren't we all a little psycho, when we need to be? Your husband, for instance, wasn't exactly a saint now, was he? Blackmail, theft, turning a blind eye."

"He could never have done any of those things. Michael was a good man. He obviously spotted your fraud, or whatever it is you're doing, and he tried to stop you."

"You really have no idea, do you? Your husband did find out about us, you're right about that. Well, let's say, he found out about one of our widows."

"Widows?"

The Lady ignored Rosie's remark and carried on talking. "So, what did he do about it? Did he investigate us for the company? Did he contact the authorities to track us down? No, he didn't. Instead, he tried to blackmail us into giving him a share for keeping quiet. It was money that was meant to go to the widow to try to give her back some semblance of a life, but your angel of a husband tried to get some for himself. I think I would call that a little pyscho, wouldn't you?"

"My husband was a decent man. He would never take money from anyone."

"If that's what you choose to believe then fine. But Mrs Hall, this could end right now if you tell me what I need to know. No one else needs to die. Not you, not Kiara and not her children. But for that to happen, I do need to know what you know."

"I don't know anything."

"Come now, Mrs Hall, we both know that is not true."

Without realising where it had come from, Rosie saw the gun that suddenly appeared in The Lady's hand.

"Your husband's death might have been just a spur of the moment thing for me, but to say he didn't deserve it is somewhat of a fallacy, but Kiara's husband really was innocent, he had done nothing. He was an accident and now, because of that, Sophia has to live with an innocent's death on her conscience. Personally, I have no feelings about it, but every time an innocent person dies, she dies a little with them. So, let's not cause her any more pain. Tell me what you and Kiara know. Do you know who Sophia is? Where she lives, anything about her?"

Rosie sat back down on the chair, leaning back into the headrest as far as she could to keep as much distance between The Lady and herself.

"I, we, have never heard of a Sophia."

The Lady looked intensely into Rosie's eyes.

"I think I believe you. But what about our widows, what do you know about them?"

"Until today I knew nothing about what you were doing. I only know you killed my husband. And Kiara's husband…"

"And?"

"And that lady, and the man in Scotland."

"Jane Powers. I never killed her. Kiara has to carry the blame for Jane's death. The man was me, I'm afraid. But even with someone as skilled as I am, accidents can happen. But I think you know more than that. You've come here today because Kiara has asked you to do something for her." She raised the gun up to show Rosie that time was running out.

"Okay, yes, we also know about MJ. We don't know exactly her involvement in all this, but we know she is involved somehow. And then there's a lady, someone in prison…" Rosie saw the look in the lady's eye change slightly and realised she had hit on the truth. "That's Sophia, isn't it? The lady that's in prison, she's the one you are talking about."

"See, you do know much more than you were letting on, don't you?"

Suddenly, Rosie felt vulnerable. She had spoken too much.

"What are you going to do to me?" Rosie asked.

"Do? To you? Nothing, my dear."

Rosie didn't know how to respond to that. Whether to believe The Lady or not.

"I don't know anything else, I promise. I'd never heard of a Sophia before you said her name. I was going to look in the company archives to see if I could find anything out. It might have led to her, I don't know, but I won't look now, I promise. I'll walk away. I'll call Kiara and tell her to walk away as well, I promise." Rosie was frightened. Up until that moment, she'd had no real care if she lived or died. After she lost her husband, she had felt all alone in the world, but then she'd met Kiara. And suddenly she had a friend who was going through the same thing she was. And she wanted to see this through. To get justice for both of them.

And she wanted to protect her new friend from these people. "Just let me call Kiara, please. Let me talk to her. She'll listen to me, I know she will."

"You don't need to call anyone, Mrs Hall. I just needed to know if Kiara and you knew who my Sophia was. I can't have anyone stop her from being released. We've come too far and are too close now for that to happen."

"I get it, I do. But we don't know anything more. Until a moment ago, I never even knew about a Sophia, did I...?"

Before Rosie could finish her sentence, The Lady raised the gun and put two bullets into her, one through her chest and one through her eye.

"Such a shame. Sophia should never have allowed it to get this far, she should have had me talk to you both before now and then perhaps this would never have needed to happen. Such a waste."

With that, she turned and walked into the main office. She looked over at the two workers in the corner, but neither of them seemingly had heard the muzzled gunshots as both were wearing headphones and listening to music whilst they worked. She doubted they had even seen her enter, but she knew that if they had that they would never be able to recall what she looked like. No one ever did.

She walked down the stairs and out into the main street. As she turned the corner, she bumped into Ellie coming the other way, knocking a coffee from her hand.

"So sorry, my dear," she said as she carried on walking away.

"That's okay," Ellie said as she wiped the drink from her jumper with her free hand.

Later that day, when Ellie was interviewed by the police, she didn't even remember bumping into a lady, let alone what she looked like.

CHAPTER 29

The taxi dropped Kiara just outside the city centre where she'd left her car. She'd spent the entire journey looking out of the car window to see if she was being followed. Having found out that The Lady had been with them at the gallery, she was sure that she was being followed now, but as she had no idea what The Lady looked like, it meant every car on the road was a suspect. The alternative was that The Lady had chosen to go after Rosie to Michael's office instead. She pushed that thought from her mind for two reasons; firstly, why stick with Rosie when she was the obvious target? Secondly, if she went after Rosie, then her new friend could be in trouble, whilst she was travelling away in the opposite direction rather than watching out for her. She decided to give Rosie a ring from her car to make sure she was okay, and then, assuming that The Lady had left them both alone, she would drive straight back to Worthing and check on the girls and her in-laws.

After the taxi dropped her off at the car park, she waited behind the payment kiosk for a couple of minutes, checking every vehicle that came and went by the entrance. Not one of them was being driven by anyone who looked like she could be The Lady, although it wasn't lost on her that this was the problem; any one of them could have been her.

As soon as she was on her way, she engaged her cruise control, and spoke into the car's smart system. "Dial Rosie Hall."

It rang three times before a message came through the car's speakers. "Hello, this is Rosie. Sorry I can't make it to the phone.

Please leave a message and I'll call back as soon as I can, or if you know the gallery's number, then try that."

"Rosie, it's Kiara. I was just checking you're okay. I was spooked when I got in the taxi, I swear she was watching me; actually, I'm not 100% sure she isn't behind me right now. Anyhow, call me when you get this message and let me know how you got on at Michael's office, thanks."

She assumed that Rosie was hard at work at the Seico office and had her phone on silent so as not to be caught out poking around their system. The next call she needed to make was to Nick Taylor to check on the girls.

"I was worried about you," Nick answered on the first ring. "I've tried calling you about half a dozen times, but it kept going to voicemail. I was worried something had happened."

"I'm sorry, I needed to stay offline for a while and just get to grips with what I needed to do."

"So you're okay then?" Nick said, sounding relieved.

"Honestly, I'm fine. I'm heading back now. I just wanted to make sure the girls are okay."

"All's good our end. It's been nice to have youngsters back in the house again."

"And my in-laws?"

"Absolutely fine. Peter has been asleep in the chair since you left, and Judy has been keeping herself busy helping Jennie around the house. She's desperate to go out for a walk, but I told them they have to stay put until we know more."

"Thanks. Knowing they are okay gives me time to do this."

"To do what, exactly?"

"I need to see MJ. She's caught up in this somehow and it's time she told me everything she knows."

"Kiara…"

"Yes?" The pause that followed gave away that he had done something. "What have you done?"

"This isn't a game, you know that, don't you? People have been killed. Your life, and your family, you're all in danger."

"What have you done?" she asked again.

"I went to see my brother-in-law. He's a bigwig in the police force."

"I know you said you were going to call the police, but I'd hoped you'd give me a bit more time to build a case first. I'm just scared they won't believe me."

"Kiara, I had to, it's gone too far already. People have been murdered. And you could be next. Anyway, you might not be surprised to know that they are well aware people have been killed and they are now looking for you as a suspect. I told them everything you told me. They've called the Bristol police station already to find you both."

"Well, I've left now, so they won't find me. But actually, I am worried about Rosie. She was going to her husband's office to try to look at the company records. I called her a minute ago and had to leave a message. I tried to stop her going, but she wouldn't listen to me."

"I know that feeling," he replied.

"Can you maybe call your brother-in-law and tell them where to find her?"

"Where's the office?"

"It's near where she works, at the Bristol Art Gallery. It's Seico, the same company I work for, but their Bristol office."

"I'll call him now. But I think you should come straight back here. Let them do their job."

"I will come, soon, I promise. I just need to see MJ. I want to speak with her before she knows what I've been doing."

"I really think you should come straight back, Kiara."

"I will, I promise. Just give me until tonight."

"Wait a minute, don't cut off. There's someone at the door. I think it might be the police, I can see lights from the window."

"Nick, don't tell them where I am, please…"

"Mrs Fox." The next voice on the line was not Nick's.

"Who is this?" Kiara asked.

"Mrs Fox, my name is Bruce Simpson, I'm with the Sussex Police. We are piecing things together, and Nick has told me everything you told him. I want to help you, Kiara, but I need to know where you are."

"If you're a friend of Nick's then he'll have also told you I just need to do one more thing and then I'll hand myself in."

"Mrs Fox, Kiara, this is important. You need to tell me where you are right away. I believe you had nothing to do with the deaths, but you are in danger, that I do know. You need to pull over wherever you are and wait for us to come to you."

"I'm sorry, I can't. I just need to do this."

"Kiara, your friend has been shot. She's dead."

"My friend?"

"Rosie Hall."

"That's not possible. I was with her only an hour or so ago."

"She's dead, Kiara. She was killed at her husband's office. His PA found her at his desk just a few minutes ago and called us. So, you see, I need you to come in, now."

Kiara went cold. Rosie dead. *Was it her fault.* When Rosie first contacted her, she could have put her off. Or told her to go back to the police station right away. But instead Rosie went back to Michael's office, to help her. Did she try hard enough to stop her? Did she really even want to stop her? She couldn't bear the thought that she could be the cause of her death. She'd have to deal with that thought later, but for now she had to see MJ, these killings had to stop.

"Kiara, are you there?"

Kiara put the phone down.

She knew her girls and her in-laws would be safe now. They had the police looking after them now, so The Lady had no reason to risk going after them.

Whoever these people were, they would expect Kiara to be running for her life, especially after Rosie's murder. They would certainly not expect her to hit them head on. But that was exactly what she was going to do.

CHAPTER 30

Kiara wasn't sure where MJ was or how she could find her. She had called the offices, both London and Brighton, but no one had heard from her in days. She could drive to London to MJ's house, but the odds on her being there, just sitting around, were slim. Also she was sure the police would be looking for her as well and Nick would tell her if they had picked her up.

But Kiara needn't have worried. MJ was looking for her as well.

Kiara's phone rang. She looked at the screen on her dashboard to see who was calling, expecting it to be the police again, but the number flashing up was unknown. She pulled the car over to the side of the road and pressed receive.

For a few seconds the caller didn't speak. Then in a whisper the voice simply said her name.

Kiara realised it was MJ on the other end.

And then they spoke together.

"Where are you?"

A pause.

"We need to meet."

Another pause.

"You called me, so I guess you talk first," Kiara said, trying her best to keep her voice level.

"It's really important I see you," MJ replied.

"To put a bullet in me as well?"

"So, you know that I'm involved in this, then. The Lady said you did."

"The Lady?" Kiara asked, knowing who MJ meant, but trying not to let on.

"Yes, that's how we refer to her. After all these years, I still don't know her name. She's the one who tried to kill you, it wasn't me, I promise you that. I never wanted anything to happen to you.

"And my husband?" Kiara's voice started to rise. "Was that you or was that your Lady?"

"If I could have stopped her, I would have. I tried, I really did. I thought she was just going to talk to you. I had no idea she was trying to kill you. Asher was an accident, she messed up with that."

"My girls saw it all. How the hell will they ever get over seeing their dad die like that? It's barbaric, MJ. It's fucking barbaric." Kiara's voice started to crack as the tears poured down her face.

"I know. I was there with them, wasn't I? I'll never be able to get it out of my mind, either."

"How could you have done this to us? You were meant to be my friend."

"I know," MJ said, trying to find the right words. "No one was meant to die. And Mia and Jas should never have had to see that. I tried to get you to pay the claim, so many times. But you just wouldn't."

"Oh, so it's all my fault, then? My husband's dead because of me doing my job. And Rosie was murdered because I wouldn't just do what you told me to do and pretend everything was all right. And how many more are dead? Are they all down to me?"

"I didn't mean that. I just meant I tried, that's all. No one was ever meant to be killed. Sophia promised me that. But The Lady… she's evil."

"Sophia? Is that who you are working for, is she the one doing all this?" Kiara said.

"Look, we can't do it like this. You're in danger still. And so am

I. Sophia has tried to stop her, but even she's lost control of her now. Please, just come to me and I'll tell you everything."

"Oh, sure. I'll come to you so your Lady friend can just pop a bullet in my head. Sounds like a great plan of action."

"That's not how it is. She's after both of us now. I am in this deeper than anyone, way more than you could even imagine. Not only is The Lady after me, but I'm part of a plan that has left over a hundred men dead over the years, including my own fiancé. So, whatever we do now matters. I'm telling you the truth. I've no reason to lie any more, have I?"

Kiara had no choice but to believe her if she was going to get to the bottom of all this. But, in truth, she really did believe her. She could hear it in MJ's voice; she was desperate and she was scared. Kiara trusted her instincts, she always did, and her instincts were telling her to trust MJ now.

"Where are you?" Kiara asked.

MJ let go of the breath she had been holding in.

"I'm heading to Brighton now. I'm not far away, only about ten minutes. Where are you?"

"I'm near Worthing…" She realised she was saying too much, that she almost gave away the location of the twins. She backtracked.

"Meet me in Shoreham," Kiara said.

"Can you pull over somewhere? Somewhere we won't be seen?" MJ asked.

"You know Shoreham from when you lived near here, right?"

"Yes."

"The old cement works near Upper Beeding, off the South Downs."

"Yes, I know it."

"I'll be there in fifteen minutes," Kiara said as she pulled back onto the road and took the turning south to head back to Shoreham. She pressed end to finish the call before MJ could say anything else.

As Kiara drove towards the derelict cement works, she realised she needed to call Nick Taylor so he could tell his policeman friend where she was. If this was a trap and no one knew she was there, then it was game over.

Nick picked up on the first ring.

"Kiara, where the hell are you? Everything's going crazy here. I've got half the police force in my house questioning your in-laws and the twins. There are armed response teams all over the roads looking for you…"

"Listen, Nick, I'm close to finding out who they are. It's much bigger than we thought."

"Kiara, enough of this now. You need to get back here right away," Nick whispered into his phone as he walked out his back door into the garden. He could already sense two police officers following him.

"Is that her?" one of the policemen said. "Sir, please hand over the phone."

"The cement works, Nick, I'm heading to the old Shoreham cement works," Kiara quickly said before ending the call.

"Shit!" Nick said.

"Give me the phone, sir," the officer said.

Nick pushed past him and ran into the house.

"Bruce!" he called to his brother-in-law. "She's heading to Shoreham, the old cement works."

"Got it," Bruce replied as he picked up his radio and started relaying the message.

"Was that Mum?" Mia asked as she and Jasmin came into the lounge trailed by Jennie, Peter and Judy. Two police officers followed closely behind the group.

"Sure was, buddy," Nick replied to Mia.

"We're not children," Mia said, referring to Jasmin and herself. "We know Mum's in trouble. So, either you tell us what's going on or we are going to get out of here and go look for her."

"Look, my darlings, it's okay, honestly. Mum just needs us to…"

"Fine!" Mia said without letting him finish. "Treat us like kids, then. You ready, Jas?" she said to her sister.

"You betcha, sis," Jasmin replied, putting her rucksack on her back.

"Girls, listen to what Nick is telling you," Judy cut in.

"Gran, we are fifteen years old, we're not babies. You lot seem to think we are kids, but we are not. Mia and I know Mum's in trouble and we are going to find her. We're not losing her as well now."

"Too right, sis," Mia cut in.

Judy had no words to that. Neither did Peter. Both just looked at each other, unsure what to say. Nick, on the other hand, with older children of his own, totally got it.

"They are right," he said to everyone. "Girls, we think your dad was killed by accident, but by someone who was, and still is, after your mum."

"Nick!" Jennie cut in.

"Jen, they need to know. For their own safety, as well. Girls, we have the police involved and they are not going to let your mum get hurt. Kiara is one of my oldest friends and I promise you we'll do everything to keep her safe. But if she thinks you two are running about then she'll panic and make some stupid mistakes, which could be terrible for her. So, I need you to stay here, with us. Let the police do what they do and let me look after you. Please."

Mia and Jasmin looked at each other and, without a word between them, agreed. Their grandparents both looked on, wondering how their little twins had suddenly grown up so quickly.

"Okay, as long as you don't lie to us any more. We have to know what's happening."

"I can do that," Nick replied.

"Okay," they said in unison.

"So, was that Mum?" Mia asked again.

"Come here, kids," Nick said, taking them into his arms and giving the others a worried look. "Yes, it was. She's gone to meet someone from her office and the police need to get there and take her somewhere safe before anything happens. They'll find her, I promise. She's going to be all right."

The girls pulled away from Nick and both held their tears back.

"Fine, we'll stay here," said Jasmin.

"Just make sure you find her and keep her safe!" Mia said, addressing the two policemen who had followed them in.

CHAPTER 31

Shoreham Cement Works

Kiara pulled into the layby on the north side of the road in front of the old cement factory. It was situated on Stenning Road just outside of Shoreham and occupied land on both sides of the road; it was huge, totalling over sixty acres. When it first opened at the end of the eighteen hundreds, it was home to over three hundred employees who transported cement down long chutes from one side of the road up and over to the other. As the years went by, the local children called it the porridge factory as the cement resembled the cereal that would keep them warm on their winter walks to school. Nowadays, it was derelict, left to decay and covered in asbestos, a blot on the otherwise beautiful South Downs.

Kiara could see no other vehicles nearby, so she pulled forward to the south side of the street, where the main factory had once majestically held court, and parked behind a ten-foot square sign that told locals that these days trespassing would not be a good idea. She had chosen to meet MJ there as, not only was it close to where she had been, but she knew she could find plenty of places to hide away if MJ brought any backup with her.

She had not needed to worry about that as, just fifteen minutes later, MJ pulled up, also on the factory side, and parked in front of the same sign, not knowing that Kiara was watching her from just a few feet away, hidden behind an old rusty skip.

MJ climbed from her car and walked slowly towards the factory building, her eyes taking in her surroundings as the light from the early evening started to make the whole site that little bit more frightening.

"Kiara, are you here?" she called out, trying to be heard, but also finding herself trying to whisper despite the place being empty of anyone but the two of them.

Kiara wanted to wait and watch her a little longer. After her experience at the Powers' mansion in Edinburgh, she was no longer ready to just throw herself in headfirst.

MJ kept walking forwards until she had passed the sign, before noticing Kiara's car parked behind it.

"Kiara, come on, this is ridiculous. I'd never hurt you, surely you know that?"

Kiara couldn't help but react. "You killed my husband, didn't you? And then you tried to have me shot. So, don't be surprised if perhaps I can't take that at face value."

MJ turned to face where she'd heard the voice from.

"I never wanted any of that to happen. None of that was me."

"You were part of it. *Are* a part of it."

"We can't talk like this." MJ held her arms in the air as if in surrender. "Look, I'm not carrying anything. I'm on my own. Please come out. I need to tell you things. We're both in danger, me as well as you."

Kiara stepped from behind the skip, so she was facing her friend.

"I'm so sorry for everything, really I am."

"So, how did it all happen then? What the hell's going on, and what's your part in it?"

"Can I?" MJ asked, signalling walking forward. Kiara just shrugged her agreement. MJ walked up to her and stood just a foot away so that they could see each other eye to eye.

"So?" Kiara prompted her to talk.

"I used to be a nurse. You might not have known that. I studied in King's College in London. I lived close by and shared a flat with Sophia, who was on the same course as me. She didn't know anyone in London as she'd grown up in Italy and had only been here a few weeks. So, we were flatmates and then became best friends. I'd never met anyone as strong or focused as her. She arrived in England barely able to speak the language and, somehow, managed to work through a nursing degree. And she was beautiful, and I mean utterly drop-dead stunning. Everyone wanted her, and not just the boys. She ended up dating, then marrying, one of the hospital's top surgeons, another gorgeous-looking specimen. It was all very textbook when I say it out loud: beautiful nurse marrying successful handsome cancer surgeon; the perfect couple. Except they weren't. He was a pig. The day we graduated, she moved out of our flat and in with him and the abuse started almost immediately. It was physical and emotional. The change in her was shocking. This strong, focused girl suddenly wouldn't see anyone, not even me, she stopped looking for work and seemed to just shrink away. I didn't know how bad it was until the day he tried to kill her. It was over nothing, something about her forgetting to pick him up from work, and he almost beat her to death. It was brutal. He even tried to set fire to her. Can you believe that shit? But it went wrong for him, and she got out, he didn't. Even though he had beaten her senseless before the fire started, she was still convicted of murdering him. That was what it was like back then, no one wanted to believe this hero of the people, this young handsome surgeon, could be a wife beater. The judge was so intent on blaming her for his death that he wouldn't even allow her lawyer to show the jury photos of her other injuries."

Kiara stood and listened as MJ described what to her would have been a living hell. Kiara was a strong, independent woman, she always had been. She couldn't imagine living with an abusive man and being treated like that, especially when she herself had been in what truly could be described as the perfect marriage to the perfect partner.

She'd heard about people like that, of course, but the thought of actually letting someone do that to you just made no sense to her. MJ picked that up in the way Kiara looked at her.

"You think you would just walk away, do you?" MJ said, the tears now falling down her face. "Sophia and I had more in common than just studying together."

"MJ, you didn't go through something like that as well, surely?"

"I wasn't always like this. Outspoken, a businesswoman. I never understood why Sophia let him do that to her. But you don't until you're in it. I loved Ivan. We were going to be married. But, bit by bit, he used to say things, stuff that would make me feel bad about myself. Always criticising me and putting me down. And then the hitting started. At first it felt like it was an accident, he would raise a hand and hit me and pretend he only meant to scare me. But then it would happen again. And again. And I would feel so stupid. But I thought I loved him, I really did. Sophia knew what was happening when I went to visit her in prison. It was obvious to her, she'd seen it and lived through it. She knew he'd eventually either kill me or utterly destroy me. So, she gave me a way out. She had a friend who had just got out of prison, and she said she would help me stop him."

"The Lady who killed Asher and Rosie?"

"Yes," said MJ, "The Lady."

"And she killed your fiancé?"

"No, she didn't. I did that," MJ replied boldly. "And he fucking deserved it. She showed me how, though. She had this poison. I don't know exactly what was in it, but I had to give it to him in a drink every day for nearly a month. It was untraceable in the body, but day by day, it was killing him. He eventually died in agony and no one knew why."

"Just like Martin Powers did," Kiara said, remembering her conversations with his secretary. "And we never found out what caused it."

"Yes, it was exactly the same poison and given to her by the same Lady," MJ replied.

"And Jane Powers was paid the life insurance claim. I suppose you did the same with your fiancé? You insured him first and then claimed on the policy when he died."

"Absolutely right I did. And I deserved that money after everything I went through."

"And did your fiancé, Ivan, you called him. Did Ivan deserve to die like that?"

"If you had seen what he did to me you wouldn't even have to ask that. It wasn't just what I've told you, either, he did much worse. So yes, he deserved every second of that pain. As did Martin Powers. As did all the other bastards that The Lady and I helped get rid of. All the widows ended up rich and safe. And I would do it all again," MJ said, fully emboldened by her speech.

"But Asher never laid a finger on me. He never even raised his voice at me. In fact, I think I shouted at him more than he ever shouted at me. So, why did he have to die? Why did I have to become one of your widows?" Kiara said, bringing MJ back to the conversation that she needed to have. "And Rosie's husband? Sure, he was playing some silly games, but he wasn't an abuser, was he? So, why did he have to die?"

"They didn't have to, neither of them. Sophia never wanted that to happen. She was devastated by them. So was I. We're not monsters, Kiara."

"Then tell me why, for Christ's sake. I need to understand why my husband was murdered."

"You wouldn't let it go, would you? I kept telling you to pay Jane's policy. I was begging you to. But you just wouldn't listen to me."

"So, Sophia told this Lady to kill me then? And Asher just got in the way?"

"Sophia never told her to kill you. She told her to warn you off, that's all. I told them you wouldn't be frightened by anyone. I said we needed to just stop now. We'd helped hundreds of women already, so why couldn't we just stop now?"

"Hundreds!" Kiara said in shock.

"But The Lady wouldn't listen. She's evil, I'm telling you. She's worse than all the men we killed. She says she does it to protect Sophia, that she would kill to protect her. And not just Asher and Michael Hall. There was also that guy in Scotland that tried to help you. And there were others, I'm certain, before she even met Sophia and me."

"So, Sophia thought she could control her, but now realises that she can't. So, what, she tells you to warn me to be careful and then you run and hide away? Is that the plan? If it is, it's ridiculous. We can't hide for ever. We need to face this Lady and stop her. That's what we need to do, not bloody run away."

"I'm not as strong as you, Kiara. I can't do this. And you won't see her coming, either. She's like a ghost, she'll sneak up on you and then…"

"I'm not running away. And your Sophia, I need to see her. I've got questions she needs to answer. I want to know who else has been killed because of her."

"Kiara, please, just get the twins, and get away."

"Where is *your* Sophia? You said she's in prison. Which prison?"

MJ knew she would eventually have to tell her.

"Middlesex. HMP Bronzefield in Middlesex. But she's due to be released any day now. She's done her twenty years and she's about to be paroled. That's why this has suddenly all happened. The Lady won't let her rot in prison any longer. If what we've been doing gets out, then they'll never let Sophia go. She'll die in there if you tell the police what's she's done."

"Good. She killed my husband, she deserves to die in prison."

"Kiara, didn't you listen to a word I said?"

"I assume you have a way of contacting her?"

MJ looked uneasily at Kiara.

"So you do. Does she have a phone? Or is there someone in the prison you speak with."

MJ just stood looking at her, not wanting to give her what she was asking for.

"Give me her fucking number!" Kiara shouted at her.

MJ pulled her phone from her pocket and sent Kiara the secret number that she had never shared with anyone.

Kiara's phone pinged to confirm it had been received.

"Sophia never wanted any innocent people to die. Please understand that. She has been a victim through her whole life as well. It was that maniac who killed Asher, not Sophia, she was the one who did this."

"I'm not sure anyone's ever called me a maniac before."

The Lady appeared out of nowhere, taking both MJ and Kiara by surprise. She stood close to them, a gun in her hand pointing directly at Kiara's head.

"I've been called a lot of things. A ghost, as you said, certainly. A kind old Lady, sometimes. I've even been called an assassin by some. But maniac is a new one, and not strictly true, as it happens. I would suggest a maniac has no control over what they are doing, whereas I am in complete control all the time." She said this whilst walking forwards and placing the barrel of the gun squarely against Kiara's temple.

Kiara knew she should be scared. Who wouldn't be when someone was holding a gun to your head? Especially someone you knew would have no hesitation pulling the trigger given the opportunity. But she wasn't scared. She was annoyed. She was fucking angry. This Lady had killed her husband, threatened her children and tried to kill her on more than one occasion. Kiara turned her head to face the woman eye to eye.

"You're a brave one, I'll give you that," The Lady said.

MJ was frozen to the spot.

"What do you want?" Kiara said coolly.

"I want you to die," The Lady replied.

"Then pull the trigger," Kiara said, too angry to care what she said to this crazy person.

"Please," MJ begged her. "Don't do it. She won't tell anyone, will you, Kiara? Tell her you won't."

Kiara didn't even feel The Lady move the gun. But she heard the shot ring out so close to her ear that for a split second she thought her eardrum had exploded. Out of the corner of her eye, she saw the look of shock on MJ's face as the bullet struck her in the chest, forcing her backwards and onto her knees.

Simultaneously to the gun being shot, flashing lights and blaring sirens rang out from the road as a dozen police cars roared down Stenning Road towards the cement works. In the split second that The Lady was distracted by the noise, Kiara struck her as hard as she could in the stomach, doubling her over, and then she turned and ran as fast as she could away from her. She reached the old skip and dived behind it as a bullet pinged off the rusted metal and embedded itself in a fallen tree stump.

"Shit!" The Lady said in a stolen breath as she pulled herself upright from the punch she had taken. With Kiara still so close, she desperately wanted to carry on the chase, but the police cars had all pulled up now and doors were starting to open. She would not allow herself to be caught and face a prison cell again. She raised her gun and, in quick succession, fired two shots at the police, both hitting the targets she aimed at and sending a policeman and a policewoman to the ground, blood seeping out of them both. The rest of the police officers dived for cover as none of them were prepared for a gun fight. Bruce couldn't let two of his team die like that, exposed to the gunman and bleeding out. He broke cover and ran to them as fast as he could manage without leaving himself too exposed to the next bullet. The Lady raised her gun to fire. Just as she took her aim and was about to squeeze the trigger, a large rock came hurtling at her from behind the skip and caught her on the side of her head. The gun still went off, but the bullet flew wide. Bruce dived to the ground and watched as Kiara dashed from behind the skip and ran at almighty speed behind a huge sign telling trespassers to stay away. The shooter, who Bruce still couldn't make out, but later swore was just an old Lady, wiped the blood from her forehead and ran back into the grounds, past the old skip that Kiara had used to stay hidden and into the derelict cement works directly behind.

With that one brave action, Kiara had saved the lives of Bruce and his two officers. He would later tell Nick Taylor that his friend was a bloody hero.

Kiara reached her car and was relieved to realise she hadn't locked it. She fumbled the keys from her pocket and started the engine. She pulled away, clipping the side of the sign and, in a cloud of dust, headed back onto the road and away from all the police cars, which sat idling whilst their drivers remained hidden from the person taking shots at them.

"Paramedics to the scene now, we have two officers down. And send the friggin' armed response unit right away, we have someone taking shots at us!" Bruce shouted into his radio. "The shooter is in that building," he called to the officers around him. "Armed response is on the way, until then I want you all to pull back behind your cars and wait it out, no one – and I mean no one – is to follow me, that's an order."

Bruce pulled himself to standing and, one by one, he dragged his two officers back to the closest police car and left them in the hands of their colleagues. Both had been shot and were bleeding badly now; he prayed both would survive, their only hope being if an ambulance arrived in the next few minutes. Looking back, he could see another body near to where Kiara had been standing. He knew he should stay hidden, but he couldn't leave someone out there to the mercy of the lunatic with the gun. Keeping his body as low as he could, he ran, zig-zagging along the way, until he reached MJ's body. He realised when he got there that he needn't have bothered; whoever she was, she was already dead.

"Shit," he said quietly to himself. "What the hell has Nick got me into?"

CHAPTER 32

Kiara drove away from the porridge factory as fast as her car would let her. The road away was narrow and winding with lots of blind corners, but she put her foot to the floor nonetheless and gunned the engine. She needed to face Sophia, the real lady behind all this. She wanted to be the one to tell her that it was over, that she would rot in prison forever for what she had done. She knew she should let the police tie this all up and that she had no business doing anything more, but in truth she had to face the lady who had destroyed her life. She had to look her in the eyes once and for all and tell her about the lives she destroyed, that they were not just names from a story, but real people, who had dreams and hopes of their own. If she didn't meet Sophia before this was over, she would live the rest of her life full of bitterness and the need for revenge. This was her way of trying to move on, and she had to take the opportunity now, not just for her own sanity, but also for the sake of Mia and Jasmin.

As she turned off Stenning Road and joined the A23, she slowed down enough to drive with just the one hand on the wheel and log into her maps app on her phone with the other. It told her that the drive to the prison would take just over an hour. She hit go and the satnav on the phone told her to continue straight for the next two miles before taking the exit. Secondly, she dialled Nick Taylor's number.

The phone only rang once before Nick picked up.

"Kiara, what the hell's going on? Are you safe? Is Bruce with you?"

Kiara paused before she answered. She needed his help again. So, she had to work out exactly what to say. She wished she had thought about that before hitting the dial button.

"Can you hear me? What the hell's going on?" Nick shouted into the phone. His voice carried around the house and drew Mia, Jasmin and Kiara's in-laws into the room and over to him. "We heard the police radios talk about a shooting. What the hell's going on there? Are you okay?"

"I'm fine, I wasn't hit, but I was the lucky one."

"And Bruce?"

"When I got out of there, I saw him pulling some of his officers behind a car, so I guess he wasn't hit either."

Nick's shoulders relaxed, as did Judy's and Peter's. Mia snatched the phone out of his hand and her and Jasmin ran to the other side of the room. "Mum, are you okay? Have you been hurt?"

Kiara could hear the anguish in her daughter's voice and wished she could be there holding them both close to her.

"I'm fine, Mia. I got away. I can't come back just yet, there's something I need to do now. But I'm okay, I promise. Tell Jas I'm okay, all right?"

Nick stood next to Mia, his hand out.

"I need to pass you back to Nick. Come home, Mum, please."

"I will, darling, I promise, just bear with me."

Mia handed the phone back to Nick, expecting him to be angry with her for taking his phone away. But he wasn't. He just took the phone and smiled at her before walking back to where the others had waited.

"You there?" Kiara asked.

"Yes, I'm here."

"Look, I can't tell you everything just yet, but I will, I promise.

I need a favour first and then I need you to get the girls away from the house until you hear from me again."

"What do you need?" he asked, ready to help her in any way he could.

Kiara gave him the briefest lowdown on everything that had happened, including the fact that the police had the place surrounded now. She explained that The Lady could have got away again, she was certainly resourceful enough. Nick asked what was so important that she wouldn't come back to them right away.

"I want to get into the prison and talk with Sophia, face-to-face. It's important to me to see the person who caused Asher's death. Without that I'm not sure I'll ever be able to get any form of closure in my life."

"I'm not sure I understand why you think meeting her will help."

"What if The Lady does get away, then what, do we spend the rest of our lives in hiding? But I bet she knows where The Lady would go. So if I'm ever to truly believe my girls will be safe then I need to do this. I need to look her in the eyes and know she is not lying to us. That is the only way this is ever going to be over."

"I know some people from my work in the courts, a couple are fairly high brow, but I don't imagine that even they will be able to get you into a prison at such short notice."

"Could you at least try, please?"

"Don't you think it would be better if you met us at the police station and they kept us all safe until they catch the shooter?"

"She's too smart for them, Nick. I've seen her in action. She can almost vanish in front of your eyes. I can't explain it, she's like a chameleon. I need to find out how Sophia gets hold of her. I need to find her and lead the police directly to her without her knowing we are coming. It's the only way we'll ever be safe. I think this Sophia is our only hope of that happening, and that's only if MJ was telling the truth and she wants this to end now as well."

Kiara pushed him to make a decision. "You said you would do anything to help me, this is how you help me."

"I can't do this. It's too big of an ask. You need to come back now. You need to be here, safe, with your children."

Kiara cut off the phone in frustration. If she had been back at the house with them she would have seen the pain in Nick's face as he turned her down. He wanted to help, he would give his own life for her if he had to, but he had promised the girls he would do everything he could to protect her, and in his mind her going to meet Sophia was the most dangerous thing she could do.

"Shit shit shit!" she screamed aloud into the car. *What to do, what to do.* Then she remembered her phone pinging back at the cement factory. MJ had sent her Sophia's number. She picked the phone up again and with her free hand found the message MJ had sent her. She clicked on the number and waited for it to ring.

It rang twice before it was answered.

"Is that you, Kiara?" Sophia asked.

"How could you know that?"

"I don't know, intuition perhaps. I figured MJ would eventually give you my number."

"I need to meet you. Face-to-face. Now."

"I understand."

"Do you?"

"Yes, I think I do."

The conversation went quiet for a few seconds as both ladies considered their position at that moment.

"Come now," Sophia cut into the silence. "I can arrange an emergency visit for you."

With that, Kiara hung up the phone and put her foot back hard onto the accelerator.

"Mi dispiace Kiara, mi dispiace. I'm sorry."

She didn't hear Sophia's final words before the call ended.

CHAPTER 33

The Lady had run into the old cement factory, over the broken glass, around the discarded furniture and all the way to the other end, before stopping at the back wall out of breath. She was incredibly fit, especially for someone of her age, but the three-hundred-metre dusty building had sucked all the air from her lungs. She wiped away at the blood that was slowly creeping down her face from the rock that Kiara had thrown at her and took a second to regain her composure. She had to get away from there as far as she could. But her car was no longer an option as it was hidden away in the factory over the other side of the road and there was no way she would be able to get that far without being caught. That and her being the only one not in a police uniform would limit her ability to blend in. The other thing going through her mind was what to do once she'd got away. She could go back to Worthing, kill the lawyer and take the kids. That would definitely draw Kiara out. But what was the likelihood that the police had not already warned them and that they would now be under close protection? She also needed to warn Sophia that Kiara knew everything, and that her release from prison could be in jeopardy.

How did it all go so badly wrong? she asked herself. For years, they had run the Widows programme in complete secret, helping hundreds of abused women escape their lives and have the chance of a better future. Not that this was really her reason for doing it. She actually didn't care much about the women they helped, in fact she found them weak and pathetic and not at all worthy of her help. She did it to support and protect Sophia, nothing more. *And I'll keep helping her*, she thought, *for as long as she needs me.*

She had to pause for a second when she thought that. *Do I mean that, though? How far will I actually go to protect her? Would I go back to prison for her, would I really do that?*

Deep down, she knew the answer before she even thought of the question. Standing there, her own life now in jeopardy, it was time to face the truth at last. Yes, she would have done anything for her, once, back in the beginning. But now, with Sophia questioning her and even threatening her? *No*, she thought. *No, I wouldn't.*

She could, of course, blame Kiara for the change in her relationship with Sophia. Before Kiara started to dig into the Widows Project, everything was on course for Sophia's release, and their relationship was as strong as it had ever been. But could she really blame her for this? She had to be honest with herself, and if she thought about it, she actually respected Kiara's tenacity and professionalism; she had only been doing her job, and she was good at it, perhaps as good at her job as she herself was at what she did. *Perhaps Kiara is not the enemy, perhaps it is more nuanced than that*, she thought. *Perhaps Sophia herself has a much larger part to play in how things are now turning out.*

That didn't mean that Kiara wasn't a target if the opportunity arose, but now her focus had to be making sure she was not caught herself. She had always been clear on one thing: if she ever needed to escape being caught then she would ultimately kill whoever was in her way, even if it was the one person she loved.

"Come out, keep your hands up, the whole building is now surrounded. We have armed police on every exit. Put your weapon down and come out slowly, with your hands up." The voice bellowed through the void of the factory as if there were speakers in every corner, bringing her back to the present moment.

The Lady had no intention of putting her gun down or putting her hands in the air. She had no doubt that the armed police were on the way and would be there within minutes, but she'd heard no more vehicles or sirens since she had run into the building and that told her that whoever was on the loudspeaker was just trying to buy himself and his officers some time. She needed to get out of the building before the armed police actually turned up and had her outgunned. The door at the far end, just inches from where she was standing, was not only padlocked from the inside, but she could just about see in the darkness that it had also been claimed by layers of rust that would no doubt have welded it shut. She turned around to find another exit, but the only options were the broken windows, which were feet off the ground and in no way accessible. The only other exit was the one she had used to come in, back towards the police. She had no choice but to risk it. She broke into a slow jog, her gun raised in case anyone came through, and headed for the door.

Outside, Bruce stood to the side, his loudspeaker in one hand and his police radio in the other. *"Where are the bloody armed response?"* he whispered into the radio.

"Under a minute away," came the reply.

Shit! he said to himself again.

He'd never been to the cement site before and had no idea how many exits there were. He'd seen the shooter run into the building, but for all he knew, they could have run straight through an exit door at the rear. He doubted they would come out of the same entrance they had gone into, as he had been clear that the place was surrounded, and it would be obvious that the entrance was the first place he'd station his men. So, he decided to take the chance, leave his position and creep around to the rear of the building and see how many exits there were, so that he could be ready when the armed response team actually made an appearance. Crouching low, so not to be seen, he left his position and moved around the building and kept going up the side, looking out for doors, but seeing none. Eventually, after what seemed like minutes, but was really just seconds, he made it to the end and found a large metal door. He did not want to give his position away, but he needed to try the door to see if it opened. As quietly as he could, he grabbed the handle and tried pulling and then tried pushing it. But it wouldn't budge. He could see a thick layer of rust stuck around the rim and realised the door was not going to move. He carried on past it, around to the other side, keeping his eyes fixed to see if there were any other ways out. As he kept moving, he wondered if, in fact, the entrance the shooter had taken was the only way in and the only way out. It would certainly make their job of containment much easier. As he carried on down the side of the building, he heard cars screech up from the road even before he noticed the lights flashing all around. *About friggin' time,* he thought to himself. *Now we've got you, you bastard.*

Meanwhile, at the entrance, The Lady pushed herself through the door, gun held up, expecting to meet at least one policeman, ready to take their life without a second's thought. But there was no one there. She stopped for a second and looked around. The only action she could see were the six police cars parked near the entrance with the police hiding behind them in fear, and she could just about hear sirens in the distance, which she assumed were the armed police unit that she had been told were already there.

Lowering her gun, she moved quickly forwards, back to the rusted skip and then beyond it, tracing her way in a big ark towards the nearest police car. As she crept up to it, she saw two officers crouching behind it. They both turned as they heard her approach, but neither jumped into action, as the sight of an elderly lady standing there was more of a shock to them than a threat.

Before either could react, she raised her gun and placed a bullet in the foreheads of both of them.

The noise from the shots were instantly drowned out by the

dozen or so cars that screeched up off the road into the cement factory grounds, lights blazing and sirens pounding.

With the arrival of the armed response unit, the whole site came to life. Bruce was back at the entrance and shouting orders both into his radio as well as to the men and women who came running to support him.

"The shooter's in this building, I believe there is just one, but I never saw him close up and it's certainly possible that there are more than one. I've circled the building and there are no more entrances or exits, so the place is contained."

"Okay," replied the officer now in charge. "Get your men back to the road."

"Got it," replied Bruce, raising his radio. "My team, in your cars and back on the road, blocking both ways, let's keep the area locked down, no one in and no one out."

"You as well," the policeman said to Bruce.

"I'm staying here. I need to see this bastard taken."

The other policeman looked at Bruce and was about to take a hard line and move him back, but seeing the look on his face, he decided it was best not to push him.

"Okay, but you stay behind us. My team, take positions all around. There may not be any obvious exits, but all those windows are broken, and we have no idea if there are ladders or even a mezzanine in there that the shooter could access.

"Sir," came the replies in unison as the twelve-man team fanned out.

Bruce stood back, giving himself enough room to hopefully stay out of the line of fire, but still close enough to see the action happening.

The Lady looked into the police car and saw the keys still in the ignition and the engine running. Suddenly, the police all around her sprang up and climbed into their cars. She realised that now the armed response was there, the general squad would start providing backup only and would use their cars to block the road. It couldn't have been more perfect for her. She pulled a cap and jacket off one of the dead officers, then climbed into the car and reversed it, just making sure she was blending in with all the other cars. She knew it wouldn't be long before someone would spot the two dead bodies she was leaving behind, but by then she would already be speeding off down the road in the stolen police car and no one would be the wiser.

Over the radio, she heard the commands as they came through. The armed unit was in place, and they were ready to go in through the front entrance and start bringing the siege to an end. Meanwhile, Bruce was continuing to order his team to block up the road. Without realising it, he gave her yet another piece of good news.

"Officers Baker and Bloom, patrol car six, take the further position south and block the road, Officers Green and Harris, patrol car nine, take the furthest position north and do the same."

"Sir," came the reply from Green and Harris.

"Car six, did you hear me? Go south."

He spun around and watched as both cars drove away in the direction he ordered. Internally he was already planning the bollocking he would give Baker and Bloom the moment the op was over for not giving him a reply. But for the moment, he had to turn his attention back to the cement building where the door was being pushed open and the action was about to begin.

CHAPTER 34

s The Lady sped down the road in police car number six, she pulled her phone from her inside pocket and dialled the secret number that only one other person knew existed. It was time to find out how broken their friendship was, and if her friend would actually betray her.

Miles away in her small prison cell, Sophia's mobile rang. She knew the call was The Lady. She took a deep breath before answering.

"Where are you?" Sophia said into the phone, skipping the usual light banter that they would share at the start of every conversation.

The Lady told her everything that had happened. Almost everything. She decided not to tell her that she had murdered MJ in cold blood.

Sophia sat in her cell, the phone glued to her ear, but her mind elsewhere. It had happened at last. The Widows Project was unravelling, as she always knew it one day would. There was no way you could kill all the men that they had killed and defraud an insurance company out of hundreds of millions of pounds without someone seeing it for what it was. And Kiara Fox had done just that.

"So, more innocent people died today because of us."

"They were the police."

"They were still innocent!" she shouted at The Lady like she was a child not understanding the simplest orders. "They were not abusers. They were good people doing their jobs."

The Lady said nothing.

"So, Kiara escaped from you again. I'm pleased at least for that mercy."

She didn't voice it, but she was also secretly pleased that Kiara Fox didn't die today. She may have been the catalyst of all this happening, but the real traitor was Sophia, she saw that clearly now.

"Yes, she got away," The Lady replied.

"And MJ? Tell me the police didn't catch her when you drove away."

She decided that sugar coating it was pointless now and it was time Sophia faced the reality of what had been happening.

"MJ is dead. I had to kill her. She was telling Kiara everything about you. I had no choice."

"Oh my God. She was one of us. She was my best friend."

That hit The Lady like a dagger.

She had been protecting Sophia from the pain of people dying for years, but now her anger boiled over and her need to protect Sophia drained away completely.

"Why did you have to kill her?" Sophia said again, this time so softly that The Lady had to strain to hear her.

Sophia suddenly seemed to have little fight left in her.

"She was trying to protect Kiara, I told you that. And she would have helped them find me, which I could not allow. And she would have definitely implicated you in all this. Then what, you spend the rest of your life in prison? Dying in there, locked up alone in your cell. Do you really want that?"

"To keep my best friend alive, yes, I would take that. I don't have a choice now, do I? But I can stop you from killing anyone else in my name." The anger and strength returned to Sophia like a hurricane. "I know more about you than you might think. I can still help the police find you and lock you up forever for what you have done."

"You'll be signing your own life sentence if you do that."

"My life was over the moment my face melted away. I've nothing to lose any more. But I am going to stop you. If it's the last thing I ever do, I'll make sure you die in here with me."

The Lady cut off the call before Sophia could say anything else.

All those years she had dedicated her life to keeping Sophia safe in prison. And all those years she'd helped her run the Widows Project. And now, in the blink of an eye, Sophia had made it all seem so pointless.

The Lady had to get away, she would not let herself be locked up again. She had stashed enough money of her own from all the insurance payouts that she could afford to go anywhere, and no one would ever suspect who she was or what she had done.

But before then, she had one more job to do.

She took the road out of Brighton and headed to a small housing estate outside of Gatwick Airport. It was her main base, where she kept spare passports, cash and other tools of her trade. She'd make a quick stop there, and then one more, before she went to somewhere warmer, and safer.

CHAPTER 35

Kiara pulled up to the prison. She'd received an email with the unusual invitation of an evening visit to one of their long-serving inmates. Sophia had done what she had promised.

She had no idea what she would say when she came face-to-face with her, but whatever she thought of the woman, she would do whatever she had to do, even beg her, if it meant keeping the twins safe.

After getting through the main gates, she was guided into the visitors' car park, before then being escorted into the main building. After a brief, but thorough physical search, Kiara was shown into a small meeting area. Apart from herself and a guard stationed outside, she was all alone.

She sat down at a long desk. On the other side of a screen there was a chair similar to the one she was sitting in, and a phone, also duplicated on her side. A door set into the wall on the prisoners' side of the screen opened and a lady walked in. She was wearing a long cloak over her prison suit, with the hood pulled up. Once the guard had left them alone, Sophia pulled her hood down and stood still in front of the lady on the other side of the barrier.

Kiara was taken aback by the juxtaposition of woman standing there. On the one hand she was one of the most beautiful women Kiara had ever seen. And she seemingly stood as strong as the triathletes Kiara had raced against in all her Ironman competitions. And yet she was also hideous. The left side of her face was all but melted away, the faint outline of cheekbones showing through the damaged skin. Kiara knew about the fire that had caused the damage, but now looking at her she could only imagine what the poor woman must have gone through to suffer such extreme damage. She tried to keep her focus on Sophia's eyes, but she found herself drawn back to the left-hand side of her face, as everyone ultimately always did.

"Kiara," she said as she sat down and raised the phone to her ear.

"Yes," Kiara said back, her own phone now almost glued to her hand in anticipation.

They looked at each other, both unsure what to say and neither able to compute the mixed emotions they felt. Both women should have hated each other. Sophia had played a key part in Asher's death and turned Kiara's life upside down, and Kiara was the cause of Sophia's Widows Project coming to an end and her possibly spending the rest of her life in prison. Yet looking at each other in that sad and dreary space, they both felt sorry for the person in front of them. Neither of them had chosen this journey, yet here they were, thrown together under such extreme and brutal circumstances.

Sophia spoke first. "I never wanted your husband to die. I never wanted anyone to die."

"I don't think that's true," Kiara replied. "I do believe you never wanted to hurt Asher, but wasn't your whole Widows thing based on murder? Wasn't that the point of it?"

Tears started to form in Sophia's eyes. Normally, she would have hidden that, but the time had passed. There was no need any more for her to keep up that façade.

"I meant, I never wanted any *innocent* people to die. Although the definition of innocent seems to now be lost on me, and my Lady... friend."

"Yes, her. The real reason Asher died."

233

"Is she alone in that, though?" Sophia said. "Or am I? The Widows was my project. It was me who sent her out into the world to act it out."

Kiara looked around the room to see if anyone was listening to this confession. Sophia picked up what she was doing.

"It's okay. I'm done with hiding it. I'll never leave this place. I know that now, and I don't deserve to."

Kiara looked deeply at her. She could feel this lady was sorry for everything that had happened. And she could see how much pain she was in. Yet she was here for a reason, and it was all that now mattered.

"I need to keep my girls safe. I don't care about anything else. All those men who were killed, much as it's hard for someone like me to understand how anyone could do that, I do know that they were not blameless."

"You have no idea," Sophia said, her hand instinctively going to her damaged face.

"But my girls have done nothing. They don't deserve to be having to hide away. And I can't spend the rest of my life worrying that your... friend is looking over my shoulder just waiting to pounce."

"I never wanted her to do this. I did tell her, and I told MJ..."

Saying MJ's name out loud gave both women reason to pause.

"You know she killed MJ, don't you? She shot her, right in front of me."

"I know. MJ was my closest friend, she was like the sister I never had," Sophia said.

"She was my friend, as well," Kiara said, still trying to come to terms with MJ's part in all this.

Sophia had to take a deep breath before continuing. "I told her to warn you off, that's all. You were getting too close to us. I didn't want you to find my widows and drag them into this, they had already gone through hell before we stepped in, and I couldn't have you finding out about them and ruining their lives again."

"And you?" Kiara reminded her. "You're due to be released soon, so you needed to stop me before I reported you to the authorities as well."

Sophia agreed. "Yes, I had a big incentive personally to stop you. My life has been wasted in this place. My husband took years from me, and I didn't deserve that. I didn't deserve any of the things he did to me. But I don't care any more, I'll die in here, it's all over now as far as I am concerned. As long as you and your girls are safe, that's all that matters now. I'll do whatever I have to do to stop her."

"So, where is she? Where do I tell the police to look?"

"She has lots of properties around the country, from the north to the south and all the way up to Scotland. No one knows where they are or what she has hidden away. Even I don't know all of them."

Kiara picked up on what she was saying.

"But you know some of them?" Kiara asked.

"Just one of them, actually. The one nearest here. And I would put my life on it that is the one she is heading to now."

"What's the address?"

"I have your number from your call this evening, as soon as I get back to my cell I'll message it to you. You need to tell the police how dangerous she is. She'll not hesitate in killing. She's got no heart. I knew that from the first day I met her."

"Then why did you trust her? Why the hell did you get her to do all this?"

"Who else did I have? And without her, they would have torn me to shreds in here. She protected me. She still does. But now she's gone, or will be, I'll be on my own again. With no one I can turn to and no one to protect me from the animals in this place."

"I'm sorry," Kiara said, and she realised she truly meant it.

"Don't be. I'll survive, somehow. Or not. Either way, you've got nothing to be sorry about. You're the real victim in all this."

"We've both been victims, haven't we? In different ways, perhaps, but we've both suffered. I'm not going to tell the police about you, Sophia. I'll lead them to your Lady friend, but I'll not bring up your widows, and I won't bring them to you."

Sophia was stunned. She had been sure Kiara would tell the police everything the moment she left there. "Why would you do that? After everything you've gone through, why wouldn't you make sure I never leave this place?"

"You've been locked up for most of your life for something you didn't do, and I believe you on that. You've already paid the price for the widows' crimes. And I don't think for a second you're a threat to my family or me, or anyone else for that matter."

"Thank you," Sophia said, tears running freely down her face once again.

"If anyone here heard any of this then I'll deny it all. Just promise me you'll leave all this behind you now, that the Widows programme will end here, tonight."

"My thirst for revenge nearly destroyed me, and it's caused so many losses. I'm done now, I promise you that, whatever life I have left I'll spend putting things right."

Kiara stood up to leave. "Send me that address right away, let's end this now."

Sophia nodded in agreement and watched Kiara leave.

CHAPTER 36

As she drove out of the prison car park, Kiara forwarded Nick the address that had just come through to her. Then she pressed dial to call him.

"Where are you?" he asked as soon as his phone rang.

"I've just left the prison. I saw Sophia."

"How did they let you in?"

"She arranged it herself. She told me everything. She's lost as much as me, perhaps even more in some ways."

"And you believe her?"

"Yes. I could see it in her eyes. That was why I needed to come here. I needed to know my girls would be safe from now on. Did they catch The Lady, is it all over now?"

"No, they didn't get her," he said. "Bruce was lucky he wasn't killed, he told me you saved his life, and the officers he was with."

"So, she did get away, then?" Kiara asked.

"Yes, but not before running them around in circles, and killing two of his officers. They were only young, they'd hardly had a chance to even start their lives. We've got to catch her, Kiara, before she kills anyone else."

"I think I know where she might be. Check your messages when I cut off. Give the address I just sent you to Bruce. Tell him it's one of her safe houses and is likely to be where she is."

"Okay. And you? Will come here now?"

"Where is here?"

"We're at Lewes Police Station under lock and key. The girls are fine, as are your in-laws, but they need you with them."

"I'm on my way. I can't do anything else now. I've done everything I can, just get Bruce to send his best people there."

"Did you tell Sophia it's all over now? That she's never going to leave that place?"

"I told her it's over."

"Kiara? Did you tell her we are on to her and she's going to die in there for what she's done?"

"I'll be with you as soon as I can," Kiara replied before ending the call.

CHAPTER 37

The Lady needed to change cars as soon as she could. The police car had to have a tracker in it and, if they hadn't already started to look for it, then they would at any moment. She pulled into the short-term car park at Gatwick's south terminal, which was the closest main car park she knew that was on the way to East Croydon where her safe house was. She knew that the cameras would pick up the car as it drove in, so she kept her face turned away and drove the vehicle right up to the top level, as far away from anyone as she could. She wiped the steering wheel and the dashboard clean with a tissue she'd found in the driver's door so that her fingerprints would not be left behind. Then she left the keys in the ignition, gave them a quick wipe down and left the car.

She took her time walking down each level, watching people as they came out of the lifts and headed to their cars. She spotted her victim easily: a tired looking Uber driver who had just done a drop-off, having no doubt carried his passengers' cases into the lift as a parting good gesture to get his star rating up high. That nice gesture was the reason he never made it out of the car park alive.

"Excuse me, young man, are you a taxi driver?"

"Yes, I am, my love. I have a job booked, though, I'm sorry. Do you have a phone? You could order another driver and they'll get here quickly enough."

She walked over to where he was standing by his car.

"I don't suppose you could show me how," she asked innocently, taking her phone out of her right pocket, while bringing the gun carefully out of her left."

"Of course I can, my love," he said.

The general noise from the airport meant no one heard the gun go off or the man's body hit the ground. She had seen him holding the keys when he had stopped to talk to her, so she had no problem getting the car started and driving off. For good measure, she also took the scarf from around his neck and tied it around her own. With it covering her neck and half her face, it meant that the exit cameras wouldn't be able to see who was in the driver's seat in any great detail.

She stayed within the speed limit the whole way to East Croydon, and if she had been pulled over for anything random, they would only have seen an old lady driving an ordinary looking car and not thought twice about it.

As she neared her house, she sensed something wasn't right. There seemed to be a lot of activity up ahead, yet no one was walking the streets, they were completely empty. She knew instinctively that the police would be there, waiting for her to return to collect her things. There would be plain clothes officers in the surrounding streets and then armed police in vans right up to her door. As soon as she crossed into the general area, they would box her in.

Sophia had done the worst thing she could have done to her. She had at last truly betrayed her. She had given the police the address of the place where they could find her.

The loss of the house was a blow, as it meant another one of her identities would be lost forever, along with a nice stash of cash and some spare weapons. She could certainly live with that loss as she had other places she could go to and there were always enough papers and cash to let her carry on with her plans to leave; however, she wasn't certain she could live with the betrayal. That was truly devastating, and something she knew she would never get over. She understood that Sophia had been angry with her. And, of course, the argument they'd had was one of only a small handful over the years. But she thought it would fade away soon enough and that one day she'd be able to see Sophia again and perhaps even pick up their friendship where it had left off. She'd never had a friend before, not a real friend, Sophia had been her first and only one. And now she had betrayed her in the worst possible way.

She took the next turning and drove out of the housing estate, not even bothering to look back.

Later that day, Bruce delivered the news to Nick and Kiara that the house was definitely the right one. They had found all sorts of stuff in there, from passports and cash to a healthy stash of automatic guns and hunting knives. He asked Kiara if she was sure this was an old lady they were after, as everything they found pointed to someone much younger and fitter, perhaps not even a Lady after all.

"So, you really didn't catch her, then?" Kiara asked.

"If it was the right house, as I said, no, she never turned up. We've left plain clothes police on the beat, all over the area, in case she comes later, but to be honest, I think she is smart enough to stay away. She must have known we were coming. I need to keep you and the girls safe, Kiara. She is still out there and there's no telling when she might come back for you."

"I am not sure she will," Kiara said. "She won't want to chase me down forever, she knows that that would just risk her getting picked up again. We know she was only after me to stop me from finding out what had been going on, but that's too late now. I really think it's all over."

"Do you really want to take that chance?" Nick chimed in.

"I feel like you're holding something back," Bruce said to her. "In fact, you've told us hardly anything. We know that the lady in Scotland…" he took out his notebook to check the name, "Jane

Powers, killed her husband before committing suicide. And that this Lady, whoever she is, helped her set it up, and then you say she tried to take the life insurance money, but you found out and tried to stop it. But what about the lady Nick said you visited in prison, what was her name, Sophia something?" He looked through his notes again. "What was her role in all this?"

"She was no help, I'm afraid. I had seen her name on some old office notes that were similar to the Jane Powers case, and I just wanted to check her out. But she didn't know anything about any of this. And I believed her."

"Why would you just believe her, she's in prison, she could easily be caught up in this."

"My instincts told me she knew nothing."

"Your instincts," Bruce said sarcastically.

"Yes, my instincts, and they are more helpful than all the police in the world," Kiara told him.

Bruce looked at her harshly. He knew she wasn't being totally honest with him, and he really didn't like her implication that he and his officers had somehow failed her.

"So, how did you get The Lady's address in Croydon then? Was that also in a work file?" he asked her sarcastically.

"Yes, I think it must have been. I have a good memory for detail and it just struck me as odd that this address seemed to have nothing to do with anything else."

"And you're prepared to stand up in court, under oath, and say that rubbish, are you?"

"My client has said all she wants to say," Nick added, stepping in between them.

"Really, Nick. After all these years."

"Sorry, buddy, but Kiara has retained me, so client privilege and all that."

"Well, we can't protect you if you don't tell us everything."

"I know," Kiara said.

She was so torn. She needed to protect her girls and this seemed like a crazy chance to take. But, somehow, she felt deep in her heart that The Lady wouldn't come back after them. And she knew that she could not keep her girls locked up hiding, and forever in fear of their lives. So, as soon as she was able to, she told them that they were no longer in danger and they could move back to their house in Brittany Road, Hove. It also meant that they could all, the girls, her in-laws and herself, start the grieving process for Asher.

CHAPTER 38

One Month Later

The police had no choice but to give up the search for The Lady. There were no descriptions of her that were helpful, and even Kiara, who was being truthful on that, ended up having to give them over half a dozen variations of how The Lady actually looked.

With so many murders, especially in the police force, they would never totally give up their search, but there was little chance of actually ever catching her. They had also interviewed Sophia in prison to establish her role in everything, but just as Kiara had told them, there was no link to any of this and ultimately they had to remove her as a person of interest.

Kiara stood outside HMP Bronzefield in Middlesex and waited for Sophia to be released. As the police had no way of linking her to the murders, her sentence came to its natural end and she was released on the date that had been agreed at her last parole interview.

Kiara watched from across the road as Sophia, dressed in her long cloak with the hood up covering her face, stepped out of the gates.

Kiara climbed from her car and started to cross the road, just at the same time as a small red sports car came careening around the corner. The driver must have seen Kiara as the car purposefully make a sharp turn to avoid hitting her, but then readjusted and drove on, hitting Sophia so hard that her body was thrown up into the air and came crashing down on the bonnet of another car parked close by, leaving her body broken and her head cracked open. The red car carried on driving, speeding off down the road. The car was found abandoned two miles away, it's windscreen and bonnet covered in Sophia's blood.

Later on, the police interviewed a handful of people who saw the car being abandoned, but all of them gave different descriptions of the driver they saw walking away and jumping onto a bus.

Sophia died on the spot, her broken body bringing almost instant death. The only thing that the coroner could remark on his file was that, for some strange reason, she seemed to have just the smallest smile on her face.

That evening, Kiara and the girls went to Nick and Jennie Taylor's house for dinner.

Kiara showed Nick a text she had received earlier on that night as she was driving over. He read it out loud after they had gone into his study for a bit of a quiet moment away from the twins and Jennie.

That was my final act, her betrayal of me had to be punished. You and your family are safe, my job's done. But don't come looking for me. The last thing you want is to be walking down the road wondering who that old Lady is following you."

"Wow," said Nick. "Do you think she means it?"

"Yes, I do. And I doubt the police will ever find her. I imagine she's left the country by now. She's certainly capable of it."

"Will you show this to Bruce?" Nick asked.

"No," Kiara said, before pressing the delete button. "It's time we let this go."

"So, what's now for you, then?"

"Well, the girls and I need to find a way to move on, don't we? We'll never get over what happened to Asher, we all lost so much that day. I'm not sure I'll ever be able to get over losing him. But

I've got to be here for the girls, they are my priority now. I've given my notice in at Seico, I can't go back there. I know that they were somehow part of this, but I can't prove it, and I can't risk bringing The Lady back, can I? So, I need to somehow just move on."

"So, that's it, then, you walk away?"

"I have to."

"If you need a job, you know there's always a position at my firm for an investigator, we'd love to have you on board."

"Thanks, but I think my days of working for big organisations has come to an end. I think maybe it's time I went my own way."

"Watch out, world, the Fox is loose," Nick replied with a smirk.

"Well, maybe she is," Kiara replied with a smile.

Epilogue

After Sophia's death, Kiara met with Bruce and had told him everything she knew about the Widows Project, about Jane Powers' suicide, about Asher's murder and the fact that she had no idea who The Lady was. She also didn't know the identities of the hundred or so widows that Sophia had created. Those details had died with MJ and Sophia. The police tried to tie Seico Insurance into the investigation, but someone had managed to get into the company system remotely and destroy whatever evidence had been left behind. Kiara knew who it must have been, but she was never going to tangle with The Lady ever again, not if she was to keep her girls safe from harm. So, she refused to help the police any further.

At first they tried to press Kiara on what else she knew about Seico, as she had been a senior investigator there, but she stood fast and refused to say anything more. They had discussed arresting her for obstruction, but after Nick Taylor had pressed the point that Kiara had saved the lives of Bruce and two of his team, it was decided that perhaps she had been through enough already and they closed the investigation on her. Although the hunt for The Lady continued.

Asher's funeral had taken a few more weeks to arrange, as his body had been held up until the investigation into Sophia and all the murders was finished. It had been a sombre affair, as he had been taken from them in the worst way imaginable, and Kiara and the girls weren't able to celebrate his life in the usual ways people did at funerals of people they loved. They simply needed to get it over with and then hide away as a family and try to come to terms with everything that they had lost.

Once everything was settled, including Kiara being able to claim on Asher's life insurance policy, she managed to rent out their family house in Brittany Road and buy an old cottage on a couple of acres of land in the small village of Hurstpierpoint, near the girls' school. She wanted a change of pace for the girls, a place where they would have some outside space to use up their energy, somewhere they could be closer to the calming effects of the English countryside. For herself, a new home felt safe, for her and the family, and with it still being close to Brighton it meant she could try to build a new life for them.

She also needed to get back to the sport she loved the most, as it was the only time she truly felt at peace. She had booked herself into an Olympic triathlon in the summer and this new slower life would give her the time and space to get back to her training, both by running and cycling around the country lanes and then heading down to Brighton beach for her early morning swim. The location of the new house ticked all her boxes.

She had decided not to take Nick up on his offer of a job at the law firm. She knew it would be great working with him, but if she was going to build a new life for herself, then that had to include working for herself as well. She was still the best fraud investigator out there and there was no reason once people realised she was freelance that she could not pick up some small local jobs to keep the pennies coming in, which, once added to the rent from Brittany Road, would be enough to keep the girls at Hurst College and pay the bills at the new house.

"So, it's definitely a no, then? There's really nothing I can say to change your mind?" Nick asked her.

"Sorry, but I think I'm done working for other people. Within a few days, you'll have wished you'd never asked, I promise. Maybe you can throw me the odd case, though. Just nothing too dangerous, please."

"I think we can do that," he replied.

"Hey Nick," the girls said in unison as they walked up.

"Hey girls, how are you doing? I love the new house, you could get totally lost in that garden."

"It's cool, isn't it?" Mia replied.

"Have you seen the little lake behind those trees?" Jasmin asked. "And Mum's new office?"

"New office?" Nick replied, giving Kiara a surprised look. She just shrugged and smiled.

"Come on, we'll show you," Mia said, both girls taking a hand each and leading him through the mini forest to the small lake behind it.

Right at the edge, stood a home office. It was made out of repurposed wood and had been built by a local specialist carpenter, which gave it the feel of having been there for years, and allowing it to blend in with its surroundings, despite having all the mod cons of a new build. On closer inspection, Nick could see it had been perfectly built and contained everything a modern home working office needed; lots of space to house the large, modern desk with three computer screens and overlooking the beautiful countryside. Plus there was plenty of space for Kiara's two triathlon bikes, one hanging from the wall and the other the floor underneath it; both ready for her to jump on and hit the trails whenever she needed to. There was also a small running machine in the corner for those days it was too muddy or windy to go out, plus a separate shower room for the times she decided to brave the mud after all.

And then, in the far corner, in pride of place, was Asher's bright gold tenor saxophone.

"That was Dad's," Jasmin said, walking over and running her hands over it.

"And that's his record player, and his old jazz collection," Mia chipped in.

"I never knew Ash played an instrument," Nick said, looking back at Kiara.

"He didn't really," Kiara said as she walked in the room to join them, "he just liked the thought that one day, when we both hit retirement, he could have some lessons whilst I was pounding the streets training for my latest race." She said it with a hint of sadness, knowing that they would never be able to enjoy getting old together.

"I've started lessons now," Mia said.

"And don't we know it!" Jas replied.

"He would have loved it here," Nick said, smiling. "I remember how much he loved the garden in your old house. This place would have been a dream to him."

Kiara walked over to the window and gazed out at the lake trying to hold the tears back.

Early the next morning, when the girls were still tucked up in bed asleep and Kiara had returned from her very early morning run, she went back down the garden to the office to have a shower without disturbing the main house. Afterwards, she sat behind the desk and stared out of the window just as the night sky was starting to lighten. She looked down at her desk and saw a few files sitting there. It was still way too early to work, but she felt comforted knowing that she had something to do when the girls were at school rather than just sit there and stare at Asher's photos on her desk and wonder what life was going to be like for her in the future.

Everyone, except perhaps the girls, kept telling her that she was too young and too beautiful to be on her own and that she'd have to one day get out there again. And she knew Asher would want her to as well. But the thought of it always made her cry. She missed him so much, every day, and she wondered how she could ever get past that. At least having the business would keep her focused and her mind away from an unknown future.

Since setting it up only a few weeks earlier, she had already received a string of calls from companies asking about her availability. She had already taken on a few small jobs: a couple of small fire claims that had looked suspicious and a triple car accident that just screamed of fraud. She had also been asked to look at a possible suspicious life insurance claim, but she was well done with those and turned it down before she even heard the background to it.

Deep down, she really wanted something juicy to get her head into, something that would really challenge her again, but she was still new as an independent, and she was tucked away in the countryside rather than being based in the big city. So, she wasn't sure anything exciting would reach her for quite some time to come.

It turned out that she had nothing to worry about on that score.

The phone on her desk rang, bringing her out of her reverie.

"Hello," she answered on the third ring with trepidation, expecting it was from her in-laws as who else would call her at that time. Her stomach turned as she waited for the bad news that one of them was unwell and was going to hospital again. The stress of losing their son had taken a heavy toll on the health of both of them and they had aged a lot since his murder.

She was relieved when the voice on the other end was neither of them.

"Is that Fox Investigations?"

"Yes it is," she replied. "Do you know what time it is?" she asked the caller, the annoyance in her voice clear for him to hear.

"Yes I do, I believe it is just after five thirty in the morning there. Which means it's seven-thirty here, so my day began an hour or so ago. I do hope you don't mind my early call, but I was told you are an extremely early riser and that if I wanted your undivided attention then I should call you before your twin daughters wake up and demand a cooked breakfast. I believe they are going back to school today after a long time off, that must be daunting for you all."

It had not been so long since Kiara had been hunted by an assassin who took the life of her husband and had almost taken hers. So, getting a call from a complete stranger before the sun had even risen, especially one who seemed to know too much about her routine, put her fully on alert. She opened the WhatsApp application on her laptop and started to type an SOS to the local security company, who, thanks to the help of her friend Nick Taylor, now kept a close eye on her and her family.

"Who the hell are you, and what do you want?" she asked sternly down the phone.

"Mrs Fox, please forgive me. I didn't mean to worry you. My name is Tyrone Waterstone. I'm CEO of a company called Worldwide Marine Insurance, based in Johannesburg, South Africa. We share a good friend, my London lawyer Nick Taylor. He told me about your recent loss, I am so very sorry, I can't even begin to imagine what that must have been like."

"What is it you want?" she asked, still not totally convinced of who he was.

"Nick talks so highly of you, he told me that you are the best insurance investigator in the business. He said you were someone who does not let go of a case until it is solved. And that is a virtue I desperately need if my business is to survive the next few months. If you need to, you can call Nick before we talk further, he's usually at his office by nine-ish, and I am sure we could arrange a Zoom call for us all."

Kiara breathed a sigh of relief. It was just a business call, and it had come as a recommendation from one of the only people left who she felt totally able to trust. She deleted the SOS message before it was sent.

"I'm sorry for my reaction, Mr Waterstone. You simply caught me off guard. I'll speak with Nick later anyway, but I'm okay to talk now if you like."

"That's great, and absolutely no apology needed, in fact if anyone should apologise then it should be me. I have called you far too early and had no right talking about your family as if I knew them. I guess Nick has talked about you so often that I forgot we have never even met before."

"It's fine, honestly, I'm good. How can I help you?"

"Kiara, we are a South African marine insurance company. We specialise in cargo insurance, covering goods being shipped from one country to another. One side of our business, the major area, is insuring the movement of oil across the major oceans. Specifically we have a large client, one of the largest in the oil industry, and we have been insuring them for around fifteen years now, always claim free. But in the last eighteen months, we have had to pay out a number of large claims and just one month ago another claim was reported, this one very sizeable. We haven't paid this one yet, but we will probably have to and now I am worried more will follow."

"If you have paid them I assume you've completed your investigations and found them to be genuine?" Kiara asked.

"Well, that has been slightly problematic. Our client has certainly been very open and has let us send in our own team. But we have found nothing to suggest that our client is involved in the losses. I do trust our client, they also have to take a large financial hit themselves each time, as their own policy excess runs into the millions as well."

"So, what exactly are they claiming for?"

"Basically, each time the oil has been offloaded at its destination port, it has been found to be in good order, no water contamination or anything like that, which we often see with shipments like this. However, each time, it has arrived at a different weight to when it first left port. This means somewhere along the journey oil has been removed. But we have found nothing in the ship's logs to suggest any other vessels close enough to them for that to happen. The first claim showed that at the loading port the weight of oil was fifty thousand tonnes, but at the final destination it was only forty-five thousand tonnes. The loss to us of the five thousand tonnes was around three million dollars. So far, in the last eighteen months, we have paid out over twenty million dollars in claims. We have looked at all the loading and unloading procedures and nothing seems out of place. So, we are at a complete loss as to how it's been happening."

"Twenty million dollars?" Kiara said in surprise at the amounts he was talking about.

"Last year, the global theft of oil was in excess of a hundred billion dollars. Our losses are small in comparison, but for a company our size they are of course significant and could really affect our financial strength and ability to keep trading."

"Forgive me, Mr Waterstone, as fascinating as this is, I am not entirely sure what you think I can do for you."

"It's Tyrone, please."

"Sorry, Tyrone. But I am not sure what you think I can do to help. I don't know what Nick has told you, but I've never worked in large corporate cases before and certainly never something like cargo theft or oil tankers. I would have no idea where to begin."

"And that is why you are the perfect person for the job. I need someone who is not willing to just give up at the first hurdle. I also need someone who will have to ask the dumb questions. It's those questions that are not being asked at the moment and are leading us to lose millions of dollars per claim."

Kiara stopped talking and tried to work out if she could really do this, or if she even had the emotional state to take on such a big project at the moment.

Tyrone, sensing he was losing her, continued with his pitch.

"Nick said you were desperate for a case that you could get your teeth stuck into. So, what could be better than this? If you help me find out what is going on then you would save me tens of millions of dollars in claims and, quite frankly, it could stop my business going down the drain, which right now is where we are heading. Kiara, I need you, I really do."

"It would be complicated for me," she replied, still thinking on the opportunity. "This job could mean a number of trips for me as I would have to be on site part of the time, so I would have to get help with my girls now they are going back to school, with drop-off and pickups, plus the sports clubs, dinners; there's a lot I would have to arrange."

"I'd make it worthwhile, I assure you. Seven figures."

Kiara was taken aback. That was crazy money. She thought about what she could do with that sort of cash behind them. It would not only help her at the moment, but it would also be a massive boost to the girls' university fees; that is, if she could get them back onto that page.

"You'd be saving us millions in fraudulent claims, if I am right," Tyrone said, knowing that the number he had thrown at her was going to be too much for her to turn down. "And your girls can take some of the trips with you as well, if that helps. It could be an adventure for you all."

"I really need to think about it."

"I understand. But please don't take too long. I can't stomach many more claims like this, I really can't."

"Let me talk to the girls tonight and see how they feel about me leaving them so soon after..." she couldn't finish the sentence *losing their dad*, it was too painful even to think about, let alone to say to a stranger. "Can you give me a few days to think it over?"

"Unfortunately I can't. But I can give you twenty-four hours. And then I will need to find someone else. But it's you I want."

"Okay. I'll come back to you within twenty-four hours.

Meanwhile, to help me make up my mind, would you be able to send me some details on the claims you've paid out?"

"I'll have them emailed to you right away," he said.

After the call ended, Kiara looked at the clock. It was 6am already and the girls would be waking up now. She just had time for a quick shower before they called her.

As the hot water poured over her, it removed the mud on her ankles from the run up Wolstonbury Hill and left streaks on the shower floor. Kiara stood there under the scalding water and tried to come up with a million reasons for not taking on the case. In truth, she had plenty of reasons for saying no. The problem was that she was desperate to say yes. Not just because of the money, which would certainly make things easier for her and the girls for some time to come, but also because she needed to stretch her mind again. She was sick of just sitting around all day and thinking about what could have been. To fill her time, she'd been taking on some insignificant jobs for the smaller motor and household insurance companies in the area, plus a job for a local payroll company who suspected their CFO was not accounting for all the tax he should be. But she really was getting to the point where she couldn't face another case from someone claiming to have lost a gold watch on holiday or a family who pretended to have damaged their TV by dropping a glass of water over it, or indeed having to spend hours on the phone waiting for HMRC to even pick up her call. It was mind-numbing and pointless work that she thought she had left behind years ago. She needed more than that, she needed something that would get her adrenalin pumping again. But what the hell would she say to Mia and Jasmin? She really had no idea how she was going to tell them that she had to jump on a plane to the other side of the world.

"Asher, what the hell am I going to do?" she said to the empty room for the hundredth time since she'd lost him.

Milton Keynes UK
Ingram Content Group UK Ltd.
UKHW031840070824
446673UK00001B/3